Prize Murder

PRIZE MURDER

Nicholas Rhea

Constable • London

Constable & Robinson Ltd
3 The Lanchesters
162 Fulham Palace Road
London W6 9ER
www.constablerobinson.com

First published in the UK by Constable,
an imprint of Constable & Robinson Ltd 2006

A copy of the British Library Cataloguing in Publication
Data is available from the British Library.

ISBN 13: 978-1-84529-375-8
ISBN 10: 1-84529-375-4

Printed and bound in the EU

Chapter One

When Brent Fowler opened the unstamped envelope marked *Strictly Personal*, he was pleasantly surprised to find an unusual invitation. Printed in colour with *Private and Confidential* as the heading plus a ten-figure reference number in the top right-hand corner, it said:

Dear Mr Fowler,

You are one of only six people from this region who have won our superb 'Shooting Party' prize. It is a country house lifestyle experience which has been arranged at Mossgate Manor, a moorland estate in North Yorkshire, and will take place from 6 p.m., Friday 18th March until lunch on Sunday 20th March. Accommodation, tuition, firearms and ammunition will be free of charge and guests should bring suitable outdoor clothing. You will not be asked to pay any fees, and transport will be provided to and from Mossgate Manor.

If you wish to accept the prize, you are asked to be in the public car park at the Arndale Centre, Manchester for collection at 3.30 p.m., Friday 18th March. Your people carrier will be identified by the name 'Mossgate' on red window stickers. It is essential you keep this prize notification with you at all times; it is your document of identification.

Further information and details of the weekend will be supplied by telephone to your home after you have had a few days to consider this opportunity. A limited number of lucky guests may be offered an extended visit of up to five extra days.

A REMINDER: keep this letter close to you; you will be asked to quote your reference number as proof of identity. This prize is strictly personal and cannot be transferred to anyone else. You are asked not to divulge the contents to other parties as we do not wish to attract unsolicited applications.

If you do not wish to accept this offer, please let us know when we call you. There will be no repeat invitation; this is a once-in-a-lifetime opportunity.

There was an illegible signature at the end of the letter but no address.

'What's that about?' His mother smiled across the breakfast table as Brent read and reread the letter. Whatever it said, it had made him very excited. Brent felt he could tell her; after all, she wouldn't invite herself along!

'This letter – I don't believe it, it's one of those prize competitions, like something from *Reader's Digest*. I haven't bought a ticket or entered any competition like this, not that I know of, so I don't know how I've won. Anyway, the prize is a weekend of country house style living on an estate in Yorkshire, all expenses paid. Do you think there's a catch in it, Mum? Like wanting me to buy a time-share or something? It's not the shooting season now but it's called Shooting Party.'

'If you don't have to buy anything, it sounds all right,' she said. 'It sounds as if somebody knows about you, Brent, somebody who's put your name forward or bought a ticket for you. You've always said your dream was to work on or even own a country estate and have guests with shooting parties and gun dogs. Somebody must have realized you have that kind of potential, somebody who knows you well enough to submit your name. After all, you are a bright lad, especially with your A-levels.'

'That sort of life is a dream, Mum, nothing else. It's out of my league, there's no way I could afford it. It's like ordinary kids dreaming about playing for Manchester United or being astronauts – most will never even get into their local team or learn to fly. I dream about that kind of life, that's all. Just a dream.'

'Well, someone must have recognized your abilities and made sure your name was included in the draw. That letter was delivered by hand, especially for you. The envelope's got your name on and it's not a circular. So what do you have to do?'

She listened as he read the entire contents and glowed with pride. She had always known Brent was capable of better things and this could change his entire life. And hers. It was a wonderful opportunity, the sort of luck he really needed.

'You must go, Brent, it's too good to miss. As it says, it's a once-in-a-lifetime opportunity, and it's all free, you don't have to worry about the cost. And who knows what it might lead to? You can't lose, can you? It's a prize, with no other commitment. It could lead to something much better than being a swimming-pool attendant!'

'It's only for a weekend so I could get the Friday afternoon off, I'm due some overtime,' he said. 'Yes, I think it would be very nice, something different, a real change for me. You won't mind if I go?'

'Mind? Good heavens no! I think it's a wonderful chance for you. I'll be fine on my own. Besides, you spend far too much time alone in your room with that computer. So when they ring, you must say you'll go.'

'I will,' he promised her. 'And if I do well, I might decide to stay those extra few days. I can check before I go, at work I mean, about getting more time off at short notice.'

'You might meet some very important people, Brent, people who can help you in the future. Opportunities like this don't happen every day. You have to make the most of them when they come to you.'

The follow-up telephone call came one evening when a man called Mr Shields rang to ask if Brent had considered the offer. When Brent confirmed he had and that he wanted to accept, Mr Shields began to explain the basics of the weekend. There would be extra delights such as meeting the Lord of the Manor, having dinner in the big house on Saturday night and a guided tour of the estate on Sunday morning; he also asked if Brent was a vegetarian or had some other special diet and he replied that he did not. Mr Shields said a very relaxed party atmosphere would prevail throughout the weekend and, after chatting to him, Brent thought it all sounded very exciting.

'I've accepted, Mum. It sounds really wonderful.'

As Brent hurried upstairs to his computer in a state of excitement, his mother read the letter which he had left on the kitchen table. It did sound wonderful. She'd always believed her Brent was worthy of better things. After all, he was approaching thirty and there must be greater opportunies than working at the baths.

This letter could mean her son was about to meet his destiny and fulfil his dreams. Hers too.

Detective Chief Inspector Paul Sanders of SIOUX Department of the Greater Manchester Police was chairing a small meeting in his office.

'Three more men reported missing from home this week,' he said. 'None with convictions and none under suspicion of child molesting. Can we or can we not say they have been spirited away?'

'I'd say not,' said Detective Sergeant Lynn Rogers. 'Enquiries suggest they've left home simply because they wanted to, even if they didn't tell families and friends where they were going. They're adults, all entitled to leave home without us getting involved.'

'And none had links with Dean Street Leisure Centre?'

'No, they weren't regular attenders or volunteers.'

'Anything more on that character Jacob Hampson who works there?'

'Nothing. He's got no form. According to criminal

records, he's as clean as a whistle even though various branches of the force are beginning to show an interest in him. He has money but doesn't seem to have a job. That alone is usually enough to raise suspicion. Unless he has a family legacy? A fortune from somewhere? Apart from the fact that he runs a strange church, the Church of the White Kelts, we've nothing on him, and running a church is not illegal. He's not come into our sights for any other reason.'

'So we're no closer to finding out who's behind those suspected murders of paedophiles? There's no evidence to suggest he's involved, is there?'

'None at all. But whoever is responsible is very clever, well able to keep their activities away from scrutiny.'

'Right, we've no bodies either, so we can't prove they've been murdered. All we have is a theory without much foundation. Maybe we should think about setting a trap of some kind?' suggested Sanders. 'It could be dangerous, so we can't use a civilian. It would have to be a police officer.'

'A trap might work, sir, as a means of gaining evidence that murder has been committed. We can't allow people to go around killing or kidnapping criminals even if they deserve it, if in fact that is what's happening.'

'I'll put my thinking cap on, Lynn. Meanwhile, keep me informed if any more suspect men go missing and keep the teams digging into Hampson's background.'

DCI Sanders closed the meeting and went away to consider his next move.

Some time after Brent had opened his letter, Detective Inspector Montague Pluke, the officer in charge of Crickledale Sub-Divisional Criminal Investigation Department, was standing on a lofty moorland hillock of granite. It was the highest point hereabouts and he had climbed it because it provided an ideal observation platform. His wife, Millicent, was nearby and both were gazing across the treeless landscape of the central portion of the North York Moors. They were the only human life among thousands of acres of knee-deep heather but they could not find what they sought.

'It must be here somewhere,' muttered Pluke.

Several miles to the east was the North Sea but, due to a persistent haze, that was beyond their view. Had it been clear along the coast, they could have seen the blue sea even from this distance, but sea frets, or roaks as they were known locally, were common along the Yorkshire coastline at many times of the year. To the south, beyond more miles of deep heather, there were other dales and moors with Fylingdales Ballistic Missile Early Warning Station's truncated pyramid sitting like a piece of white Lego on its distant lonely site. The famous three white balls had long gone. To the north were yet more acres of thick heather and these were occasionally interrupted by many deep but very minor dales while a considerable distance to the west, beyond another series of heathered peaks and troughs, were more deep dales and lofty hills. They were the Yorkshire Dales and the Pennines, seventy or more miles distant. Some of their distinctive features were visible from Pluke's elevated position on the other side of Yorkshire.

Although the surrounding landscape was smothered with heather and bracken, Pluke knew that this dense carpet concealed much of interest – remnants of history such as old burial sites known as howes, ancient packhorse routes and footpaths marked by stone crosses, evidence of glaciers and even relics of Stone Age settlements. As he stood on his piece of granite and stared across the once-purple sea of vegetation, the vista seemed to present a hopeless quest. How on earth could he find anything in what was truly a jungle of tall and thick impenetrable ling? This species of heather – the ling – was tough and wiry but beautiful with its purple blossom later in the year. Bell heather flourished here too, but not in such quantities.

'I'm sure it's here somewhere.' Unwilling to abandon the search, Pluke was sweeping the vast open spaces with a powerful pair of binoculars. 'All the available information points to this locality.'

'What you need is a piece of lucky white heather,' said Millicent.

'It won't be in flower yet, it's only March,' he said. 'August is the time for the ling to bloom, the bell heather blooms earlier, in July. By mid-August, though, this moorland will be a carpet of purple, hundreds of square miles . . . and there may be white among it. But ling hides such a lot, Millicent, all sorts could be hidden here.'

'You must keep looking, Montague. If this was a police search for evidence of a crime, you'd never give up, would you?'

'No, my dear, of course not. It may mean quartering the landscape and systematically checking every square yard, it's not as if I can follow a stream or be guided by stone walls. Where on earth does one begin?'

Watching Montague in his great distress, Millicent was sure a sprig of white heather would have made all the difference but on this occasion Pluke's carefully cultivated luck appeared to have deserted him. That was surprising because he had completed all his usual good-luck rituals before embarking on the trip. He had put his right foot forward as he'd started today's journey, and he'd ensured his lucky rabbit's foot was in his pocket. He'd touched some wood and had checked that the horseshoe was correctly positioned on the house wall – and then, as they had left the outskirts of Crickledale, he'd seen two magpies in a tree. 'Two for joy,' he'd shouted with obvious happiness and excitement as Millicent drove him to this lonely and remote location. This outing was not a police duty trip, however; after ten days in the Lake District, their favourite holiday haunt, Montague Pluke was enjoying the final weekend at home. It had made a nice long break from his demanding work as a high-ranking detective and he had decided to make good use of his final days of free time by locating the mysterious horse trough known as the Holy Trough of Blackamoor.

11

It was reputed to exist on these moors. It had an ancient history which dated from the time monks travelled on foot between distant abbeys but he knew it might date from an even earlier period. The Stone Age perhaps, or the time of the Druids and Celts. According to old accounts, the trough had an almost mythical status because of its ability to constantly replenish its supply of fresh water while standing in an apparently dry section of the moor. According to the legend, no stream or ghyll fed the trough and falling rain was not its source of supply. If the story was true, it was indeed a most unusual example of a horse trough: according to medieval records, it appeared to maintain its level due to miraculous means, hence its status as a holy trough.

There is little doubt it was a remarkable example because in spite of its reputed elevation more than a thousand feet above sea-level, it was constantly full of fresh water. Was that miraculous? In many ways, it was like Lake Gormire near the foot of Sutton Bank, not far from Thirsk. That freshwater lake has no inlet stream and no outlet, and yet it is always full and never overflows. In the belief that the Holy Trough of Blackamoor was miraculous, pilgrims came from afar to take its waters, believing they cured most ailments. At one stage it acquired the status of a wishing well. The truth was, of course, that this water did not cure ailments – in fact, all it achieved was not to make people ill when they drank it. Most of the people at that time drank polluted water which made them ill, consequently pure water, as found in the trough of Blackamoor, was regarded as something quite magical. Almost without exception, other troughs were serviced by streams, becks or springs which had been diverted into them, and so the Holy Trough of Blackamoor was very special. His intention was to find it, even if some experts regarded it as nothing more than a myth.

Pluke's fame came from his dedication to and knowledge of horse troughs. They were his all-consuming hobby; he devoted almost as much time to that subject as he did to being a senior police officer. One of his notable successes was his famous book *Horse Troughs of Crickledale and District since the 16th century – fully illustrated by the author*, and he was also an expert on civic horse troughs, not only those in local towns but those which enhanced town centres and city halls across the realm.

It was often said that 'horse troughs were the lifeblood of the Plukes', a phrase attributed to an illustrious ancestor, Justus Pluke, who had also specialized in troughs. There was no doubt that Montague's expertise had helped to continue that high-profile and long-established Pluke family commitment. It was Montague's earnest desire to locate, renovate, record and photograph every horse trough in North Yorkshire, then East Yorkshire, West Yorkshire and South Yorkshire before expanding his endeavours further north into Durham and Northumberland, west into the Lake District and south into Derbyshire. He might even consider Lancashire if he had the time.

He regarded this self-imposed duty as a lifetime commitment, one he would continue with greater gusto when he retired with a modest pension. He might even compile an encyclopedia of horse troughs from around the world, or a ten-volume book of European horse troughs, or more books about English civic horse troughs from the Middle Ages, or horse troughs along the Great Wall of China or in the foothills of Everest. The scope was endless.

But any account of horse troughs within the North York Moors would be incomplete without proof of the existence of the renowned and almost legendary Blackamoor Trough. Blackamoor was an old name for this part of the moors.

'It must be hereabouts, Millicent.' He tried to sound very resolute. 'And if it is, I must find it. One cannot ignore such a persistent legend, it is the Holy Grail of North Yorkshire troughs, in fact it is probably the most unusual trough in the whole of England if the stories are true.'

'Are you sure this is the right place?' she asked daringly.

'We've been here more than two hours with nothing to show for it.'

'I'm sure it's the right place. All the records show it was just off the monks' trod which crossed these moors from Rosedale Abbey to Whitby Abbey, and the road we used to drive here follows that route. Other clues are that it lies midway between White Cross and Raven Cross. If you examine the route of that old road and mark the map with straight lines between those points, that is where we are now.'

'But old records were never very precise. When you read stories of people walking between places, their accounts seldom match each other. I think we need to expand our search, to find another vantage point, one nearby.'

'The main problem is that this heather is so deep and thick, it could be concealing the trough. It's not as if we have a stream or ghyll to guide us to it.'

'There's that howe over there.' She pointed to a Stone Age burial mound a couple of hundred yards away. Like the rock upon which they now stood, it was protruding above the heather. 'That's higher than this rock. Shall I go and look around from up there? It might give us a better view.'

'I'll come with you,' he offered. 'I'm convinced we'll never spot it from here.'

A few minutes later, they were standing on top of the howe, once again with Pluke sweeping the area to the north with his binoculars while Millicent shielded her eyes with her hand and stared towards the south. It was like looking for the proverbial needle in a haystack.

'There's been a fire over there.' Millicent pointed to a large patch of burnt moorland about a quarter of a mile away. 'A whole area of heather has been burnt away.'

'It's a swidden, sometimes called a swizzen.' Pluke aired his knowledge. 'It's the result of controlled burning. It's done every year, often in March before the grouse start their nesting. The landowner burns off about a sixth of a given area of heather, then the following year it will be the turn of another sixth and so on, so that over a period of years, the entire moorland is burnt.'

'Goodness! But why?'

'It destroys the old heather, clears and refreshes the ground and encourages new growth. New shoots of heather grow quickly and they're stronger and healthier than the old; the new shoots are needed to feed the grouse too, and in former times local people would remove the turf after the burning and use it for domestic fires.'

'So turf is not the same as peat? I know a lot of moorland farms had peat fires,' said Millicent.

'That's right, but they had turf fires too. Turf burns more slowly and gives out a lot of heat with a very pleasant scent. The thick heather stems which survived the flames were collected for kindling to light home fires. Those stubby stalks were called cowls, they were collected in big bundles called boddins, the local way of saying burdens. Boddins o' cowls, as the local people called them. The whole exercise of controlled burning was, and still is, a necessary, useful and very effective means of maintaining the heather and the moors.'

'It sounds rather dangerous to me,' she shuddered. 'You'd think accidents might happen.'

'They can – and did,' he said with authority. 'Sometimes a sudden wind can whip the flames away from the men who are protecting the moorland around the swidden, and the heather burns easily. It can blaze very furiously and quickly, especially in a stiff breeze, and the fire can run fast. There have been cases of men dying while burning swiddens, being overtaken by a running fire. There haven't been many deaths, it must be said, because the burning is always very carefully supervised by experienced workers and that's the way things are now. In every case, though, great care is taken when firing a swidden, but sadly accidents can still happen. One must be realistic about that.'

'That must be a dreadful way to die,' she said. 'It looks as if the heather over there has been carefully burnt off – there haven't been any reports of accidents, have there?

15

But look, it has exposed lots of rocks and boulders, Montague. I think you should look at it through your binoculars, your trough might be among those boulders, you know. From this distance, it's hard to distinguish things with the naked eye.'

'Yes, we must explore that burnt section,' he muttered as he turned his attention to the swidden. It was very prominent among the surrounding moorland due to its dark and sombre appearance among the sea of heather. It resembled a miniature forest of bare, grey and dead heather stalks which protruded from the ground where the fire had swept along.

The patch of moorland, around forty acres or so, was also riddled with stark grey boulders and stones, some on the surface of the moor and some half buried. Some were little bigger than a household brick while others were the size of a small car. Several were trough-sized, he noted. When the heather was fully grown, most of those smaller or half-buried rocks would be hidden from view but now everything was exposed as this patch of moorland began its new cycle of growth. Many people, especially townsfolk and tourists, found it hard to believe this kind of treatment was beneficial to the moorland, but the coming spring would rapidly reinforce that age-old wisdom.

He ranged his binoculars across the bare ground, halting at every large rock or boulder just in case it was really a stone trough, and he systematically scanned the entire swidden. It was remarkably rectangular, its length running from south to north, and its breadth from east to west. It was a well-conducted example of swidden burning which had not affected any of the adjoining moorland, save for the inevitable few scorched clumps along the banks of the boundary streams. Then he halted his binoculars.

'Oh my goodness, Millicent, oh dear . . . I must go over there.'

'You've found the trough?'

'No, not the trough. It looks like somebody lying in that swidden. Dead, if my eyes don't deceive me.'

Chapter Two

Some days earlier, Brent had had no difficulty finding his transport in the Arndale Centre car park. With a case full of clothes suitable for the open countryside along with a smart dark suit because his mother had reminded him he would be having dinner with His Lordship, he had nervously approached the vehicle, a grey eight-seater. A Ford Galaxy. A man standing outside had noticed his arrival and opened a door. Brent saw it contained five other people, all men.

'Brent, is it?' In his mid-thirties and surprisingly well-spoken, he was a large man with a shaven head showing signs of dark, stubbly hair. He was dressed in a white sweater and jeans. Brent had seen him around the leisure centre and swimming pool, but had never spoken to him until now. 'I'm Jake.'

Brent had fiddled around in the inner pocket of his fleece to locate his important prize letter with its personal identification code, but the man had brushed aside his efforts. 'No need, Brent, I recognize you. Put your case in the back. All right, lads, we're all here. Let's get this show on the road.'

Jake climbed into the driving seat and started the engine without making any other introductions. Brent did not know the others and sat alone in one of the nearside seats. Moments later, they were driving out of Manchester towards the M62, heading towards the A1 and eventually the North York Moors. A drive of about three hours.

'Excited, are you?' called Jake when everyone was settled. 'Looking forward to this trip?'

Brent could see Jake's eyes in the rear-facing mirror. 'Yes, very. I've never been to those moors before. I don't know of Mossgate Manor. Have you been, Jake?'

'Not me, no. It's new to me is this one. New to us all in fact.'

'So how did we get to win this prize? I never bought a ticket, and no one knows I'm keen on country life. I'd love to work on an estate, to work my way up, maybe to run it one day . . . I'd never earn enough to buy one.'

'Who can tell what might happen? Everybody needs a bit of luck in life and we've all got dreams, haven't we? Just thank your lucky stars it's your turn, Brent.'

There were murmurings of what sounded like agreement from the others, all otherwise silent in their seats. Jake continued to chatter but made no effort to draw them into conversation or to make introductions. Brent thought they must all be strangers to one another. Probably like him, they were just a little nervous and puzzled about all this. Brent felt sure they'd become well acquainted before the weekend was over or even before they reached Yorkshire.

'So how was I included in the draw?' persisted Brent.

'Somebody with influence must have heard you were a great fan of country estates, Brent, and the kind of life they offer. You'd mentioned it to Ali. She might have put your name forward, put your name in the hat in a manner of speaking.'

'Ali?'

'The girl at the leisure centre, the one you like to talk to at break times. Nice girl. She mentioned you and your dreams so my boss thought you'd like a chance to win this trip.'

'Yes, I think I did talk to her about my dreams, that's right.'

'So you've won, good luck to you. You might get a chance to meet my boss during the weekend. He'll tell you all about it, he makes all the contacts and sees to the arrangements.'

'I'm really amazed I've won, I can't really believe it.' Brent turned to watch the ceaseless traffic outside. 'But it's all so wonderful, such a thrill.'

During the journey, none of the others spoke to him and, if he was honest, they didn't look a bit like the sort of people you'd expect to want to win a shooting party on a country estate. In fact they looked more like foreigners and they'd even been chatting in a strange language. And they all wore white T-shirts and jeans. Maybe they were here to study English rural life?

'So what's the intelligence from Derbyshire?' asked DCI Sanders during another meeting.

'Not a lot, sir,' said Detective Sergeant Rogers. 'A silver people carrier was seen with seven men aboard, parked up. It was later seen near that mine shaft with seven men. When it left, it had six men on board. The witness, a National Park ranger, is reliable. He reckons if a body was thrown down that pit shaft, it would never be found and never be recovered. A search has been made but the pit is too deep, no caver in the world can get right down there.'

'And the timing coincides with a missing paedophile?'

'Yes, sir, a scout master called Patterson, Manchester-based but a lover of the Peak District. Vanished without a trace.'

'Any links with the leisure centre?'

'Yes, he ran evening classes there, his subject was the Peak District.'

'So a pattern is emerging?'

'Of sorts,' said Lynn Rogers. 'It's all very loose at the moment.'

'Am I right in thinking Jacob Hampson has a silvery-grey people carrier? A Ford Galaxy?'

'He does.'

'As I said earlier, we must keep a closer eye on that character. We need to know more about him and his background. Monitor his movements, make him a target.'

'I've already got a scheme in action, sir.'

'Good, and keep in touch. Be sure to tell me if more men are reported missing from home.'

It was eight days after Brent had taken his ride in that people carrier that Montague Pluke approached the body with all the care of an experienced detective.

In his voluminous old beige and black patterned coaching overcoat (a Pluke family heirloom), uncreased and baggy trousers of similar colour, his panama hat, pink socks, light beige spats and brogue shoes, he looked like anything but a famous detective. Peculiar though he might appear, he was no longer a trough expert searching for famous or missing examples of that stonemason's craft; he was now a senior detective approaching what could be the scene of a murder.

As they approached, he advised Millicent to remain at a distance, not only because her presence might contaminate the area by leaving unwanted evidence or spoiling clues, but also because if the body had been severely burnt, it would be a rather unwholesome sight. He did not want her to be upset or suffer later from nightmares. Struggling through the knee-high heather, Millicent accompanied Montague down a slope towards the edge of the swidden where they found a natural boundary. It was one of the narrow streams whose bankside vegetation had been blackened and contorted by the heat. At the far side of the narrow strip of water, the heather had been completely burnt away to leave those leafless cowls of heather. There being no footpaths hereabouts, the Plukes completed their descent and reached the edge of the ghyll with the swidden rising before them. Standing on the banks of the shallow water they could not see the far side of the burnt area, only that part closest to them. That patch of ground rose until it disappeared over the summit and, at this point, Pluke could not see the body.

It was just over that summit, close to a large rock on land which sloped gently away at the far side. He must cross the beck and then some of the turf but he would mark his path just in case this proved to be the scene of a crime. His route would then be used by others, to limit as far as possible any contamination of the scene.

'The body is just over the crest of that hill near a large rock roughly in the centre of the swidden,' he explained. 'The rock's a good landmark, I'll head that way and make an assessment of the situation. The moment I've done that, I'll return to let you know what I find.'

Millicent remained at a distance as Pluke, after leaping across the narrow ghyll, headed for the northern edge then turned towards the big rock. As he approached the top of the rise, he could see the body. It was lying to the east of the rock, almost in its shadow; it was face down with the head towards the north. It was a male person, fully clothed. Even from a distance, Pluke could see the highly visible results of the fire. Scorched clothing – jeans and the burnt remains of a light blue T-shirt, very brown skin where it was exposed, most hair burnt away, fingers burnt off, feet and toes protected by white trainers. Each arm was lying close to his side, and the legs were together. There was a moderate amount of fire damage which suggested a rapidly passing flame. It had not been an intense and long-lasting fire, that was evident. The body was far from being destroyed. He was young, late twenties? Thirty even. Slim and he'd had dark hair. The age was little more than a guess but Pluke was considering the size and general appearance of the casualty.

He stood motionless for several minutes as he gazed upon this awful scene, his memory absorbing everything he could see. The big sheltering rock to the west of the body. The huge acreage of burnt heather which was the size of several football pitches with close-growing cowls sticking up from the ground like miniature leafless trees.

21

There were lots of stones and rocks which had been exposed by the fire. Near the body's head was a small cairn of stones, each about the size of a large potato. He reckoned there were around two dozen stones, all probably collected from this moorland. They had the same general appearance as the stones littered about the swidden, not slate like the Lake District but sandstone or granite. The cairn was undoubtedly the work of human hands.

The patch of ground upon which the body lay did not bear much heather. It was a tiny area of grass but such pieces of grass-covered land, only a few feet wide and a few feet long, were a feature of these moorlands. Scattered about the moor, they were just large enough to accommodate a sheep or even a human body and were popular with the moorland sheep who often slept there. This man was lying on one of those patches; if the thick heather hadn't been burnt, the body would have been surrounded and hidden by it. It would have been quite invisible, even at close quarters.

Now, thanks to the fire, it was fully exposed. As Pluke studied the scene, he realized the body had been carefully arranged. It had been placed there. It had not fallen into that position or been merely abandoned. He could see, beyond any doubt, that the casualty was dead but was he a victim of the fire? Or had he collapsed while hiking? In clothes like this? He supposed someone might go walking in jeans and a T-shirt with trainers on his feet, but they were not very sensible for hiking or rambling, certainly not here and certainly not at this time of year. Was he someone who'd been sleeping or resting in the heather, only to be overwhelmed by the flames? Someone who'd died from natural causes in this lonely place? Or had he died from other means? If the fire hadn't cleared the scene, the body might never have been discovered. Thick heather could conceal such a lot and undiscovered bodies, humans and animals, could quickly disappear due to decomposition and the work of nature. The scattered bones of many a dead sheep were proof of this. Pluke was sure this body had not been dumped *after* being burnt but he must not lose sight of the fact that it could have been here some time *before* the swidden had been fired. Forensic tests beneath the body might reveal useful information, and he knew that tests on the body would show whether death had occurred before, during or after the burning. A post-mortem would also show whether death was due to some other cause.

So was it a murder, with the killer trying to dispose of the body in this way? Or was it nothing more than a tragic accident? Suicide even? He felt not.

In his view, the neat arrangement of the body and its method of disposal suggested murder. So when had this swidden been burnt? Pluke needed answers to a lot of questions. With his thoughts ranging across many possibilities, he approached the body, knelt at its side and touched it briefly on the cheek. It was cold with death but brown like mahogany and leathery due to the heat and smoke. Preserved, like a kipper. And then he saw the little hole in the skull. Near the temple. The right temple. A bullet hole. It looked like one caused by a small calibre bullet, probably from a .22 firearm by the look of it. That caused him to search around to see if there was a gun of any kind, or the remains of one, lying nearby.

There wasn't one within sight but there were hundreds of acres of heather around him. So could this be suicide? Not with the arms lying close to his side. The hole in the temple was a common indication of self-destruction so he must consider the possibility but with no sign of a gun it was improbable. Unless someone had come along and removed the gun? Or was it hidden under the body?

Or had someone removed the gun without even noticing the body? That might be possible with the heather in full growth. If a gun had been dropped nearby and caught by the fire, it would have been made useless but removing it, in whatever condition, may have been a means of concealing the suicide. Would someone do that? Remove the gun while not informing the police of the discovery of the body? That was most unlikely, considered Pluke – but not impossible. A family member might want to do that. In the world of jealous families and in the world of crime nothing was impossible, but after due consideration he did feel suicide was unlikely.

There were some signs of decomposition, he realized, but he wondered how the smoke and heat had helped preserve this body. Or was a modest rate of decomposition due to the fact the body had not been here very long? The weather was cool too, being March, but in recent days it had been wet. All manner of possibilities ranged through his head as he crouched beside the body, but he did not attempt to search the pockets or take any further action such as turning over the body. If the gun was underneath, it would have to remain until the forensic pathologist had examined the corpse in its present position.

All that kind of thing was for the experts to deal with – a great deal of valuable information could be obtained from a dead body.

This was not an emergency because there was nothing he could do for the victim but it was time to contact Crickledale Police Station. Saturday mornings weren't the best of times to catch people in their offices, but he must do what was immediately necessary. Report the presence of the body, express his opinion that the death was suspicious and then assume his professional role as Detective Inspector in charge of Crickledale Sub-Divisional Criminal Investigation Department. The body was within his jurisdiction, he realized.

He returned to Millicent who was waiting patiently beside the ghyll with her mobile telephone already out of her haversack and clutched in her hand. The haversack stood on the ground at her side; it contained their maps, waterproofs and some light refreshments but they might not now be required. She knew by the expression on Montague's face that the body required his professional

24

attention. He was back on duty now, the trough hunt being relegated to the back of his mind.

'Press the green button then figure two.' She passed the telephone to him. 'That calls Crickledale Police Station, the numbers are stored in its memory.'

'Thank you, Millicent. I fear we have a suspicious death in the swidden,' and he briefly described his discovery.

'Then you must do what you must.' She waited and watched as he called his office. When the duty constable responded, Pluke asked to be connected with the tiny Control Room where Sergeant Cockfield pronounced Cofield was in charge.

'Ah, good morning, Sergeant,' shouted Pluke into the mobile. 'Detective Inspector Pluke here, calling from the Blackamoor region of the moors.'

'Good morning, sir,' bellowed Cockfield pronounced Cofield. 'It sounds windy, wherever you're ringing from, unless you're almost out of range.'

'It's not windy but not the best of places for communications of this kind,' admitted Pluke. 'You sound a long way off. Static interference or something. But I am calling because I have found a body on the moors, and I regret to say it is a suspicious death.'

'Not another one, sir! You've a habit of finding bodies when you're supposed to be enjoying your weekend off.'

'I have put myself back on duty, Sergeant, but I will require the usual assistance for a case of suspected murder. Forensic scientists and a pathologist, scenes of crime team, a doctor to certify death, task force to search the scene, photographers to record the scene, Incident Room to be established and teams of detectives to conduct house-to-house enquiries. And I need the services of Detective Sergeant Wayne Wain. Will you arrange all that, please? I shall remain at the scene, Sergeant, until reinforcements arrive.' He then provided the map reference with details of how to approach it.

'Very good, sir, I'll set things in motion. Do you have

more details, something we can start work on right away?'

Pluke provided an account of the circumstances so that all the incoming teams would be aware of the situation. He stressed the remoteness of the area, the possible cause of death and that the crime scene had been cleansed by fire. He also added a note about the small cairn of stones, stressing he wanted it photographed and preserved, along with any other evidence found nearby. Pluke asked the sergeant to arrange a check of missing persons records, particularly those in this area, to see whether any men, especially those less than thirty or even forty, had been reported absent from their usual haunts or places of work. Sergeant Cockfield pronounced Cofield assured Pluke he would do everything that was necessary and that the support services would report to Pluke on site as soon as possible. Pluke warned him that the teams would have to park their vehicles on the roadside, some two hundred yards from the scene. Not even a 4x4 vehicle could cope with those boulder-littered heather regions.

'There,' said Pluke to Millicent. 'That's all I can do for the time being. I need not detain you any longer, Millicent, and suggest you take the car home. I will remain until my staff arrive and when we finish for the day, I will ask Detective Sergeant Wain to drive me home.'

'A good idea, Montague. I'll leave you with something to eat from our bag, and you'd better keep the mobile phone. You can operate it, can you?'

He could not drive the car – or to be precise, he could drive it but he was considered such a danger on the road that his police colleagues had forbidden him to drive official vehicles. For like reasons, Millicent drove their family car because he frightened the life out of her whenever he took the wheel. And, she had to admit, she had never seen him in action with a mobile phone. She wondered if he could operate it any better than he could use the television remote control box. He still couldn't copy or play a video.

26

'You press the green button to make a call.' She showed him the actual button. 'Then press number one for our private phone and number two for your office, those numbers are programmed in. Press number three to dial any other number and press the relevant keys. And press red to end a call.'

'That sounds easy enough,' he replied as he accepted the mysterious device. 'Thank you, Millicent. I'm sorry our day out has come to this sudden and rather unpleasant end.'

'Not to worry, Montague, you must do your duty. I will go home and expect you for dinner this evening? Eightish?'

She did not tell him she would pop into town this afternoon to do a little shopping. Montague hated shops and shopping so with him nicely out of the way and a useful murder enquiry to keep him occupied, she could indulge in a little carefree trip of her very own. She enjoyed life when Montague had to work at weekends; it made such a welcome change from hunting horse troughs.

'If there is any change in that arrangement, I'll call you,' he said. 'I shall do so by pressing green then one. I think I've got it!'

And so she began to trek through the rough heather back to her car on the roadside about two hundred yards away. She might even keep her eyes open for the Blackamoor Trough en route.

Montague would be so pleased if she found it.

Within the hour, support service vehicles began to assemble on the roadside closest to the northern end of the swidden. They brought news that no one matching the brief description of the victim had been reported missing locally, but Pluke decided there should be no further activity on site until Dr Meredith, the forensic pathologist, had

27

examined the body and the scene. It was vital he completed his work ahead of the inevitable disturbance created by the murder investigation. The police doctor was among the first to arrive, having been working near Crickledale, and he certified that the body was dead.

He departed before the arrival of Simon Meredith, the forensic pathologist, a slightly built man with thinning fair hair, a matching moustache and half-rimmed spectacles. Shortly before eleven thirty, he plodded through the heather with his small black case of mysterious instruments and bottles and he greeted Pluke.

'Good morning, Mr Pluke, you've managed to find another one then?'

'Sorry about that, Mr Meredith. I assure you I had no intention of discovering a dead body in suspicious circumstances, in truth I was seeking the famous Blackamoor Trough. This was pure chance.'

'A Pluke fluke, as one might say. You do seem to have an uncanny knack of finding bodies as you hunt your troughs, Mr Pluke, and it's usually at weekends when I'm trying to catch up with my painting and decorating. It's usually people walking dogs, not detectives, who find bodies. So, what have we this time?'

Pluke explained, giving Meredith a full account with due emphasis on the swidden-burning practice, and then the scientist said he would examine the body.

As the assembled police officers waited near the little ghyll, Pluke guided Meredith across the swidden by the route he had earlier taken, using the big boulder as his marker, but he remained at a distance while Meredith carried out his assessment. First he studied the scene, making rough notes and a sketch in a reporter's notebook, and then he squatted at points around the body to peer at it from different angles. Finally, he tilted the corpse to look at the ground and anything else beneath – there was no gun or other weapon – and to see the face, allowing it to fall back into its position so that the police photographers could record every detail. They made good use of both digital cameras and videotape and it took several minutes for Meredith to satisfy his professional curiosity.

'The body was definitely in this position before the fire started,' he told Pluke. 'I have noted the hole in the skull and although it has all the appearances of a small calibre bullet wound, I cannot confirm that that is the cause of death until I have examined the body in laboratory conditions. I can confirm, however, that the victim was dead prior to being placed in the path of the fire; the ground beneath, which is a clear patch of moorland turf with no heather stems, has not been affected by the flames and I see no evidence of suicide, Mr Pluke. No weapon is nearby and I shall be most interested to learn whether your searches reveal any spent ammunition. Perhaps he was murdered some distance from here? So yes, you have a murder investigation on your hands and you need to determine whether the fire was a means of disposing of the remains and concealing the crime, or merely incidental.'

'Many people have died of natural causes on these moors in the past, Mr Meredith,' said Pluke. 'In some cases, their bodies were not found for years and, I suspect, some have never been found at all. If this area of moorland had not been burnt, the body might never have been discovered, and certainly not so quickly.'

'Exactly, Mr Pluke. That is something to consider. Was he killed here or elsewhere? Another puzzle. Now, once your officers have finished with the body, it can be removed to my laboratory and I will let you have my report as soon as possible. Before I leave, though, I will take a sample of earth from beneath the body and another sample of burnt turf, just in case it becomes necessary to analyse it. He might have been lying dead on some other surface, Mr Pluke, some other patch of ground perhaps. In a barn maybe. Or beach. Or garden. Or on a carpet. There may be particles of dust or fibres from such a site on his clothing or body, in the hair for example, or what remains of his hair. We might even be able to identify his place of death . . . and I stress *might*. The ground is now cold, by the way, so I'd say the fire was not burning overnight or earlier this morning. Now, does anything strike you as odd with this scenario?'

'Yes,' said Pluke. 'The fact that the fellow is not dressed for hiking or rambling, and also that he has no jacket, sweater or overcoat. Just a T-shirt and jeans. And trainers. It is most unusual to be on these moors at this time of year without adequate clothing, and I think that dispenses with the idea he was a serious hiker or rambler. He may have been taking a little light exercise but he has nothing with him such as binoculars, vacuum flask, bag of any kind . . . there are no other remains apart from his. I would draw your attention to that little cairn of stones too. Interesting to say the least. There are no roads or footpaths nearby and on top of that, the head wound is in an odd place, if it's not suicide. Most people who are murdered are not shot in the temple like this man. And I feel the body has been arranged where it lies, not just dumped. If he had been shot and fallen dead, he would not have landed in such a neat state. You will note the body is arranged face down with the head towards the north and arms by his side.'

'All very valid points, Mr Pluke, and I agree with you, although I must say the little pile of stones puzzles me. Surely lots of people build this kind of thing on the moors, and on mountain tops? Hikers and climbers do so, you find cairns of varying sizes on all manner of summits, it's a tradition for climbers to add one when they conquer a peak. I doubt if this has anything to do with the body.'

'I would venture to disagree, Mr Meredith. In the very distant past, ancient peoples built cairns where bodies had met a violent death. It was to prevent their ghosts haunting the locality or pursuing the killer. I cannot ignore the possibility that the killer might have built that cairn.'

'Well, you're the expert on such things, but in my view it might be nothing more than a pile of stones built some time ago by a child during a family picnic.'

'That's always possible,' agreed Pluke. 'But whatever its source, its presence at the crime scene must be noted.'

'Then so it shall be,' acknowledged Meredith. 'Now, Mr Pluke, I think we agree that the body has been placed here by a third party or parties? I agree with you that the body has been carefully positioned so I'd say he did not die here. He was dead before he was placed here; death seems to have been by shooting which occurred before the fire started, and it must therefore have been at another scene. That is my opinion, albeit provisional until I have completed my laboratory examination and tests.'

'That's enough for us to be going on with at the moment,' agreed Pluke. 'But if the body was carried here, we must remember there are no paths or tracks to this scene, so how did anyone carry him here? It is almost certainly beyond the strength of one man to carry a dead body such a distance over rough terrain.'

'Exactly, Mr Pluke. How – and why – did the body of a young man in casual clothes come to be lying in the middle of these moors, with or without the fire? We shall remove him by stretcher – so perhaps that is how the corpse was transported?'

'It takes at least two to carry a stretcher,' said Pluke.

'So more than one person was surely involved in this? That is interesting. Now, do we know his identity?'

'Not yet, we've not searched his clothing for evidence but we've no reports of locally missing persons who match this description.'

'A search of his clothing can be done in the laboratory, we need those conditions to ensure we collect any debris from his clothes and remains. Your coroner's officer can search for documents and other evidence, although I suspect nothing will be found. I'm sure whoever did this does not want him named, that's why he was dumped in such a remote place. And, you will note, his fingertips have burnt away which rules out identification by fingerprints. DNA might assist, of course, providing we can get a lead as to his possible identity.'

'What about the time of death?' asked Pluke.

'Almost impossible to say with any degree of accuracy,'

31

admitted Meredith. 'It could be as long ago as a week or even ten days bearing in mind the rate of decomposition, the weather and the effects of smoke. He was dead before the fire started and it shouldn't be difficult to find the person or persons who lit or supervised that fire. Then you'll know when the moor was burnt. I may learn more from the post-mortem and from deposits on him and his clothing. Bring the body to my laboratory when you're ready. Now I must be getting along. Goodbye, Mr Pluke.'

When scenes of crime, the task force and the police photographers had all finished with the body, a windowless van, already parked on the roadside, conveyed it to Meredith's laboratory. Pluke then called for members of the task force and scenes of crime team to begin their fingertip search of the swidden and surrounding heather-clad moorland, explaining that the murder weapon might be a .22 rifle or pistol but definitely not a shotgun.

It might have been discarded by the killer so it could be anywhere within the 553 square miles of heather moorland – and it might be very close to the body or miles away. Task force members were asked especially to seek any rounds of spent .22 ammunition but there could be other evidence too – anything they found would be regarded as material until the contrary was proved. Pluke reinforced his wish that the cairn of stones be preserved too, and photographed. Then the stones must be treated as evidence and retained, for scientific examination if necessary. A thorough search of the swidden would not be too difficult as the heather had been burnt off, but to search among the neighbouring acres would present its own tough problems – and that heather couldn't be burnt off because it would destroy any evidence it may conceal. And so began a long, tedious but very systematic scrutiny of this part of the moorland.

Pluke's next job was to authorize the establishment of the Incident Room and that would be the responsibility of Detective Inspector Horsley. Having attended the scene and discussed things with Pluke, Horsley confirmed he had sufficient information and personnel to have the Incident Room up-and-running within an hour or so. The question was where? Any suitable premises could be utilized but ideally it should be as close as possible to the scene of the crime. Because it required access to modern communications systems, including the Police National Computer, the Driver and Vehicle Licensing Centre's records at Swansea, various databases and specialist websites, a fully operational police station was usually the best option even if it was some distance away.

And so, because there were no suitable buildings on these heights, Crickledale Sub-Divisional Police Headquarters was nominated. Horsley went away to set up his Incident Room which would include liaison with other police forces, supplying information to the Force Press Officer, initiating routine enquiries, checking names for criminal records or missing persons, filing and analysing all statements, storing data on computers and establishing the Action Book which would record and monitor the work of all teams of detectives, whether on house-to-house enquiries or dealing with more specialized actions. The Incident Room would be the nerve centre of the investigation, becoming more important as time passed and activity at the scene was necessarily reduced. Pluke suggested that most of the thirty detectives who had presented themselves at the scene, and who were now standing around in little groups beside the ghyll while awaiting orders, could be usefully deployed on house-to-house enquiries – not that there were many houses on these heights. However, Hurnehow village was nearby and there were others within four or five miles or so in any direction, along with farms, cottages and estates. He asked Horsley to arrange suitable enquiries in the neighbourhood, chiefly to establish whether anyone had seen a solitary man walking on the moors within, say, the last fortnight, or any odd incident on the moors. He might also consider setting up road blocks to ask motorists, delivery drivers and regular road users the same question.

And so, as matters became more organized and a plan with a sense of purpose began to develop, Pluke was happy to see Detective Sergeant Wayne Wain heading towards him through the thick heather. Tall, dark and handsome with a head of thick black hair, the sergeant always attracted a host of women but now he was alone, tramping through the heather in his smart dark suit. Wayne was Pluke's deputy.

'Good morning, sir.' He was sweating profusely. 'If you don't mind me saying so, you do find bodies in some peculiar and out-of-the-way places. This is the middle of nowhere!'

'How can there be a middle of nowhere, Wayne?' asked Pluke in all seriousness. 'I would think such a thing would be mathematically or geographically impossible!'

He referred to Wayne by his first name because it sounded exactly the same as his surname; normally, Pluke never addressed other officers by their first names, he considered it far too informal so far as maintaining good relations with his subordinates was concerned.

'So what have we got now, sir?' Wayne quickly changed the subject whereupon Pluke explained in great detail the progress to date.

When he'd finished, Wayne said, 'Good. Well, I arrived slightly later than the others because I popped into the National Park offices on the way. I thought it might be sensible to find out who this swidden belongs to. The map reference you gave to Control was a great help.'

'Excellent, Wayne, well done. So you've found the answer?'

'I have, sir.'

'Good, then let us find out who set fire to this moorland, and when.'

Chapter Three

This is what happened when Brent arrived on the moors.

'This is as far we go.' Jake turned to him as the people carrier came to a halt somewhere in the middle of a dark and featureless stretch of moorland. Jake and his five companions prepared to disembark and so Brent, wondering why they had stopped with no sign of any house and certainly no mansion in the vicinity, did likewise. The five had said nothing to him during the three-hour trip, not even when they'd stopped for a snack, although they had chattered among themselves in a language he did not understand. Jake used the same tongue when speaking to them, and he seemed very fluent. Having spent this short time with them, Brent wondered how they would cope with an entire weekend in an English setting, even if it was broken up with practicals, tuition, visits and meals. Why on earth had these people wanted to win such a privileged weekend?

'Where are we?' As he climbed out of the rear with the headlights still blazing, Brent tried to look into the inky blackness but there was nothing. No lights. No houses. No trees. No people. Nothing. Just an all-embracing darkness.

'You don't need to know where we are, Brent. Now, you're coming with us.'

'To the manor?'

'No, not to the manor. There is no manor, Brent. There is nothing more for you,' and in the light of the vehicle he was horrified to see that all six men carried guns. Handguns. Small enough to be easily concealed in their clothing . . .

'Walk.' Jake prodded Brent in the back. 'Walk as far as the car lights shine.'

'But what are you doing? Why are you doing this? What's happening?'

'We are going to kill you, Brent. Out here where no one will find you.'

'Kill me?' Surely this was some kind of joke . . . a test! That's it. It must be some kind of test of character. 'You can't be serious . . . it's a joke, a test of some sort, so tell me what to do . . .'

In disbelief combined with genuine fear, he tried to run away, to escape these people in case they were mad. He could hide out there in the pitch darkness. But a large strong hand seized his collar and halted him, then propelled him forwards as the cold steel of a gun's muzzle touched his neck. The heather was snatching at his jeans: it was difficult to walk. He stumbled along, not really believing what was happening, thinking this must all be a game, some weird test of his reactions, but with the gun pressing into the back of his neck he wondered if it was for real. He started to shout and cry, hoping someone, even out here, might hear him. But there was only him and these men and the lights of their vehicle.

'Shut up. Just walk, Brent, just walk.' It was Jake's voice, now harsh, cold and strong instead of being friendly and warm.

In his sobbing, stumbling terror, Brent was propelled across the moor until they came almost to the limit of the car's headlights. Beyond was sheer darkness.

'We are from the Church of the White Kelts, Brent, an ancient Celtic faith whose aims were, and still are, absolute purity among the population. Impure people were, and are, disposed of. We cannot tolerate impurity in human beings.'

'But . . . I don't understand . . . is this a joke?'

36

'It is not a joke, Brent. To make society pure, we dispose of the impure so you must go. This is for all those little girls, Brent, those the police know about and those they don't. And it is especially for my little girl, the one you killed and threw in the canal. You didn't know she was mine, did you? Neither did the police. But from this day forward, you are not going to touch, harm or kill any more little girls, Brent.'

'You can't mean this, you can't . . .'

They stood in front of him in a semicircle, all six of them with Jake to his right. All in their white tops with their guns pointing towards the ground . . . He was quivering with fear, he couldn't speak, he didn't believe they would really do anything . . . It was just a warning, wasn't it? Then he croaked his final words.

'I'll leave them all alone, they loved me and I loved them . . . but I'll leave them alone from now on, I promise . . .'

'Yes, you will, Brent, oh yes you will. From this day, you will not touch another little girl. Only one of these guns contains a real bullet, the rest are blanks. We shall not know who killed you and neither will you,' and within a split second, the guns were raised to point at his head, each less than two feet away. 'Now,' shouted Jake as Brent turned his head in an attempt to avoid them. There was a sharp crack and Brent Fowler fell dead into the heather. It was all over in seconds.

'Don't eject the shells,' Jake reminded them in Serbo-Croatian. 'Don't look at his head to see which gun got him. Now let's carry him over to that high spot, nobody'll never find him there.'

With their eyes now accustomed to the darkness in the reduced light from the vehicle, they could see the rising ground against the lighter skyline. Two men seized a leg each, two more an arm each and a fifth held his head. They carried him deep into the heather as Jake, walking ahead, produced a torch from his pocket. They found a patch of grass among the thick heather, just the right size to accommodate a body. Carefully, they laid Brent face down with his head to the north then placed the arms by his side and closed the legs. With practiced efficiency, they searched his clothing and body, and removed everything that might help identify the remains, including his wallet and watch. And the prize letter he had received.

Finally, without a word, they hunted among the heather for stones, found enough and made a little cairn. No one asked Jake why he insisted on doing this or why he wanted the head pointing north with the corpse face down. But he was the boss. There were times he'd even brought his own bagful of small stones, just to be sure he had a supply.

'Right, that's it. Make sure you've left nothing.'

When they returned to their vehicle, they all stood outside and peed against the wheels. This suggested a reason for stopping in this remote place in case someone had seen the vehicle and noted its number, but in fact no one had passed along that road while they were busy. By the time they returned home, they had disposed of all the evidence, including Brent's luggage for the weekend. Bits were placed in wheelie bins in several towns and villages, with nothing to indicate their origin. Items with names or identifying features were burnt on isolated sites.

On the way back to Manchester, they stopped in Oldham and set fire to a silver Galaxy they had stolen earlier and abandoned there. It was just another device to throw the police off the trail.

'That circular we issued, about the silver people carrier,' said Lynn Rogers. 'It's produced a result. One was sighted in the Lake District, a few weeks ago, perhaps in suspicious circumstances. Beside a lake, with men inside. Innocent or not? We've no idea.'

'Wasn't one of those missing men keen on lakeland walks?' asked Sanders, mindful of the Derbyshire sighting.

'He was, he's the one we think has been weighted down in Wastwater – a fisherman reported seeing something dumped from a rowing boat but we can't search the bed, it's too deep. Besides, it might have been a dead dog.'

'But he was a paedophile, sir? The one who might be in Wastwater?'

'Yes, the fellow we think it could be did have convictions. There's another six from Manchester alone who are unaccounted for – these kidnappers are experts, Lynn, we need to know how they find their victims and persuade them to take a ride in that carrier.'

'The vehicle was probably stolen, sir?'

'Perhaps or perhaps not. It's odd each one seen has been silver. You can't guarantee to pick your own colour when you're nicking vehicles, Lynn. Not as a rule.'

'So they're using the vehicle legitimately?'

'Or appearing to do so!'

'We've a lot more work on this one, sir. Anything more on Hampson?'

'Nothing, but it's early days. We know he has no known background, no police record and no job yet plenty of money. A false identity perhaps? Some kind of illegal immigrant? We've a lot to do on him so let's get down to it.'

As Pluke and Wayne Wain trudged back to Wain's car through the trouser tugging heather, Pluke was told that the swidden, and hundreds of acres of moorland which surrounded it, belonged to the Hurne estate. The rights for grazing sheep on that section of the moor were leased to a local farmer called Henry Roache. He was the tenant of the estate's Home Farm. The shooting rights over the moor, which included that particular piece of land, remained with the Hurne estate, although there were concessions for the benefit of Roache in his role as tenant.

Apart from the right to shoot grouse during the season, he could also take other game in season such as pheasant or partridge should they venture on to the moors, as well as rabbits and hares. He also had the right to kill vermin such as foxes, rats, mice and wood pigeons, and he could take turf or peat from specified sites without charge. According to the girl in the National Park office, the swidden burning would probably have been arranged by the estate and completed under the supervision of an experienced member of staff. That was the usual procedure.

'Then let us proceed to the estate office,' said Pluke. 'You know where it is?'

'The girl told me to go to Hurnehow village,' Wayne told him. 'Just past the church, we'll see the gates which lead up to the Hall and there are signs in the grounds directing us to the estate office, it's behind the big house.'

Hurnehow lay in a lush hollow close to the southern edge of the moors, well away from the more windswept and barren heights. A village of sturdy stone-built houses and some three hundred inhabitants, it boasted an inn, a shop, a post office, a garage and several bed-and-breakfast places. These were all situated pleasingly around an undulating village green whose lawn-like surface was shorn smooth by the moorland sheep, and through it ran a fast-moving peat stream whose water was often the warm colour of malt whisky. Once upon a time, the stream flowed across water-splashes and fords, but they had been replaced by neat and picturesque little stone bridges. Not surprisingly, the village, and especially its green, was a mecca for day-trippers during the summer months although today it was quiet. Few tourists ventured here during March but in the summer, gift shops, tearooms and an art gallery opened, an ice-cream van touted for business, tourists wandered like lost sheep and the village car park was always full. Wayne had no trouble locating the estate's entrance. The two ornate iron gates were standing open as he drove between the tall pillars, each with a large carved stone figure of a cockatrice standing on top. There was also the silhouetted outline of a cockatrice in the estate's colourful armorial bearings which adorned the gates.

'Why the dragon, sir?' asked Wayne, indicating the

cockatrice figures and knowing Pluke was an endless source of information on obscure subjects.

'It's not a dragon, Wayne, that creature is a cockatrice.'

'It looks like a dragon to me.'

'You should be more observant, Wayne. Take a closer look and you will see it has only two legs. It is a cross between a dragon and a bird, being hatched by a dragon or a serpent from a cock's egg. You will note it has the wings of a bird, the tail of a dragon and the head of a cockerel. It was not welcome in any community, Wayne, because legend said it could kill any living thing with a mere glance.'

'Nasty, sir. So I suppose the villagers were terrified of it?'

'I am sure they were, Wayne, but the creature could be dealt with very easily. All you had to do was place a mirror just outside its lair. When it saw its own reflection, it died. All that was needed was a knight in shining armour who was bold enough to approach its lair, armed with a mirror. Its own reflection killed it. Wonderful stuff, Wayne.'

'So, once mirrors were invented, it would quickly make itself extinct?'

'Indeed it did, Wayne, indeed it did. You don't see many live ones around nowadays. Ah, I see the estate office sign ahead. Bear left before we reach the main building, it's round the back. I hope someone is working.'

Moments later, they eased to a halt outside the office door. Wayne had no time to ask Pluke why this estate would adopt such a dangerous mythical creature as its emblem, for in a moment Pluke was out of the car and striding purposefully towards the green door marked *Office*. There was a secondary notice saying, *Knock and enter*, which he did, with Wayne hurrying behind clutching his briefcase.

Inside was a counter which acted as a barrier and behind it were two desks along with an array of computers, filing cabinets and all the paraphernalia of a busy commercial concern. A dark-haired young man was seated before one of the computer screens, concentrating upon something which looked like a colourful chart or display. Dressed in jeans and a light blue sweater, he continued to work, apparently unaware of the incomers.

'Ahem,' called Pluke.

'Oh, sorry, I didn't hear you come in.' The young man saved whatever he was working on and rose from his chair. 'I'm sorry, the office is closed.'

'I need to speak to someone in charge. I am Detective Inspector Pluke from Crickledale Sub-Divisional Police Headquarters, and this is my colleague, Detective Sergeant Wain.'

'Oh, this sounds serious, you'll need my father. Dad?' he shouted.

'Hello,' returned a well-spoken male voice which came from within an adjoining room with an open door at the left of the office. 'A moment, if you please.'

As they waited, Wayne noticed more cockatrice emblems on things like file covers, letter-headings and internal memos and then a man appeared through the open door. In his shirtsleeves, he was in his late fifties, estimated Pluke, very tall with a head of dark hair and an air of confidence. He wore a cream shirt with a plain green tie and Lovat green trousers; he was an older version of the youngster who now stood to one side and watched with interest.

'Yes?' He studied the two visitors, noting the odd character in the dark-rimmed spectacles with hair sticking out beneath a panama hat and wearing an ancient overcoat which had seen better days. His companion was much younger and dressed more soberly and smartly. 'We're shut, you know, and we don't do tours of the house.'

'They're detectives, Dad, not tourists.'

'I am Detective Inspector Pluke from Crickledale Sub-Divisional Police Headquarters,' announced Pluke with all the seriousness he could muster. He fished his warrant card from one of his commodious pockets and passed it to the man. 'And this is my colleague, Detective Sergeant Wain from the same station.'

'Oh,' said the man, glancing at the document and clearly interested to know what this was all about. 'Is something wrong, Inspector?'

'To whom am I speaking?' asked Pluke, returning his card to the depths of a pocket.

'My name is Hurne, Sebastian Hurne, and this is my son, Jonathan.'

'I was hoping to speak to the estate agent . . .'

'Won't I do? This is my house,' grinned the man. 'It's Saturday, Mr Pluke, one can't get staff to work weekends these days, secretaries can't understand that our work continues long after five o'clock seven days a week and you can't always rely on estate agents to be there when they're needed. I'm taking the opportunity to catch up with my own office work and Jonathan is surfing the internet, whatever that means . . . looking for holidays, I think. So what can I do for you?'

'Have you the map, please, Wayne?' asked Pluke. 'I shall show Mr Hurne the patch of moorland in which we are interested.'

Wayne took a map from his briefcase and spread it along the counter, then Pluke found the map reference and stabbed a point with his finger.

'There is a piece of moorland about here, Mr Hurne,' he said. 'It has been burnt, a swidden as we call it. Am I right in believing your estate owns it?'

'Yes.' Hurne did not hesitate. 'It's the only swidden up there this year. I can't see why that would interest the police. You know why we do that? It's not vandalism or arson, we burn off the heather by rotation under strict control, good husbandry and all that.'

'I know the procedures, thank you,' Pluke assured him. 'But there is a problem. We have found a body upon that swidden. A man's body, Mr Hurne.'

'Good God! Burnt to death, you mean? You can't be serious!'

'Not burnt to death, Mr Hurne. The post-mortem has not yet been completed but it is my belief he was shot. It is also

43

my belief that his body was placed on the swidden before the fire was started. I ought to add that we suspect murder, Mr Hurne.'

'Lord Hurne, actually, Inspector. Did you say murder?'

'I did.'

'Oh my God . . . this is dreadful . . . you're not suggesting that I or my men or my family were involved, are you? Trying to get rid of someone? Is that what you are suggesting?'

'I am not suggesting anything, sir, I am merely trying to establish facts. I need to know who was in charge of that fire and when the swidden was burnt. And, of course, I need to establish the identity of the dead man.'

'Look, I think I ought to get up there, I can explain things far better if I am on the site. Is the fellow still there? I could have a look to see if he's anyone I know.'

'No, he's been removed so that a forensic pathologist can carry out a post-mortem, but there are police officers on the site now, searching for evidence.'

'So does that mean I can't visit the site, Inspector? It would be most helpful if I could, I am sure I could be much more use to you from there.'

'We can take you close to the site,' Pluke compromised. 'But the scene itself is currently sealed off. It will be out of bounds for some time yet.'

'I can understand that but I would like to see precisely what you are talking about. And surely you must have some idea of the victim's identity? I know the need for a formal identification in these cases but often you chaps do know the name of victims but can't say so for various reasons.'

'Not in this case. Quite genuinely, we have no idea who he is, Lord Hurne, not the slightest, we need to find out as soon as we can. He is a man in his twenties or thirties, dark hair and average height and build. We have little to go on at the present and we've no reports of anyone missing locally.'

'He could be from anywhere, I suppose. We do get

44

ramblers and wanderers on our moors. Anyone missing from your party, Jonathan?'

'Not that I'm aware,' said the son. 'I can ask around.'

'Party?' asked Pluke.

'It was Jonny's twenty-first last Tuesday, quite a thrash with lots of lovely people there. We had a marquee in the grounds.'

'We'll need to discuss that with you,' said Pluke. 'But first, it would be helpful if you could confirm your ownership of the swidden in question, and details of the burning. I agree it would be better done on site, to clarify things in my mind and remove any doubts, then we can proceed from there.'

'Then follow me,' said Hurne. 'I have a Range Rover. Jonny, you'd better come too.'

With Wain and Pluke aboard the unmarked police car, the dark green Range Rover appeared and swept before them, but it did not exit the grounds via the main gate. Instead it turned along a narrow dirt track and although Wain thought they were heading in the wrong direction, Pluke assured him this would be the correct way. After all, there was only one swidden on the moors at this time. A few minutes later, they were climbing towards the open moorland and after what seemed a very short journey, were parking on the verge of the track. In the near distance they could see teams of policemen searching the moorland but more importantly, the edge of the track was also the southern boundary of the swidden. As they halted, the entire stretch of moorland rising to their left was burnt, the little grey stalks of consumed heather looking rather pathetic. They all climbed out of their vehicles.

'Well, Detective Inspector Pluke, it seems we were talking about the same thing,' said Hurne. 'I can confirm that this is my swidden, and that I am responsible for burning it recently. And I gather those are your officers?'

'Yes, they are, but I did not approach it from here, my officers are parked on the moorland road at the northern

45

end of this swidden, about two hundred yards away from the body.'

'Then let them use my road, Inspector. It is much more convenient and it's private, tourists and members of the public aren't in the habit of using it, although some do stray into my grounds when they come off the moor at this point. They assume this track is just another route across the moor, you'd think they would carry maps.'

'That is very kind of you, Lord Hurne, most certainly it would be helpful if our vehicles were closer to the scene.'

'Then help yourselves, my gates will be open until you have finished here. Just drive through. Now, how can I help you?'

'When did you burn this swidden?'

'Wednesday morning. The heather needs to be as dry as possible, and ideally we want a good stiff breeze to keep the fire moving, preferably from the south in the case of this patch. And that's what we had on Wednesday. Ideal conditions. My gamekeeper and one of the workers super-vised the burning, Inspector, they started early. Seven thirty or so I believe. They do it every time, very experi-enced chaps, you know. It was done without any problems so far as I am aware.'

'I'll need to interview both of them,' said Pluke.

'Of course. The gamekeeper is Eddie Hall who lives in the Keeper's Cottage and his colleague was Don Haynes – he lives in the village in one of my cottages. Hall will know his address.'

'Thank you. We will find them. Now, Lord Hurne, what are the boundaries of this swidden?'

'We use natural boundaries, Inspector Pluke, as far as we can, roads or tracks and streams in most cases, things that will prevent the spread of the flames. As you can see, this swidden is elevated in the middle, there's a ridge running north to south and the moor drops away at each side. Along each side there is a small beck or ghyll, as they are known hereabouts, and even that narrow stretch of water stops the fire spreading. To the north, which you can't see from here, there is a patch of exposed moorland, bare rock in fact. For some reason, it's not been colonized by heather or bracken, and we use that as the northern extent of this swidden. It will be somewhere close to where you have parked your vehicles. The fire can't cross the rocky waste. In all, the swidden's about forty acres give or take a rood or two but don't ask what that is in hectares. So where was this unfortunate fellow found?'

Pluke gazed at the burnt ground; as it rose from this point, it didn't look the same as it had from his previous vantage point, but eventually he identified the distinctive big rock, now some distance to his left on the horizon.

'You see that big rock?' He pointed. 'On the horizon. He was lying close to that, a few feet to the right of it as we look at it from here.'

'I understand. And you say he was there before the fire passed that way?'

'So it would seem. His remains were badly burnt. I'm interested to know why he was not discovered by your men while they were supervising the burning. You'd think they would have known there was a body in the path of the fire.'

'You'll have to talk to them, but I'd say they would not venture on to that part of the moor, Inspector. They would ignite the fire from this point, from where we are standing now, and the breeze would fan it ahead of them. The east and west boundaries are those streams to left and right, so one fellow would walk along the banks of one stream, and one along the other. They'd not be able to see each other, in fact, they'd move forward as dictated by the front wall of flames. You can see from here that the streams are much lower than the high patch of moor around that rock. The fire would sweep through the heather and across the remains of that unfortunate chap without my men realizing he was there. Besides, they'd not want to stray into the path of a running fire, would they? With a strong wind behind it, the blaze can run faster than a man, you know.'

As Pluke discussed this with Lord Hurne, his son stood apart from them staring across the bleak swidden. Wain decided to speak to him.

'Jonathan,' he said. 'Your birthday party was on Tuesday, the night before the burning, I believe?'

'Yes, in the marquee but that was almost a mile from here. In our grounds.'

'Quite a way to walk. What time did the celebrations start and finish?'

'We started at five thirty, with a champagne reception, buffet food at seven and dancing from nine onwards. Free drinks all night.'

'So what time did things finally finish?'

'Seven thirty the following morning. With breakfast. Some guests went straight off to work.'

'And how many guests were there?'

'Four hundred and fifty or thereabouts were invited but I can't be absolutely sure how many turned up. Some dropped out for various reasons, or just never arrived, and I suppose there were gate-crashers. I'd guess we catered for three hundred and fifty, give or take a handful either way.'

'A lot of people. We'll need names and addresses, we have to check that our fire victim isn't one of your guests. I can tell you he didn't look like a rambler or hiker, or someone taking a casual walk. His clothing was not that kind. He could have been at a party. Was the dress code at your party very formal?'

'Not at all, everything from tails to jeans. People like to relax, especially the younger element,' said Jonathan. 'I find it very worrying that the victim might have been at my party. I hope it isn't one of my friends or guests, or someone from the village. You don't know how long he was lying there before the fire, do you?'

'No, although the forensic pathologist might come up with some idea of the time of death, but I doubt it, not very precisely, not with the body being burnt as it was. We need to know if anyone vanished from your party, whether someone never arrived home or never turned up at work next morning.'

'I'd never know, would I? They could leave at any time without me realizing, unless they came to say goodbye. But, so far as I know, most of them stayed until the very end. I can say I've not been told of anyone who didn't return home or get to work.'

'Would you be prepared to come to the mortuary and look at the victim? It will not be a pretty sight, I can assure you, but you might be able to recognize him if he is an acquaintance.'

'If you think it will help.'

'Good. And I saw you working on a computer when we arrived. Does that mean you can check your list of guests for us? Without us trying to find your office staff at home or waiting for the office to open on Monday?'

'Yes, it was all arranged from our office. I can access the list for you and print it out. I helped to organize my own party.'

'Good, that will give us a very good start.'

Lord Hurne and Pluke then rejoined Wayne and Jonathan with Hurne promising every possible assistance during the investigation. Pluke said he would have to return to make further enquiries – these were preliminary questions, a form of scene-setting exercise. Hurne said he understood. Pluke suggested Wayne returned to the estate office with Jonathan to obtain the guest list, then take him to the mortuary in the hope he could identify the victim.

While Wayne was undertaking those essential tasks, Pluke would interview Eddie Hall, the gamekeeper, and his colleague Don Haynes. He'd also speak to Farmer Roache at Home Farm and would check at the scene for an update on the search for evidence.

'We will rendezvous back at the scene, Wayne. I'll get my officers to bring their vehicles here too, it will be much more convenient for everyone. Thank you for that, Lord Hurne.'

And so the enquiry acquired a welcome flourish of positive activity.

Pluke found Eddie Hall in his garden. The gamekeeper, a dour red-haired Scotsman in his mid-fifties, listened with some amazement to Pluke's account. Pluke told him the victim appeared to have been shot, without describing the method of shooting or the probable calibre of the bullet or shot. Hall shook his head.

'Well, Inspector . . .' His rich burr sounded wonderful to Pluke's ear. 'Ah cannae say for sure whether that chappie was there or not when we fired the moor. Ah jest walked along the one wee burn and Don the other, we never went up to the ridge and ye cannae see up there from where we were. Ah've not the faintest idea who he might be.'

'You have shooting parties on those moors?'

'Aye, but only in the grouse season. That ended on 12th December, all oor grouse shooters are accounted for, Mr Pluke. Since August. He's nae one of those, but if he'd been there since December there'd not be much of him left, would there?'

'True. But he's not a hiker, he's dressed more casually than any rambler,' said Pluke. 'We're checking to see if he could be one of Jonathan's party guests.'

'Aye, well, that might be so. They do some daft things, those young bucks, when they've had a bevvy or two, high spirits an' all that, but Ah dinnae think they'd shoot one another, not even accidentally.'

'I'm concerned as to how long the victim might have been on the moor before we found him,' said Pluke. 'I agree with you he won't have been there since December. Have you seen any activity up there in recent weeks?'

'We're always busy in the grouse season, Mr Pluke, but outside that there's always ramblers and hikers about the place, some coming doon fre' the heights by yon piece of moor even if it's not on their rightful path, I mean the piece of moor that's the swidden now, but I've seen nothing over the last week or two. Heard no shots either but you don't, not down here in the village. You could drop a bomb up there and we'd nae hear it. But if he'd been put there at night, he'd be expected to have been well hidden till the next grouse season . . . not many folks go up there at other times and nature would have reduced him to a few wee bones. And we wouldnae ha' seen him while we were burning . . . Do you think somebody put him there hoping he'd be burnt to a cinder? Gone for ever! Lucky you spotted him, eh?'

'Yes, I suppose it was. Now, tell me, Mr Hall, was the date of the burning known in advance? If so, who would know about it?'

'Well, Mr Pluke, we always burn in March, we don't burn later in case we destroy the grouse nests, and I think most of the estate workers would know we were due to do it any day now. I don't think the exact date would be known in advance – it all depends on wind direction and fine weather.'

'So it would be a rapid decision on the day?'

'Aye, it would. I had no idea of the exact date myself until the morning in question and Don wouldn't know until I called him in to help.'

'So the people at the party would have no idea the moor was going to be burnt around the time the party was due to end?'

'The locals would know it was due sometime around now, but incomers would probably have nae idea at all.'

'Thank you. So local people attended the party?'

'Och aye, the whole village was invited and a fair number turned up.'

Quite clearly, Eddie Hall did his best to help Pluke but there was no doubt in Montague's mind that the gamekeeper had no idea the victim's body had been lying there whilst he was supervising the burning of the heather.

Pluke got the same response from Don Haynes. Haynes

was a mature estate employee who normally looked after carpentry and fencing requirements but on occasions he turned his hand to other tasks, often helping Hall with aspects of gamekeeping. Pluke received promises from both men that if they had any ideas about the identity of the victim, they would contact him. Henry Roache told a similar story. Although he had the right to graze his sheep and shoot over the piece of moor which was now the swidden, he had not been up there for several weeks. However, he had been grouse shooting on several occasions between the Glorious Twelfth of August and 10th December but since then had not been close enough to the moor to note any activity by tourists, ramblers or local people. Although he ran his sheep on that part of the moor, he had not been up there in recent weeks; he'd do a count shortly before shearing them, but that would not be until the late spring. Certainly, he had not walked up there during the past week and although he knew the estate would have been burning off the heather around that time, he did not know the precise date. He listened to Pluke's description of the victim but shook his head.

'I can't say I know that chap,' he said. 'Unless it's one of Jonathan's party guests from away. That's the most likely explanation.'

With little to show for his efforts, Pluke decided to return to the scene of the search, a walk which allowed him a little time to consider his progress.

In the estate office Jonathan Hurne quickly printed out the guest list, which included home addresses and telephone numbers, rapidly scanning it to see if the names would jog his memory about anyone who might have been behaving oddly. But he drew a blank, and stressed there had been no antagonism among his guests – at least, nothing of which he was aware. Wayne Wain said he would pass the list to Inspector Horsley in the Incident Room whereupon Jonny said he could email it so that Horsley's teams could reproduce it very rapidly. Wayne said he'd get Horsley to ring him with his email address. Horsley would then be able to immediately allocate tasks to his teams of detectives; each of those guest names would be carefully checked and any males between eighteen and forty years of age must be *seen* to be alive. Secondary assurances would not be acceptable – the fellow must be seen in person by a police officer as proof that he was living. And that included everyone, even local guests.

Then, after Wayne had contacted the mortuary via his mobile phone, they drove there and Simon Meredith welcomed them. Wayne explained about the twenty-first party at Hurne Hall then introduced Jonathan as a possible identifier of the deceased. He and Wayne were led into the operating theatre where the burnt remains lay on a plinth, albeit covered with a sheet except for the face. The victim had been placed on his back.

Meredith said, 'In my opinion, he is between twenty-five and thirty, five feet ten inches tall, average build, a white man with dark hair and good teeth and in life, very healthy. I found no scars on his body such as those which might result from an operation or injury, no tattoos or other identifying marks. His fingertips have been burnt away which means we can't obtain fingerprints although the soles of his feet were undamaged thanks to his shoes, good sturdy trainers. He has a broken toe, by the way, the big toe on his right foot. It has healed with a bend. I don't think it would be painful now, but it is quite distinctive. A point of identity perhaps? Whether or not naked footprints can be utilized as a means of eventually proving his identity is something I shall need to discuss with your scenes of crime officers. Perhaps if we get a name, we can check his bathroom for signs of bare feet. Just a thought. There's always DNA of course. I can arrange those checks from my samples. I'll hand his clothes to your scenes of crime team too, to see if they can be traced, but there was nothing in his pockets, no watch or ring, nothing to provide a clue to his identity. Removal of identification evidence is the hall-mark of a professional killer. The trainers, by the way, were Nike. Size nine. I fear they will have been mass produced although they could possibly be traced to the point of sale, and then to the purchaser if he used a credit card.'

He did not mention the cause of death in the presence of Jonathan, but then asked Jonathan if he was prepared to look closely at the remains. Jonathan nodded. Meredith led him across to the plinth, and for a moment or two the young man gazed unemotionally at the burnt face, screwing up his own features in an attempt to produce some kind of image in his mind. Wain thought he was trying desperately hard but after two or three minutes, he shook his head.

'Sorry,' he said. 'Sorry, I just can't recognize him as anyone I know.'

Jonathan was led away by an attendant who had been hovering in the background. She took him into a waiting room and gave him a cup of tea while Wayne discussed the cause of death in confidence with Meredith.

'It was definitely caused by a .22 bullet,' said the pathologist. 'I've retrieved it and it's been sent to our ballistics laboratory. I hope they can say whether it's from a pistol or a rifle, a repeater or a single-shot weapon, but if and when you do find the weapon, it could be matched to it. It entered the brain from the right and I'd say it was slightly to the front of the victim; the angle of entry suggests that. He might have seen who shot him and turned his head instinctively the instant the shot was fired, but clearly too late to save himself. I don't know if it was fired at very close range, sometimes there are deposits on the skin from gunpowder if the muzzle was very close but the moor fire put paid to all that.

'It's difficult to estimate the time of death but I would say around a week ago at least, perhaps ten days. There is some insect infestation and the stage of decomposition suggests that, although smoke from the fire has preserved him to some extent. There was some decomposition before the fire reached him, so I think he was there some time before the fire. Some days, I mean. Four or five. Certainly longer than mere hours. He had stopped breathing long before the smoke reached him, there are no deposits in his lungs. I found no evidence of drugs or alcohol either but the passage of time may have affected anything of that kind in the blood. This has all the appearances of someone attempting to conceal a murder by burning the remains of the victim, but I'll be honest when I say it might not have happened in this case. The delay between the death and the fire suggests the fire may have been entirely coincidental. Without the fire, of course, the body might not have been found. So you must consider whether nature was supposed to dispose of the remains or whether that was the job of that fire.'

'You echo my concerns precisely, Mr Meredith,' said Wayne. 'I'll inform Detective Inspector Pluke. You'll send the usual written report?'

'Of course.'

And so Wayne returned to rendezvous with Pluke, dropping Jonathan off at his parents' home en route. Jonathan did not speak on the return journey but Wayne felt the experience had shocked him. Did he really have no idea of the victim's identity? Or was he being devious? Wayne would have to keep an open mind on those questions.

He drove to the private road within the estate grounds where he would update Pluke and hopefully learn what, if anything, the search teams had discovered.

Chapter Four

Mrs Fowler went to the leisure centre on the Monday morning after Brent's weekend away to ask if he had been in touch because he hadn't come home on Sunday night. If he'd decided to stay at the shooting party, she thought he would have told someone at the pool. He would need permission to take more time off and she was sure he would have rung her too. He was like that, thoughtful and considerate.

'Sorry, Mrs Fowler,' said the manager. 'We've had no word from him. He asked if he could have Friday afternoon off – no problem, eh? No problem at all, we owed him a few hours. He told us he'd be back as usual on Monday. When he didn't come in, we thought he might be ill, so we weren't too bothered. Monday mornings are usually quiet in the kitchen.'

'Kitchen?' She frowned.

'Oh, didn't he tell you? We had to move him from the poolside – complaints, you know, from parents. So we transferred him to the cafeteria, washing up. Same building, different department.'

'Complaints?' She frowned again.

'From parents, about what he was doing to little girls, pretending to help them to swim and breathe and things. So we've moved him away from them, for his own good really. We wouldn't want him arrested, would we? We had to do something, you can't let these things go unchecked. Not nowadays. Not that I believe your Brent would do such a thing, he's always been a good reliable worker, but we had to show we were doing something to keep the parents happy. He never said, eh?'

'No, he never said a thing. I thought he was still a lifeguard, he always seemed to enjoy his work.'

'I'm sure he enjoyed his work at the poolside and in the water, Mrs Fowler, but perhaps not in the way he should have done. A bit careless with his hands maybe? Sorry to break this to you like this, but honestly I thought he would have said something.'

'He's shy about discussing his private matters,' she said. 'I hope he's not been a nuisance to those girls but some parents will complain about anything. Brent can be very affectionate with children, he loves them, you know. I keep saying he should get himself a grown-up girlfriend, marry and have a family and not spend all his time in his bedroom with that computer . . . but thank you, if he rings up I'll let you know.'

'And if he gets in touch with us, I'll tell him to contact home.'

'Yes, thank you.'

She went home to see if the post had come but there was no letter. She couldn't contact the shooting party organizers because he'd taken the piece of paper with him. She had no idea of their address or telephone number, or even what they called the firm. She went into the spare bedroom where he had his computer but she had no idea how to work it. Did he keep a diary on it, she wondered? Or what else did he use it for? He'd never told her. She looked on the desk, there were copies of *The Field* and *Country Life* but nothing to say where he'd gone. Everything was neatly tidied up and he hadn't left any note with an address or phone number. It was most unlike him not to get in touch. She wondered what to do next.

Perhaps he would ring later today? She would wait a little longer before she decided what to do.

'Anything more on silver-coloured people carriers, Lynn?'

'No, sir, no more reports. And no more men reported missing.'

'I wonder if they've run out of victims?'

'There's always Brent Fowler, sir, he's still around. And he works at the leisure centre.'

'Tell front office to let me know instantly if and when Brent's reported missing, Lynn. We'll have to try and establish just what's going on. He's never been prosecuted, though, even if he's been a long-term suspect. He was questioned about that child murder too, but we couldn't prove anything.'

'Should we warn him?'

'About what? We've nothing positive to go on, we can't really warn people about rumours or speculation. We could keep a discreet eye on him though, if we've the personnel available. I think we should run a check on silver people carriers too. Try all models through the PNC. Any Ford Galaxy for starters. Check for all those registered in the Manchester postcode area, then we can run their owners' names though our computers. See if it throws up anything more about Hampson too, he might own more than one vehicle.'

'Yes, sir.'

The first Saturday after Mrs Fowler had been to the leisure centre, a clutch of police vehicles moved closer to the scene on Blackamoor and were now parking within the Hurne estate's grounds. This had become the centre of operations as all the vehicles were fitted with radio, and some with computers. There was even a mobile canteen – Inspector Horsley, in his role as Incident Room supervisor, was as efficient as ever. The Incident Room, of course, remained at Crickledale Police Station.

Upon returning from the mortuary, Wayne Wain located Pluke and updated him on Dr Meredith's opinions and findings. To discuss those matters, they walked across the moors well away from the swidden, keeping clear of a large area of surrounding moorland which had now been enclosed by yards of yellow plastic tape to identify it as the scene of a police investigation. With Pluke up-to-date, they located Detective Sergeant Tabler, the officer in charge of the scenes of crime team, whereupon Pluke asked whether there had been any progress with the search. Tabler told him that already hundreds of spent twelve-bore cartridges had been found among the heather to which Pluke responded that it was to be expected, this being grouse shooting country. In addition, hundreds of brass caps from used cartridges had been found on the swidden. The cases of those cartridges, some probably many years old, had been consumed by the fire. There had been a mass of rubbish among the unburnt heather too, such as discarded beer cans, bottles and plastic wrappings. Most of it had been dropped by tourists and ramblers over the years and every piece had been logged. The swidden itself bore very little rubbish, most having been burnt. It did, however, produce some incombustibles like beer bottles and drinks cans.

'No ejected .22 shell yet?' asked Pluke, who had told Tabler that the pathologist had confirmed death was due to a bullet of that calibre.

'Nothing, sir, and to be honest there's very little we can link to any crime. Most of the stuff we've found is what I'd expect from this moorland. Ramblers' and tourists' junk, most of it.'

'If there is no .22 shell, it could mean the victim was killed elsewhere, or of course, it could mean he was killed here but the shell not ejected. That can happen with non-repeater weapons. You'll have to keep searching, Sergeant. Most if not all killers leave something at the scene. I know it's difficult, especially when searching among growing heather, but I know you'll do your best.'

'If there's any evidence here, we'll find it.'

'There's another factor,' Pluke reminded Tabler. 'How was the victim's body placed here? If he was carried, which is what I believe, how was it done, bearing in mind the location and terrain? Was a motor vehicle used? Or a stretcher? A horse even? Bodies are very heavy and unwieldy things to lug around, Sergeant, so I think more than one person was involved. And they took great care to lay out his body. There may be some evidence of that.'

'If he was dragged to where he was found, sir, I'd have expected the route to be marked with broken stems of bracken or heather – and the same might apply if a vehicle had been used, but we've found none beyond the swidden. Heather stems broken by a large heavy weight would have shown up even after the fire. There's a good case for thinking he was carried and laid there, as you said.'

'So if he was killed away from the scene, where did it happen? Somewhere nearby, or a long way off? How can we ascertain that? We need to find that place because it's the true scene of the crime. Nonetheless we need to examine the ground here for things like tyre marks, footprints or even hoof prints. You might find that sort of thing in softer patches of ground among the heather.'

'I've got that in mind, sir.'

'Good, I'll leave you to get on, Sergeant. Now, Detective Sergeant Wain, you and I need to discuss our next move. Let's go for a walk.'

They left the knot of vehicles and walked towards Hurne Hall with Pluke intending to emerge via the ornate gates and continue into the village. He needed to gain a wider appreciation of the lie of the land, how the Hall related to the village, the village to the surrounding moors, and the surrounding moors to the swidden which was the focus of their interest. He wanted to bounce ideas off Wayne too because he felt, even at this early stage, that his enquiries were fruitless. Although the investigation was very young, he had made a worrying lack of early progress. After a few yards, he halted. Down to their left, on a level slightly lower than the track upon which they walked, stood the clutch of buildings which comprised Hurne Hall. They could easily distinguish the outline of the huge stone-built Hall, its gardens, the surrounding

60

buildings which had once been stables but which were now garages and outbuildings with a variety of uses, and the acres of farmland in which it was located. Only a very short distance from the wilderness of the moors, the Hall was like an oasis with its lush fields and productive gardens.

'How important is the Hall in relation to our enquiry?' Pluke asked Wain.

'Well, sir, it's the nearest building or collection of buildings. There are no others within two or three miles across the moor in any direction, except the village. This is by far the nearest, with the village being only a few hundred yards further away as the crow flies.'

'Is it significant that the place where the body was found cannot be seen from the Hall or the village? There's no building in sight from there, no human habitation. Not even a remote farm.'

'It must be relevant. The people who placed the body there might have thought they were further away from habitation than they really were.'

'Strangers to the district, you mean? So how relevant is the birthday party, Wayne? Was the body disposed of while events were going on at the Hall? Do we know where people parked their cars that evening? Do we know the site of the marquee? Where did guests stay? Were some accommodated at the Hall, or did they find rooms in the village? Did they camp somewhere? Use caravans? Or is it possible that whoever dumped the body on that swidden had no idea there was such a large gathering not very far away? What was the weather like on the night of the party? Moonlight perhaps? Dry or wet underfoot? Or was the body placed there some days ahead of the party? The pathologist thinks it might have been. On the other hand, the death might not have any links whatsoever with either the party or the Hall. Could the dumpers of the corpse have found their way to that rock without torches or lights of some kind? Vehicle lights even? Or are we thinking they might be very well acquainted with this part of the moors?

And even with this approach to the swidden through the Hall grounds? A very local person or persons perhaps? One of the villagers?'

'It means we have a lot of people to eliminate from our enquiries, sir, the Hall and all the people who live and work there. The guests and all the villagers.'

'Absolutely right, Wayne, but it must be done,' said Pluke with the hint of a smile. 'There's another factor while you are questioning people at the Hall. Rifles and pistols. Most country houses have a gun room well stocked with firearms. We must examine any .22 weapons to see if they have been used recently. I will ask Inspector Horsley to obtain a list of all firearms certificate holders in this locality, then we can run a check on those authorized to possess .22 weapons. And we need to ascertain whether any of the guests are authorized to possess .22 weapons, or had access to them.'

'So I'm going to make myself unpopular with Lord Hurne and his family?'

'I am sure your charm and professionalism will overcome any animosity, Wayne,' said Pluke. 'Not that I expect resistance from him or his family. I am quite sure the Hurnes will be most co-operative. Lord Hurne has already indicated his willingness to help in a very positive way.'

'Some who offer to help during murder enquiries are not as innocent as they might appear,' observed Wayne.

'Exactly,' agreed Pluke. 'We must never forget that.'

'So what will you be doing while I'm busying myself around the Hall?'

'I shall acquaint myself with the village and its people,' said Pluke. 'I need to ascertain whether there are any undercurrents we should know about, any gossip which may be relevant, any problems with the villagers' relationships with the big house and, of course, whether anyone saw anything unusual last Tuesday night or indeed upon any other recent night. I shall not pursue house-to-house enquiries in the village, however; that is for our teams of detectives and I am sure Inspector Horsley will have that well in hand. My purpose is to gain what might be termed an overview if my knowledge of modern terminology is correct.'

'With that kind of huge party going on, people would have some difficulty knowing what was unusual, what was suspicious and what was nothing more than high spirits,' Wayne pointed out.

'We mustn't let ourselves be tempted into thinking the body *was* dumped while the party was in progress, Wayne. There might be no link between the victim and the people at that party, or the victim's death and the timing of the fire.'

'It's more than a coincidence, surely, that they all occurred around the same time in almost the same place? Party? Fire? Body? Murder?'

'Don't ignore the possibility that the body might have been there some time before Tuesday evening, but I agree that coincidence in a murder enquiry has to be treated very carefully. We need to concentrate on suspicious events on Tuesday and earlier. For several days earlier, I would suggest. We have a lot to do, Wayne, to separate truth from speculation. I'll leave you here, now; there's a back entrance to the Hall just down there. Shall we rendezvous in, say, an hour and a half? Back at the car?'

'Right, sir.'

Although Pluke had passed through Hurnehow village on many previous occasions, his trips had usually been in search of horse troughs and he had never had cause to examine the village from the murder-hunt detective's viewpoint. Before asking any questions, he walked around to fix in his mind the precise location of distinctive buildings such as the church, shop, post office, garage and other relevant places. He confirmed in his own mind that no part of the swidden could be seen from the centre of the village, although he accepted parts might be visible from the upper floors of some of the outlying properties, especially when it was ablaze.

Certainly the smoke would have been visible over a huge distance but in this part of Yorkshire, such a sight would not excite comment. It was quite normal. Nonetheless, reported sightings of unusual occurrences might emerge during house-to-house enquiries.

Having established his own mental image of Hurnehow, he began his questions and, as he progressed, one thing became clear. The people in the big house were liked and respected by the village people and when Jonathan had celebrated his twenty-first birthday, it was typical of the Hurne family to invite everyone in the village. All the estate staff were invited too, along with others who had been helpful over the years such as the family solicitors, bankers, doctor, dentist, butcher and grocer, while the catering had been handled by an outside firm so that all the local people could take part in the celebrations. None of the villagers to whom Pluke spoke could suggest an identity for the victim unless it was one of the guests from afar, and none could provide even the remotest of clues as to a likely motive behind his death. 'It's not the sort of thing we expect to happen here,' was an oft-repeated comment.

It was while Pluke was walking around Hurnehow gathering his impressions that a man hailed him.

'Detective Inspector Pluke?' The newcomer was a small middle-aged man with a beard and a bald head surrounded by what looked like a monk's tonsure. He was casually dressed in a colourful sweater and green corduroy trousers. Pluke knew him from somewhere but couldn't quite place him. Had the fellow worn a hat the last time they'd met?

'Yes?'

'Ray Morgan, freelance journalist,' he introduced himself. 'You won't find many reporters working today, Mr Pluke, apart from covering football matches, but I have to make a living from local snippets.'

'So how can I help, Mr Morgan?' Pluke now recognized the fellow.

'I've heard a whisper that you are investigating a murder in the village?'

'Not exactly in the village,' Pluke explained. 'But yes, the body of a man was found nearby in what I believe are suspicious circumstances.'

'Can I ask for a brief statement from you? I presume you are the investigating officer?'

'Yes, of course. There isn't a lot I can say at this point, Mr Morgan, except to confirm that we are investigating the suspicious death of a man whose body was found on these moors. His identity is not known but he's probably between twenty and thirty, give or take a year or two either way, a white male with dark hair and he was wearing a light blue T-shirt, jeans and white trainer shoes. We are very anxious to have him identified. He died of gunshot wounds, that has been confirmed, and we are treating his death as murder.'

'That's clear enough. Can I ask which part of the moors?'

'If you go along this road out of Hurnehow towards Hillshaw, you'll see a piece of burnt moorland on your right, about a mile from here. A swidden. It is sealed off at the moment while we search for evidence. That is where the body was found.'

'And who found the body?'

'I did, while I was on my day off.'

'The moorland was deliberately burnt, a source tells me.'

'The fire was regular controlled burning of the moorland, Mr Morgan, no sinister motive can be attached to it. I'm sure you know the method is widely utilized to encourage new growth around this time of year.'

'So the man didn't die in the fire?'

'No, he was dead before the moor was set ablaze. If you ask whether the person who killed him expected his body to be consumed by the fire, then I can't speculate on that. What I can say is that the body was not consumed by the fire.'

'Would you say the fire exposed the body?'

'Yes, that's fair comment. I doubt whether I would have seen it if it had remained deep in the heather, which is normally very thick and deep at that point.'

Ray Morgan then asked the usual questions about the number of detectives engaged on the enquiry, speculation as to the motive, whether it was a gangland killing with overtones of drugs dealing or armed robberies, and then he asked what kind of weapon had been used.

'I shall not reveal the calibre or type of firearm used, Mr Morgan, nor will I say which part of his body was wounded. You may quote me as saying the victim died of gunshot wounds. You are at liberty to take pictures of the moorland in question, but from a distance at this stage. So which papers will you send this material to?'

'I supply most local and regional papers in the north of England, Mr Pluke, especially when things occur at weekends. I work as a stringer for regional television news bulletins too, but they don't operate on Sundays. You'll not get much publicity for this tomorrow, not in the Sundays. I'll send a confirmatory note to them all, and then hope we can get some better copy tomorrow, ready for Monday. I would hope the local evenings, weeklies and dailies would carry the story on Monday, Mr Pluke. But this is hardly a sensational story nowadays, is it?'

Pluke thought it unwise to mention Lord Hurne's birthday party for his son – the tabloids would make an almighty splash about that if they thought the murder was linked. But if this reporter did his job, then the link could be established. Pluke would have to be prepared for that.

'I hope you can do whatever's possible to gain good coverage, particularly of our efforts to identify the victim, Mr Morgan. It is vital we find out who he is so we can trace his movements and contacts. Anyone who knows or suspects that a young man is absent without explanation from his usual haunts should ring our Incident Room,' and he gave the telephone number to the reporter. Morgan promised to do his best, repeating his view that Sunday was a very poor day for local news. Pluke realized, of course, that the press interest was a useful development and it cheered him as he continued his perambulations around Hurnehow, although he gained nothing of evidential value. Almost everyone had been at the party from around five o'clock on Tuesday evening, and most had left for home around midnight, leaving the youngsters and house guests to continue their celebrations into the morning hours. None had reported any unusual incidents either at the party or on the moors nearby, neither on Tuesday nor earlier, although many pointed out that traffic moving late at night on this particular occasion was not unusual; at any other time, it might have attracted interest and attention.

Although Pluke pressed them to recall days prior to Tuesday, none remembered anything unusual. If strangers or ramblers had gone for a walk on to that part of the moor any evening or parked their car there, it would not have been noteworthy. Such things happened all the time. Lots of people, locals and visitors alike, walked or drove across those moors but on this occasion, no one had noticed anyone up there during the past few weeks. Indeed, some had not even noticed smoke from the swiddening process.

By the end of his enquiries, Pluke had gained absolutely no useful information whatsoever. No one had noticed anything out of the ordinary and no one could suggest a name for the victim. The description did not match anyone living in the village or nearby, and none of the local young men was known to be missing.

As he returned to base, he wondered how Wayne Wain had fared at the big house.

Lord and Lady Hurne had been most helpful. At Wayne's request they had escorted him on to the huge area of lawn where the marquee had been erected, and together they had tried to see the swidden from points around the marquee. Those points were still visible in the grass but Wayne quickly realized the swidden was invisible from each one of them. He then asked about other accommodation on Tuesday evening, such as the catering tent, toilets, a rest haven some distance from the main marquee and again, from each of those points, the swidden could not be seen. From these gardens, Wayne noticed that the swidden was further away than he'd thought – about a mile.

He began to think it highly unlikely that anyone would voluntarily walk as far as that, even if they wanted to stretch their legs or get some fresh air. There were plenty more areas of heather much closer, and of course the swidden hadn't been burnt on the day of the party. During that time, it would be just like any other patch of moorland. He began to think the chances of any of the guests being witnesses to the crime were remote. As it was March, most had spent the entire evening inside the warmth of the marquee.

When the question of firearms arose, Lord Hurne sprung a surprise by saying he did not have a gun room. He said he did not like guns in the house. He was not a shooting man, he told Wayne, although he hosted shooting parties for social and economic reasons. He would go on to the moors with his guests and enjoy the atmosphere without firing a single shot; he simply enjoyed walking with his dogs. When it came to looking after and cleaning the guests' guns after a shoot, most of them did that themselves in a room set aside for the purpose. Alternatively, Eddie Hall, the gamekeeper, provided the right assistance and sometimes beaters would be recruited to help clean the guns, but, as His Lordship explained, those guns were twelve-bore shotguns, not .22 rifles or pistols.

Wayne had a long chat with Jonathan Hurne about friends who had come to the party; some had been accommodated in the Hall's eighteen bedrooms but many had driven from the locality or obtained taxis, while those living in Hurnehow had walked. Jonathan told Wayne he had been mentally checking and rechecking his list of guests and friends, but could think of no one who looked like the victim, even when making allowances for his burnt appearance.

Wayne talked to Lady Hurne, who could not help; he talked to the housekeeper, a widow called Mrs Gladys Cooper, and the cook, Amy Collins, but they knew nothing either. Friends of the family would be listed among the guests, and so the teams of detectives would catch up with those during their enquiries. There was no need for Wayne to go chasing them for information. He did succeed in getting the names of the caterers, the entertainers and even the car park wardens; all would be interviewed through Inspector Horsley's allocation of tasks to the teams of detectives.

At the end of his allotted time, Wayne produced a negative result. No one had seen anything, no one knew anything and no one could suggest a name for the victim who had been found dead so close to Hurne Hall. There were many enquiries still to be made but now it was time to report to Pluke.

'Let us walk on the moor,' said Pluke, taking the lead. 'So what have you gleaned, Wayne?'

'Nothing, sir. All we can do is wait until all the party-goers have been checked to see if any are missing, or if any emerge as suspects. Those external employees must be interviewed too, the ones who helped at the party. We need to check the whereabouts of each young male who came to the party for whatever reason. That'll take a long time, even if we're not sure the death and party are linked.'

'Emails and computers will speed up the enquiries, Wayne; it's not as if all the guests are from the same town or village. We don't have to interview them all, officers from other forces will do that for us. Because it's a murder enquiry, they'll make sure it is dealt with very speedily.'

Pluke told Wayne of the impressions he'd gained from

his enquiries in the village then said, 'One thing is certain, Wayne. If our victim is not one of the party guests, he must be a stranger. If he is a stranger, he would have been dumped with no intention of his body being found. The fire changed all that. We must bear in mind that the body may not have been dumped in the hope it would be destroyed by the fire. It could have been dumped here simply because the killers thought it would never be found.'

'So where do we start looking for culprits, and for the deceased's name?'

'If we can answer those questions, Wayne, we will be well on the way to finding answers to this riddle. But I think we must now adopt a slightly different approach, pending the result of all those outstanding interviews. We can't wait for those, they could take days. We must take the initiative.'

'So what are you suggesting?'

'That we look outside this immediate vicinity, Wayne. At the moment, all our enquiries are concentrated upon this small part of the moors, with the party and its guests dominating our minds. Let us suppose the victim was not connected in any way with the party or with Hurne Hall. Let us momentarily dismiss the moor fire as an incidental irrelevance too.'

'Right, I'm with you.'

'How would we then conduct this investigation? The investigation of an unknown male murder victim found on this moor?'

'Well, the first thing would be to get the body identified, and that might mean a nationwide search of missing persons registers or hospitals with patients who've run away or prison escapees, the DNA database . . .'

'Absolutely, Wayne. That is being done anyway. Then what?'

'Well, this is a remote area, but we'd need to find out if anyone has been seen coming here at odd times, or at any time. We can check with regular delivery people, the postman, milk lady, people living along the roads into the moors at this point, gamekeepers, hikers, pubs along the way . . .'

'And we need to do all this while placing the fire and the party at the back of our minds but we cannot forget those aspects. They could be relevant. In effect, Wayne, we shall have two enquiries running simultaneously, each independent of the other. One very local, the other ranging over a wider area. If we later establish a link between them, then so be it. Do you agree with me?'

'I do, sir.'

'Then let us return to the Incident Room and explain our strategy to Inspector Horsley so that he can split his teams into two sections. You drive, Wayne.'

Chapter Five

During that week, Mrs Fowler waited and worried, not sleeping and hardly daring to leave the house in case the telephone rang. She called everywhere she knew, checking places like hospitals in Manchester and all across the Pennines into Yorkshire. She checked at airports and seaports, the leisure centre's cafeteria again and again, the swimming pool too in case Brent had gone back to work there without telling her, his favourite cinema, the few friends and neighbours he kept in touch with and even the library. But no one had seen Brent since last Friday, nor had they heard from him. It looked as if he had decided to stay on after the shooting party to take full advantage of the heaven-sent opportunity to further his dreams. Someone must have invited him to remain or even given him a job. Those she asked assured her that when he'd settled down after these euphoric few days, he would contact her. After all, this must have been the most exciting thing to happen to him in years so it wasn't surprising that keeping in touch with her had momentarily slipped his mind.

In spite of those reassurances, and because such a long time had elapsed since he'd left home, she wondered about calling the police but she'd heard the force rarely bothered to look for missing adults. If a child, old person or someone vulnerable was missing, they would treat it with a degree of urgency, but healthy adults could come and go as they please. She knew there were no laws to say an adult couldn't leave home if he or she wanted, even if they had dependants such as children or spouses.

But if she told the police, they might put his name on the missing persons list if she was really worried and his details might appear on a computer and be checked regularly. Checks would occur if someone was, say, found drowned or suffering from loss of memory or injured in hospital without his identity being known. But the police could not mount an organized search for someone unless it was feared he or she was a victim of crime or perhaps involved in crime. But Brent wasn't, was he? He didn't mix with criminals, he was such a nice boy, always honest and polite and in fact he'd often helped the police with their enquiries. In any case, where could they start looking for him? The world was such a big place.

Unable to sleep or relax, Mrs Fowler maintained her lonely vigil. She left the front door unlocked in case Brent came home late at night or in the early hours, and she set a place at table every day for his breakfast and evening meal, just as she always did. If he turned up without warning, she didn't want him to think she'd forgotten him. She waited for the post each morning in case he sent a postcard or a letter – she supposed he could have sent one which had got lost somewhere? That sort of thing did happen. That could be the reason she'd not heard from him. In any case, she left all the internal doors open in case he telephoned – sometimes, with the doors closed, she didn't hear it ringing. But when the following Friday came, with no word of any kind from Brent, she decided to be positive. She would start to look for him. She had waited until Friday because that was exactly a week since he'd set off with such enthusiasm. If he had spent extra time at the shooting party, he'd have to leave on Friday to make room for newcomers. That letter he'd received had said the party ran from six o'clock on the Friday until lunch on the Sunday. Friday was apparently the start of those shooting party weekends so that's when he would have to leave. That sort of reasoning made sense to Mrs Fowler.

On Saturdays, she always went into town and had lunch followed by a look around the shops along and behind

Deansgate and Victoria Street, and in the Arndale Centre. There was a police station in Bootle Street not far from the Central Library, between there and Deansgate, so she decided to go there on Saturday to see what they suggested about Brent's absence. Maybe the police would realize she was very worried about him and do something? There was no harm in asking. She decided to take a photograph of him, just in case.

And so it was that Saturday afternoon, after worrying whether she was doing the right thing and after several cups of tea for reassurance, she went to the police station. It was a huge place with a sign outside saying it was 'A' Division of the Manchester Metropolitan District of Greater Manchester Police. The young woman at the counter in reception looked very nice, but was she a police-woman or one of those community support people? The uniformed sergeant who was also working behind the counter didn't take much notice of her, he was busy doing something with a computer, staring at it just like Brent did. She hoped she wasn't being a nuisance but guessed lots of ladies would probably come in to report losing purses or umbrellas, or complain about the noise of neighbours. Some would even come to ask for help with filling in forms or wanting someone to speak at their luncheon club.

The young woman slid the glass panel to one side, smiled a welcome and asked, 'Yes, luv?'

'Oh, er, I hope I'm not being a nuisance, but my son is missing and I'm very worried about him. He's been gone a week now, well, more than a week.'

'How old is he?'

'Twenty-eight,' said Mrs Fowler.

'He's grown up, luv, he can go off if he wants to, without telling you. I know it's rude and irresponsible, but it happens. Do you know that more than five hundred people absent themselves like that *every day* in this country? Every day, mark you. And a lot of 'em seem to come

74

from Manchester. They just go without a word, never say goodbye, some don't even take a toothbrush.'

Mrs Fowler, before making this bold step, had decided not to be put off by a lack of official interest in her case. 'But I think my son's come to some harm,' she said firmly. 'That's why I want something done about it.'

'We can't arrange search parties for grown men who don't come home. So why are you worried? He's old enough to look after himself, isn't he?'

'He won a prize to a shooting party, last weekend. In Yorkshire. He said he would be home on Sunday night, last Sunday it was, but he didn't come back and he's not been seen since. He's not been to work, they've not heard from him and neither have I, or his friends. It's most unlike him, I'm so dreadfully worried.'

'All right, I'll take details and if anyone does turn up suffering from loss of memory or injured in hospital without being identified, we can carry out checks.'

She pulled a computer keyboard towards her. It was very like the one Brent used.

'So what's his name and address?'

'Brent Fowler,' and she gave her address, adding, 'I'm his mother, Mrs Fowler. Emily.'

The girl started to compile a record of the report, but when she entered the name 'Brent Fowler', the name was flagged. Mrs Fowler did not see that, but it told the operator the name was of interest to the police and that SIOUX should be contacted. The girl had no idea what it was about, but decided to go ahead with the report. She asked the usual questions which were presented on her screen, such as where he worked, who were his closest friends, what his interests were and whether or not he was driving a car or motor bike, and then asked about the circumstances and time of his disappearance. Mrs Fowler explained as much as she could about the shooting party but couldn't remember all the details.

'I have a colour photograph of him if it's any use to you.'

75

She fished it from her handbag and passed it across the counter.

The young woman accepted it and smiled. 'A good-looking lad, isn't he?' Then called to the sergeant, 'Sergeant, I think you ought to check this one.' The sergeant had left his computer and had come to her side.

'Problem, Sue?' he asked.

'No, Sarge, a potential missing person. This lady's son hasn't been seen or heard of for a week or more, name of Brent Fowler. He went on a shooting party in North Yorkshire and hasn't come back. He's twenty-eight, old enough to go it alone.'

And she pointed to the flagged item on the screen. The sergeant understood; this man's absence must be reported to SIOUX without delay. He smiled at the worried Mrs Fowler.

'Shooting party? At this time of year? They don't have shooting parties in the close season, do they?'

'Oh, I don't know anything about that, I'm not very good with countryside things.'

'Look, leave this with us, Mrs Fowler, we'll do what we can,' the sergeant smiled. 'If you are very worried, you could also contact the National Missing Persons Helpline – we can give you their number. They offer help and advice in cases where we can't assist. Anyway, we have your phone number, have we? If we want to contact you?'

'Yes, I gave it to this lady, with a photograph of Brent.'

'Good, well, we'll do our best,' and so Mrs Fowler went home feeling much better. At least Brent's name and picture would go on to their computer and that might help to find him.

When she was safely out of hearing, the sergeant said, 'Sue, you know who that missing man is, don't you?'

'Brent Fowler. Should I know him?'

'He's a paedophile, well known to CID, we've had him in several times for interfering with little girls, but their evidence has never stood up, no good for a prosecution. He was brought in as a murder suspect too, but there was no prosecution. He's never been convicted, always got away with it. That's why SIOUX want to know if he's reported missing. They'll be concerned about this, especially as they don't have shooting parties in March and he's not the first lad of his kind to go missing from here. So send the report to SIOUX. And, I might add, an All-Force email's just come through from North Yorkshire, they've found a body on the moors. A young man between twenty and thirty, they think. Shot dead. Murdered. I wonder if it could be our man Brent? Nothing's impossible. I'll ring North Yorkshire to see what's going on at the wrong side of the Pennines.'

Detective Chief Inspector Sanders did not know whether to be pleased or not about Brent Fowler's absence, especially as the lad had not been warned he might be in danger. Things certainly looked ominous so he would make some local enquiries before contacting Mrs Fowler for more details of the shooting party. At that moment, DC Rogers came in with the email from North Yorkshire Police.

'North Yorkshire Police have found a body, sir, on the moors. The description could fit lots of young men, but we can't ignore it. It could be our man.'

'So it seems he did go to a shooting party!' snapped Sanders. 'I don't like this. All right, let's see what North Yorkshire can tell us.'

With Wayne Wain driving, Detective Inspector Pluke made his way to Crickledale Police Station, now the location of the Incident Room. As he entered the station, he poked his head into the tiny Control Room where Sergeant Cockfield pronounced Cofield was in charge and said:

'It's Detective Inspector Pluke, Sergeant, just letting you know I shall be in the Incident Room for a while, with Detective Sergeant Wain. Any messages for me? From the scene or elsewhere?'

'No, sir, nothing. All's quiet.'

Not quite sure whether that was good news or not, Pluke mounted the staircase and panted somewhat as he passed his own office, popping his head around the door to see if his secretary was at work. She was the very buxom Mrs Plumpton who skilfully tantalized him with her flowing wide-necked purple gossamer-like dress which only just managed to conceal her wobbly bits. There were times, when she bent forward over his desk, that he was sure he could see right down to her knees but, speedy though she was in her tantalizing gyrations, he always managed to avert his eyes just before the critical stage. Such things were not good for a gentleman's heart, especially a gentleman of mature years. But she was not at work; for one thing it was a Saturday afternoon and secondly, she had not been recalled to duty for this murder. Not yet. Had she known about it, she might have voluntarily come to work; she was that sort of person, was the vacillating Mrs Plumpton.

The Conference Room was at the end of the corridor on the second floor and it was that which had been transformed into the Incident Room with its desks, computers and their operators, blackboard, noticeboards and telephones. It was buzzing with activity whilst at a desk at the far end sat the formidable Inspector Horsley.

'Good afternoon, Inspector Horsley,' said Pluke upon entry.

'Hello there, Montague,' breezed Horsley. 'And Wayne. What brings you two here? I thought you were up on the moors somewhere.'

'We are here because I feel we should expand the range of this enquiry,' said Pluke. 'We are concentrating very heavily upon an extremely local area based in and around the Hurne estate and Hurnehow village. My instinct, upon reflecting on how little we have learned from our early but very intense questioning of the local people, suggests we should spread our enquires over a much wider area.'

'You haven't forgotten we are endeavouring to trace and

interview all the party guests, Montague, that was one of your specific requests. They came from all over the country to that lad's twenty-first. We can't spread our enquiries much wider than that. Do I take it you don't wish me to complete those enquiries?'

'On the contrary, they are vital. We must trace every young man who was there, Inspector Horsley, to check that he is alive and, I might add, ascertain that he is not the killer. Each of those party-goers must be interviewed and eliminated from this enquiry. TIE is the word, Inspector. Trace, Interview and Eliminate. What I am anxious to do, however, in addition to that, is check all places along the various routes into Hurnehow, to see if any strangers were seen in the past week or ten days.'

'Strangers? In a tourist area, Montague? The place is full of strangers.'

'It is March, Inspector Horsley, not July or August. Strangers may have been noted. Or people behaving strangely, to be more precise. Anyway, that road beyond Hurnehow just goes to Hillshaw, it comes to a dead end there. Strangers would be noticed there, for example.'

'Right, I understand what you are saying. I'll arrange enquiries at all places along every route into Hurnehow. To be honest, there's not a lot of roads to trouble us, but we might turn up something useful. You'll want to concentrate on roadside houses rather than those down side streets? Garages too? Cafés? Pubs? Takeaways?'

'Absolutely, Inspector Horsley. Any occupied building along the roadside. And if anyone has a closed-circuit television camera, that might help. I believe some of those cameras at garages can record vehicle registration numbers? I ought to add that I am very interested in vehicles and people who came this way before Tuesday, before the party at Hurne Hall, that is. The body was almost certainly on the moor prior to the fire and before the party but we must not be tied precisely to those times.'

'I get your drift, Montague. Are we looking for something in particular? Or someone in particular?'

'No one in particular but a vehicle must have been used to dump our victim or at least to transport him to Black-amoor, dead or alive, and at least two people must have been involved in the disposal of his body. It's also likely the body was deposited under cover of darkness and so we are thinking of vehicles and people moving late at night, with extra lights perhaps, lights among the heather. Night-time security cameras might be worth a check if any operate in this area. Today is Saturday and Mr Meredith, our forensic pathologist, believes the body could have been dead for a week or even ten days. So we need to start looking from, say, as early as Tuesday or Wednesday last week. A tall order, Mr Horsley, but we are speaking of only a few roads all of which are normally very quiet at this time of year.'

'I'll get cracking immediately, Montague. Thanks to mobile phones, I can recall some officers without further ado.'

And at that point, his telephone rang. 'Horsley, Incident Room,' he barked into the mouthpiece. As Horsley was listening, Pluke looked around the room, noting a description of the victim on the blackboard, photographs of the body and its resting place, and the list of party guests on another noticeboard with some already ticked off as being alive and positively eliminated as suspects. Emails to all forces with a description and photograph of the scene and the body had been despatched soon after the establishment of the Incident Room; with the bold heading *Murder*, they were guaranteed swift action. Already, there had been some response from police forces around the UK. There were a few emailed photographs of men who had been reported missing from their usual haunts in circumstances where there was cause for concern but at this stage none could linked to the victim – they were either too tall, too short, too fat, too thin or too old. Pluke was pleased; the investigation was running very smoothly; progress was being made.

'Montague,' said Horsley, holding the telephone at arm's

length with someone still on the line, 'I think you should take this call, it's a Sergeant Russell from Greater Manchester Police, "A" Division. He's got reports of a missing man who might be of interest to us.' And he handed the phone to Pluke.

'Detective Inspector Pluke speaking, Sergeant. How can I help you?'

Sergeant Russell, it transpired, worked in the Control Room at Manchester's 'A' Divisional Headquarters, and had fortuitously been in reception when Mrs Fowler had paid her visit. He explained Mrs Fowler's reports, with due emphasis on the invitation to a shooting party and adding that her son had been missing since just after three o'clock a week last Friday.

'Friday is a very bad day to begin any new enterprise,' commented Pluke.

Russell made no comment about that but added that a photograph of Fowler was available and it could be emailed to Pluke's Incident Room without delay.

'Our victim has a broken right big toe,' said Pluke. 'Or rather, it has been broken in the past and it has mended with a slight kink.'

'His mother didn't mention that, sir,' said the sergeant. 'And it won't show up on this photo!'

After discussing the general appearance and estimated age of the victim, Pluke agreed there could be a match, then said, 'Sergeant, we have taken a DNA sample but if your man has no convictions, then there may be difficulty securing a profile for comparison, unless there's something in his home we can use.'

'His DNA profile will be in our computer records, sir, Fowler is a paedophile. I might add that our CID is very interested in this report. Fowler has been arrested and questioned on several occasions, once on suspicion of child murder, and, as you know, a recent court ruling said we can retain DNA samples and profiles from arrested persons, and that applies even if a suspect is cleared by the court. So yes, we can compare that profile with the sample you've obtained from the victim.'

'Then we must establish whether there is a match before we inform his mother of this possibility and before we take any further action. That is vital, our next move. I will ask the forensic laboratory to make sure you receive the victim's DNA profile at the earliest opportunity.'

'Thanks, sir. And there's one other point, sir,' said the sergeant. 'In view of what we already know about Brent Fowler, I have spoken to our Detective Chief Inspector Sanders in the CID at this office and told him of your murder enquiry. He has authorized me to inform you that it is suspected, based on sound intelligence, that an execution squad is operating in this region. They are taking out selected victims. Our intelligence leads us to believe that a paedophile was recently tricked into going to the Lake District on a free weekend's diving course. He was keen on diving. He was never seen again. Another one is thought to have been murdered and thrown down a pit shaft in Derbyshire. It is suspected there have been others but I have no further details, sir. DCI Sanders asked me to tell you that your victim, if it is Brent Fowler, could have been assassinated because of his paedophilia. That would fit the pattern of what is already suspected, even if we have no other bodies.'

'Vigilantes? Very nasty indeed. Clearly, I must discuss this with Detective Chief Inspector Sanders, whether or not our victim is Fowler,' said Pluke. 'I'll endeavour to get our victim identified as a matter of priority and if it is Fowler, I'll arrange an urgent meeting with your Mr Sanders. If this is the first body left by the vigilantes, it will contain vital evidence. You'll tell him?'

'Thank you, sir, and I'll send you a photograph of Fowler.'

It was a very thoughtful Pluke who replaced the telephone. An assassination squad from Manchester? Killing paedophiles? Vigilante murders? Was this real? If so, why would the killers come all the way from Manchester to the

North York Moors, a hundred and forty miles or so, to dispose of the body? Surely they hadn't brought it with them, all that way? That was taking a huge risk. It was just possible, he supposed; vehicles did carry dead bodies long distances but not usually if they'd been murdered. Murder victims were usually dumped as quickly as possible to get rid of any evidence. It made more sense to speculate that the crime had been committed close to where the body was found.

However, it was an interesting thought that if the victim had been killed in the Manchester area, then that would become the scene of the crime. Not Blackamoor. And that meant the responsibility for investigating the murder would rest with Greater Manchester Police, not Montague Pluke. Nonetheless, if the victim was Fowler, it was quite likely that he had been brought here while alive and then killed on the moors, in which case the problem remained with Pluke. But news of a possible execution squad, if it was genuine, began to puzzle Montague Pluke.

For example, how did that cairn fit into the scheme of things? And the northern orientation of the body? If someone truly despised a person who had died, they might bury the corpse with the head towards the north. That was a means of displaying their contempt. Had that been done in this case? And a paedophile? People would hate and despise him, so the body's northern orientation now made sense. As did the cairn. But would a cold-blooded killer or team of killers consider such details? And leave evidence behind?

Pluke's next task was to contact Simon Meredith at the forensic laboratory and ask him to liaise with Detective Chief Inspector Sanders immediately about the DNA profile. Meredith was very excited by the prospect and said he would deal with the matter without delay. A rapid identification was vital.

Pluke told Horsley and Wayne the exciting news and repeated the intelligence provided by Sergeant Russell; this meant his personnel were up to date.

'If all this is true, gentlemen,' Pluke continued, 'this crime is out of our league but we must not let that daunt us. Let us assume, for the moment, that our victim is Brent Fowler. Whether or not his murder occurred within our boundaries, we must trace his route, dead or alive, from Manchester to Blackamoor. We must trace those who brought him here and the vehicle they used. Our officers must concentrate on traffic movements at the material times, well into the hours of darkness and even into the following morning, especially movements on the moors around Hurnehow. We must begin immediately.'

'Leave that with me, Montague,' said Horsley. 'Now, correct me if I'm wrong, but does this development mean we can forget the birthday party at Hurne Hall?'

'No, we must not forget it, Inspector Horsley. Coincidence is a rare thing in crime investigation, as you are aware, and we have several in this instance – a body on the moors, a murder no less, a fire on the moors where the body was found and a large gathering of people from all over the place, all at roughly the same time and in the same vicinity. We can't avoid the possibility of a link of some kind.'

'Fair enough, that's how I see things,' and he bent to his task.

And as Inspector Horsley began to contact units on the moors, Pluke went to the list of party guests which was pinned to a noticeboard. Several had been ticked off as having been interviewed and eliminated from suspicion, and, of course, as being proved to be alive. As he began to read each name, Wayne joined him.

'Something interesting, sir?' he asked.

'I am wondering if any of those party guests came from the Manchester area. I know the party was several days after Fowler was last seen in Manchester but we can't ignore the possibility that the two events could be linked in some way. The fire was on Wednesday morning, Wayne, a few days after Fowler left his home town, but we must remain aware that our victim might not be Brent Fowler. We cannot jump to conclusions but we must beware of coincidences.'

'So why the interest in guests from Manchester?'

'If it is Brent Fowler, I was wondering if any of them knew him. Or knew those we suspect of killing him. Did they know those vigilantes? And if they did know Brent Fowler, did they also know this part of the moors? If so, how? Have they been here? Look at it this way, Wayne. Someone knew precisely where to conceal that body. I am confident the dumping place was not chosen by chance. It was done with care and advance planning. If those people at the party came from all over Britain, is it feasible some would be familiar with that part of the countryside? Someone from Manchester perhaps?'

'Very possibly, sir, but knowledge of this landscape isn't limited to those who live here or come to smart parties in big houses.'

'One must start somewhere, Wayne,' said Pluke. 'So trace, interview and eliminate, eh? Starting with guests from Manchester.'

'Inspector Horsley has got that in hand, sir, through local forces.'

'I know, but I should like to personally interview the Manchester guests.'

'Why can't you leave it to the local police, sir? That's what normally happens.'

'I am aware of my specialist knowledge of the moors, Wayne. I know Manchester Police will do a good job but they lack my awareness of folklore and local customs. I am not forgetting that little cairn. That is one example, orientation of the body is another. Ah, see? Names?' and he prodded the list with a finger. 'Here's one we must check. A woman from Manchester. So did she come alone to the party, Wayne? Or with a friend or partner? You see, there *were* guests from Manchester. And when I have completed my notes from this list, you and I will hit the road, as they say. We will cross the Pennines to make our enquiries. But such a lot depends on whether or not the victim is Brent Fowler.'

Chapter Six

Mrs Fowler was pleased she had found the courage to visit the police and even more pleased they had given her the telephone number of the National Missing Persons Helpline. That sergeant had been very nice, she thought, but she wouldn't ring the Helpline just yet. She'd give the police a day or two because the sergeant had said he would do his best and, after all, they were the real experts. Surely they would find Brent? If he had been admitted to hospital or lost his memory or something, the police would be the most likely to come across him. She'd wait until Monday morning to see what happened.

At home, she half expected to find Brent sitting at the kitchen table or watching television in the lounge, but there was still no sign of him and no note or card through the letterbox. She went up to his room, calling his name in advance as she climbed the stairs, but he was not there and nothing had been disturbed. He'd not been, not even for a short visit. Feeling helpless, she realized she was no further forward, except the police now knew about Brent and his name was in their records.

She rang some of the people she'd called on previous occasions and contacted the leisure centre again, thinking that if Brent was coming home to go to work on Monday, he might have contacted his manager to let him know what was happening, but no one had heard anything, not even a postcard or phone call from him. As always, they said they would ring if he did make contact. Now it was time to make something to eat, a poached egg on toast would be nice after that lovely lunch, and so she busied herself with the meal, laying the usual place at table for Brent.

While in town, she had bought a copy of the *Manchester Evening News* to see if it mentioned any unidentified young men in accidents or attacks. Sometimes they printed stories of people suffering from loss of memory or being found injured after an accident or an attack by drunks and thugs and not being recognized in spite of publicity. Even though she read the paper from front to back, she found nothing which might refer to Brent. She would watch the news on television too, but they didn't do many local stories on Saturdays, except for the football. And Brent wasn't the slightest bit interested in football.

The report of Brent Fowler's disappearance had energized the SIOUX department of Manchester CID, with DCI Sanders asking his teams to search all their records, computerized and manual, for any firm indications of who might be responsible. Unidentified groups of men had to be named, tapped phone calls analysed, vehicles traced and undercover observations reassessed. Two officers were assigned to Jacob Hampson, albeit with specific orders not to let him become aware of their interest. Much now depended upon whether the body found in North Yorkshire was Brent Fowler. That could provide the breakthrough they needed.

From the list of Jonathan Hurne's party guests, Pluke found four whose home addresses were in the Manchester area. There were a Mr and Mrs J. Sharpe from Stockport, and a couple who apparently lived together at an address in Salford, Alison Wharram and Mark Newbury. None had been interviewed by Greater Manchester Police at this stage, so he would arrange to personally speak to each of them if the deceased was identified as Brent Fowler. If the victim was *not* Fowler, he would reconsider his tactics.

'While we are waiting for the identification, Wayne, I would like to return to the moors,' said Pluke. 'We can check a few locations en route, cafés, garages and so on. And Inspector Horsley?'

'Yes, Montague?'

'Can you arrange a conference of detectives at the scene at six thirty this evening? I'd like to address the teams before dismissing them and will update you before going off duty.'

'Fine,' said Horsley. 'Oh, and by the way, we've been emailed a photograph of Brent Fowler. You asked for one, I believe?'

'I did indeed.' Pluke studied the photo carefully and showed it to Wayne, but neither could definitely say it was their victim. The fire had done too much damage but the picture would be useful when asking questions in the locality. Then he and Wayne Wain departed. As Wayne drove away, Pluke took a road map from the glove compartment and studied the most likely route to be taken if the deceased was Brent Fowler, and if his killers – at least two of them – had driven from Manchester to Blackamoor. It was almost certain they would travel east along the M62 and then head north up the A1 until they reached the junction for Thirsk. They would then take the A168 and A170. Once beyond Thirsk, they would have to pass through Crickledale before taking one of several minor and unclassified roads as they headed deep into the moors. As it was a popular tourist area, there were lots of stopping places if they needed a break for a rest, food or fuel.

'Timing is important, Wayne. According to Sergeant Russell in Manchester, Fowler was last seen at three o'clock by his mother. He was not picked up at the door and he told her he had been asked to join a people carrier at the Arndale Centre at half-past three. He tells me the CID are already checking silver people carriers because one has attracted police interest. Now, to travel from Manchester city centre on a Friday afternoon, and then to cope with traffic along the M62 and A1, is not easy, one cannot speed along as one might at three o'clock on a Sunday morning. So how long would it take to get here? To Crickledale from Manchester city centre?'

'Three hours at least, sir, perhaps four on a bad day. I'd allow four.'

'So we're talking of the possibility that our victim arrived on our moorland around seven thirty that Friday evening, but possibly earlier, six thirty or so. Within that hour. It would be dark and that fits into the scheme of things, disposing of the body, I mean, under cover of darkness.'

'Yes, I understand that. My suggested timing is without stops, by the way. Would they stop, do you think?'

'I think it very likely. I know we are theorizing but I think they would want their trip to appear as normal as possible. They would not exceed the speed limit, for example, they would not risk being stopped by the police, they would not get angry with silly drivers, they would purchase fuel with cash not credit cards which are traceable, and they might pull in at some halting places for a few minutes merely to check whether or not they were being followed or observed. And they might need refreshments. Remember, though, that they were on a criminal expedition. Whether or not Fowler was dead at this stage, they would be highly suspicious of everyone and everything. There is no doubt in my mind they would do all within their power to make sure they did not attract undue attention and that the journey appeared as normal as possible. Even so, I am sure there would be nervousness among them. And we do not know how many people were in that vehicle – Mrs Fowler said Brent was one of six prize-winners for that trip. So perhaps, to make things appear in keeping with that, there were six in the vehicle?'

'I agree with that, and if your prognosis is correct they would actually have driven through Crickledale!'

'There is only that one road out to Blackamoor from here, Wayne, so I suggest we check at all likely stopping places between here and Hurnehow.'

'So exactly what are we asking about, sir? We don't know anything about the vehicle except it was a people carrier according to Mrs Fowler – could it be the silver one mentioned by Sergeant Russell? And we can't be sure how many people were involved or what any of them looked like. It's a bit of a tall order, if you ask me.'

'If they were all from Manchester, Wayne, they will stand out like chapel hat pegs.'

'Why, sir?'

'The way they speak, Wayne. They don't speak like people from this part of Yorkshire. They don't say book, they say byoook, they don't say look, they say lyoook, they pronounce their rrrrs as urs and so on, all with very rounded vowels and some very noticeable consonants. A most distinctive mode of speech, Wayne, particularly when heard around these North York Moors.'

'So we are looking – lyoooking – for a people carrier full of Lancastrians?'

'I believe so.'

'But does this mean they were all involved in Fowler's death? Murder is usually a solitary crime.'

'Murder is often solitary, Wayne, execution is not. Remember those executions in Iraq – done in the full view of television cameras? Whatever their number, they shouldn't be hard to find in Yorkshire,' chuckled Pluke, or Plyoook. 'There'd be at least three, one of whom would be Brent Fowler, and we have his photograph.'

And so it was that Montague Pluke and Wayne began enquiries in Crickledale, visiting pubs, cafés and fast-foot outlets like fish-and-chip shops while seeking strangers from that part of England on the wrong side of the Pennines. They checked garages too, just in case such a people carrier, possibly silver, had called for petrol or diesel a week last Friday between, say, six and eight in the evening.

In all cases, they showed their photograph of Brent Fowler but drew a blank. Gradually, they worked their way along the minor road which led from Crickledale up to the moors, checking at more pubs, eating places, shops and garages, but always with no result. In spite of having the photograph, which had reproduced well on the computer print-out, Wayne Wain did not really expect anything positive from this exercise, chiefly because of the time lapse and also because of the vague nature of their questions. But because his boss felt it necessary, Wayne would comply.

And then they came to a lofty inn set in the middle of a huge expanse of open moor. Rugged and weatherbeaten, its stones darkened by centuries of history, it sat low among the heather. Already, lights were burning and the place was surrounded by cars, camper-vans and motor cycles.

'This is the sort of place where they would call,' said Pluke. 'The finest way to lose oneself is among a crowd of people, and the best place to hide a vehicle is among other vehicles. I know this place, it is the Cockatrice Inn. Mrs Pluke and I have had some very nice meals here, not that we frequent public houses on a regular basis. When seeking horse troughs on these moors, I have always regarded it as a place of shelter and refreshment. A most atmospheric place, Wayne, full of ancient history and rich with fascinating horse troughs. I might add that it is very popular with ramblers, hikers, naturalists, cyclists, motor cyclists, busloads of tourists, everyone in fact. Let me show you the place, Wayne, as we ask a few questions.'

'The Cockatrice? Is this anything to do with the Hurne estate? Their emblem is a cockatrice, isn't it?'

'Indeed it is. They owned the inn many years ago, but sold it to raise money during the 1960s. That's when large estates and landowners were suffering from the socialist politics of the period. Lots of large estates sold off unwanted cottages and other assets. Today it has nothing to do with the Hurne estate or family. And, I might add, I know of no other inn by this name, although I could be wrong. Legendary animals such as the unicorn, the griffin and dragons of various colours are used as inn signs but this could be the only Cockatrice Inn in England.'

'You were going to tell me why it's the emblem of the Hurne family, sir?'

'And so I shall, Wayne. You might remember I told you the cockatrice could kill any living thing with a mere glance, and so the only way to deal with the menace was to place a mirror near its lair. The theory was that when it caught sight of itself, it died instantly – but a very brave knight was needed to approach the lair. And, long ago, the local knight in question was an ancestor of the present Hurne family. It became his responsibility to deal with the cockatrice because it was spreading fear and death to every living thing in this district. And so the brave Sir Algernon Hurne made himself a suit of armour which was polished so that every part had a mirror-like finish and then he armed himself with a mirror. He reasoned that if the cockatrice found him, it would kill itself by catching sight of its reflection in his armour, but the creature did not appear and so Sir Algernon managed to place the mirror in such a position near its lair that the cockatrice would see its own image and die. Sir Algernon became renowned as a man who would never allow evil to harm either his family or any of the people living nearby.'

'Rather like those people who killed Brent Fowler, sir?'

'That is something one has to bear in mind, Wayne, the family tradition; that might indeed provide a motive. Now, if what Manchester Police tell me is correct, and if our victim is Brent Fowler, then I am sure those who killed him thought they were doing right. They see themselves as protecting the general public and children in particular, against a villain. Just as St George killed the dragon and Lord Lambton killed the worm.'

'And David killed Goliath?'

'And there are many similar stories, Wayne, local, national and international. They are all accounts of good overcoming evil; the story of the Hurne cockatrice is one such tale.'

The entrance to the inn was stone-flagged and worn by the tread of thousands of visitors over the centuries. Inside, it was dark because the walls were several feet thick and it had very small windows. They were built to retain the heat rather than enhance the view. The entire inn comprised lots of small rooms with low ceilings heavy with oak beams, and some of the walls had been removed in recent times to provide more space. Wayne could imagine this inn being a welcome place of shelter down the centuries when deep snow covered the moors outside, sometimes for weeks at a time. He wondered if highwaymen had ever lurked here.

'I can see why you like this place so much, sir,' he said to Pluke as they entered. 'Most atmospheric.'

'Indeed, Wayne, and it has six horse troughs strategically placed around the exterior walls. Many teams of horses would halt here as they hauled wagons of lime and stone across these heights; their attendants would enjoy the ale and food, just as pilgrims in the Middle Ages halted here for the same reason . . . This is living history, Wayne, I can feel it in my bones, which is why the Cockatrice is one of the few hostelries that Mrs Pluke and I patronize on a modestly regular basis.'

As they moved through the rooms and crowded tables towards the bar, the landlord noticed Pluke. 'Ah, Mr Pluke! Good to see you. Mrs Pluke not with you?'

'Not today, Mr Firth, I am not here to admire your six troughs nor to research the folklore and legends associated with your esteemed establishment. I am here as a police officer investigating a murder and this is my assistant, Detective Sergeant Wain. Wayne, this is Mr George Firth, the owner, licensee and mine host of this inn.'

The two shook hands as Firth said, 'Murder? Look, you'd better come into a quiet room, they can manage without me for a while.' And so he led them into a room at the rear of the premises, one regularly used for small business meetings.

'Can I get you anything to drink?' asked Firth as Pluke and Wayne settled at a table.

'No, thank you.' Pluke never accepted gratuities from other people, not even drinks; one might find oneself compromised by accepting gifts from licensees or someone who was later found to be a suspect. A police officer must be above suspicion at all times and Pluke obeyed that diktat to the letter – almost.

Firth sat down. 'So how can I help, Mr Pluke? A murder, you say?'

Pluke provided a heavily edited account of the body found on the swidden near Hurnehow, saying it was that of a young man who had been shot, probably a week last Friday. Firth said he had already heard from some of his customers that there was police activity on the moors but had no idea it was a murder investigation. Pluke continued, 'It is a difficult question to answer, Mr Firth, in view of the number of strangers who pass through here, but I am trying to trace any who might have been in this vicinity a week last Friday, between say six and nine in the evening. I am particularly interested in people, probably men, who might have had a Lancastrian accent; there'd be at least three of them, I believe, but possibly more. I have nothing much else to go on at the moment, except that they might have been using a people carrier. I might add we are working with Greater Manchester Police in this enquiry and I may be in possession of further helpful information in the near future.'

'A week last Friday? Well, I was here on duty . . . let me think . . . I'll just get my order files, that'll help me. We're old-fashioned here, Mr Pluke, I don't use computers for my accounting chiefly because most of our income is in cash. I keep the order forms on a spike each working day, then file them when I do my books. Back in a second.'

He returned with a buff-coloured file with a tag in one corner, and it was full of order forms which had been used that Friday. Each had been completed at the time the order was placed, each bore a time and each bore a table number.

And each had been crossed with a black pen to signify it had been paid.

'Between six and nine, you say?' he muttered as he flicked through the pile. They were filed in chronological order; clearly either this man or one of his staff was a capable administrator. Then he found one.

'This order was placed at quarter to seven, Mr Pluke. The first since four o'clock that afternoon – we serve food all day between 10 a.m. and 10 p.m. but it's usually very quiet between six and seven. Clearly, we did serve some on that day. Seven meals, it says here. Ah . . . .yes, it's coming back to me, yes, I remember this lot. They practically had the place to themselves for a while. Seven men, one very much in charge of things, the others quiet. I think the bossy one had a faint Lancashire accent although he was quite posh really. I could definitely hear traces of Lancashire in his voice. One of the others was from that part of the world too, if his voice was anything to go by, but the other five didn't say a word to me. I think they were foreigners, I heard them speaking to each other in some lingo I didn't understand. Those five wore white T-shirts and the boss had a white sweater. The one without a white top was different from the others, not really part of things. The bossy one asked if we had a happy hour and our barman said no. He wasn't satisfied with the barman's answer so he asked me as well, I think he was wanting cheap drinks. I said we had no need for a happy hour, we were always busy without giving big discounts, then he said we weren't all that busy with only his party in! You can't win, Mr Pluke, so I retorted that the staff needed a quiet time now and again. I told him we'd be busy later, being a Friday, and in fact we were. We were run off our feet later.'

'Did you take this food order?'

'No, one of the waitresses did, Cindy. She's not here yet, she'll be in later. At seven.'

'But you saw the men?'

'I did, Mr Pluke. I make it my business to talk to every

customer during their meals to ask if everything is to their liking. If not, I need to know, so that standards are maintained. That's how I recognized those chaps' Lancashire inflections.'

'I would imagine a good memory is invaluable in your business, Mr Firth.'

'It's vital, and I do have a good memory. I can recall most of my customers even if they come in a year later, just as dentists and hairdressers can remember the most intimate facts about their clients. I didn't serve their drinks in this case, they got those at the bar and that's when the barman was asked if we did a happy hour. The boss man didn't buy alcohol – he said he was driving. He had a glass of orange but he ordered pints for five others, and a soft drink – a Coke, I think – for a young man who didn't seem part of the group even though he was with them. I don't know who they were or why they were here and I didn't ask, I don't pry into my customers' business, Mr Pluke.'

Pluke dug into the commodious pocket of his huge coat and pulled out an envelope containing the photograph of Brent Fowler.

'Was this one of those men?' he asked.

Firth took it from him and held it to gain more light on the picture, studied it for a few moments and nodded.

'I can't be a hundred per cent sure, Mr Pluke, but yes, I'd say this was that young fellow who didn't seem part of the group. A bit of an outsider, quiet, shy sort of lad. He had the Coke, if I remember. Cindy will remember more than me, she dealt with them and was busy around them on other tables. They paid cash, by the way, the boss paid the bill, so I don't have any credit card or cheque details.'

'I need to know more about all those men,' said Pluke, putting away the photograph. 'Any detail, no matter how slight. What did they talk about? How did they arrive? Had they been here before?'

'Can I ask if they are linked to the murder, Mr Pluke?'

'Let me say we are anxious to trace them, so we can eliminate them from our enquiries, Mr Firth.'

97

He decided to make use of a modest subterfuge in case his enquiries reached the ears of the killer or killers, and so he did not tell them that the photograph was of the victim. All he said was that he wanted to know as much as possible about all the men, stressing that any detail, however slight, would be of value.

'They didn't draw much attention to themselves, Mr Pluke, and they were all well behaved but the big chap was clearly the boss. Jake, he was called. I heard one of them call him Jake.'

'And what did Jake look like?'

'Big and powerful, a presence if you know what I mean. Six foot tall and more. Six one or two. Broad. You could see him as a wrestler or shot putter. Cropped hair, dark, the beginnings of a beard, brown eyes – yes, brown eyes. Well spoken even with his Lancashire accent. Very much the boss.'

'And the others? Did you hear any names mentioned? What sort of vehicle did they have? What were they wearing? How old were they? I need as much detail as I can get, Mr Firth.'

'Apart from that lad in the photo, Mr Pluke, I can't remember much about the others, except they didn't say a lot to me or my staff. And they all wore those white T-shirts. Jake did all the talking. He bought them all another couple of pints each, got the quiet lad another Coke and he had an orange juice. They all had big meals, steak and chips, cod and chips, that sort of thing, and Jake paid in cash. All I can say is the others were all fairly young, under forty, most with good heads of dark hair. Foreign-looking, I'd say. East European, not French, Italian, Greek. More like Russians or Czechs. No names, though, I heard no names for them but Cindy might have done.'

'We'll talk to Cindy. Now, their transport? How they did they arrive, Mr Firth?'

'Well, Mr Pluke, like I said it was quiet just then, so I noticed there was a people carrier in our car park when they were here. Just the one. A silvery grey one. I think they all came in the same vehicle. I can't tell you the make or give its number because I didn't take much notice of it, but it was parked by itself, close to the front door, that's how I noticed it. Silvery grey, a bit like a Ford Galaxy, but it could have been a Renault or a Merc or anything. But they'd need a big vehicle to carry all of them, wouldn't they?'

'They would indeed, Mr Firth. Well, thank you for all this, it has been a great help.'

'Has it? I haven't told you much!'

'But what you have told us is valuable, Mr Firth. Perhaps you would give some more thought to this, I may call back for another chat once you've had time to think about it. Now I have a conference of detectives to attend before we conclude our day's work, then I'll come back after that to interview Cindy. Is that all right with you?'

'Yes, no problem. I'll stand in for her while she's talking to you, Mr Pluke. Pleased to be of assistance.'

'What did you make of that?' asked Pluke as Wayne drove him from the Cockatrice towards the swidden and the search teams.

'A very useful lead, sir,' smiled Wayne. 'I was beginning to think we were getting nowhere but now we have struck oil. It seems Greater Manchester's intelligence is right – Fowler was the victim of some kind of assassination squad involving several men who use a silvery people carrier.'

'That's if our victim really is Fowler! We're not sure yet. But the good news is that we have a name for a suspect – Jake – which could be false or fictitious. We have a reasonable description of him and evidence that Brent Fowler was with him and others in the Cockatrice a week last Friday, probably hours before he died. It seems he was brought here alive, Wayne, which strongly suggests he was killed on our moors. I'm sure he is our victim and that he was in the Cockatrice with his killers. All we have to do is find and identify them. White T-shirts, eh? And a white sweater. Almost a kind of uniform. Is that significant?'

99

When Pluke and Wayne arrived at the moorland assembly point just inside the Hurne estate's grounds his teams were already assembled, but before Pluke addressed them, Detective Sergeant Tabler told him they had found hundreds more shotgun cartridges, all evidence of earlier grouse-shooting expeditions. They'd also located hundreds more pieces of domestic litter such as plastic sandwich wrappings, plastic bottles and drinks cans, but none could be linked to the crime. Likewise, the detectives on house-to-house enquiries had not learned anything of value, in particular they had not been able to establish sightings of people or vehicles behaving suspiciously in the locality of the swidden, or along any of its approaches.

Inspector Horsley, when arranging this conference, had informed Tabler that twenty more guests from the list had been interviewed and eliminated from the enquiry. His good news, however, was that the DNA profile sent by computer from the forensic laboratory to Greater Manchester Police had established that the victim was Brent Fowler. His mother had not yet been informed because Detective Chief Inspector Sanders of Greater Manchester Police wanted to discuss the case with DI Pluke before proceeding any further. He said he would welcome a call from DI Pluke at his earliest convenience – he would be in his office until eight o'clock this evening and Horsley had assured Sanders that Pluke would respond the moment he returned from the moors.

Standing on a rock near the parked vehicles to elevate himself above the heads of his officers, Pluke was therefore able to inform them (a) that the deceased was Brent Fowler, an unconvicted paedophile from Manchester; (b) that his death was probably due to an assassination plan by several men from that area, some of whom were foreigners; (c) that a vehicle, something like a silver-grey Ford Galaxy, had been used; (d) that the men and Fowler had probably been at the Cockatrice Inn a week last Friday; (e) that a week last Friday was probably the date of his death; (f) that the scene of his death may have been the swidden or somewhere on the moor very nearby; (g) that the death could be part of a series committed by the men who'd accompanied Fowler on his last day, and (h) that as Fowler had been alive when seen in this locality, the place of his death was surely nearby, thus the enquiry would be the responsibility of Pluke and his teams. House-to-house enquiries would continue tomorrow, Sunday, and Pluke felt that the moorland search could be scaled down although it was still necessary for the fatal bullet to be recovered. Tomorrow morning's conference would mark the start of another day. It would be in the Incident Room at Crickledale Police Station. And with that he dismissed his officers, saying the enquiry was progressing well, and thanked them for their day's work.

'So,' said Pluke to Wayne Wain, 'it is now time for us to revisit the Cockatrice for a chat with Cindy.'

Cindy's real name was Lucinda Owen and she lived in Hurnehow. A small, extremely slender girl in her mid-twenties, she gave her home address and told them that she worked in the stables of a local racehorse trainer by day and as a waitress in the evenings to earn a little extra. When Wayne Wain walked into her life, Pluke noticed the effect upon her but took the opportunity to immediately begin the interview, even if Cindy's eyes seldom left the rugged handsomeness of Wayne. Pluke outlined the reason for his questions, then asked:

'So, Miss Owen, do you remember those men?'

'Yes, I do, Mr Pluke, most of them had white T-shirts on and they left a good tip.'

'Did you learn anything else about them?'

'No, nothing. They never told me anything about themselves.'

He produced the photograph of Brent Fowler without revealing he was dead and she nodded, saying that definitely he was one of them. She remembered him because he was so nice and quiet, and hadn't a white T-shirt. The big man, the boss, often made jokes with the others in a foreign language, and then laughed and said something in English about this being their last supper.

'Their last supper?' frowned Pluke.

'Well, I heard the big man say something about this being the last supper some of them might get, he said that to the one without the white T-shirt. I had no idea what they meant, I guessed it was an ongoing joke between them and thought they might be going somewhere where they couldn't get anything to eat . . . like a long overnight hike mebbe. Such as the Lyke Wake Walk. We have lots of parties in here, getting a good meal before they set off for a night on the moors. Quite a lot of them joke that it could be their last supper if they got lost.'

'Did you talk to the one in that photograph?'

'No.' She shook her head. 'No, he wasn't saying much, Mr Pluke, and besides, the big one was doing all the talking, often in a foreign language but I never heard them use bad language, Mr Pluke, no swear words like some people use in pubs.'

She could not tell him anything about the vehicle; although she was vaguely aware of the presence of a silver-grey people carrier in the car park when she had arrived for work, she was unable to give its number or other details. She could not provide any information about the other men, other than they were youngish, foreign-looking with dark hair, and they all left about eight o'clock as the place was getting busier. She said all the beer drinkers looked more cheerful than when they had arrived but she had no idea where they went upon leaving. Pluke and Wayne thanked her and left, saying they might wish to talk to her again another day, and she said she would try to remember anything else that had been said that evening.

Pluke asked Wayne to drop him off at the police station in Crickledale from where he would ring Detective Chief Inspector Sanders in Manchester to arrange a meeting before deciding his next course of action. Then he would go home because Millicent would have prepared a nice evening meal.

There might even be a glass of sherry but hopefully there would be some cocoa before he went to sleep.

Chapter Seven

When Mrs Fowler climbed out of bed on Sunday morning after another sleepless night worrying about Brent, her first job was to check his bedroom in case he had come home during the night. But he hadn't. His bed covers were as smooth as when she had made it all those days ago and nothing else had been touched. She looked into the little back bedroom too, the one he used for his computer, but he wasn't there either.

She washed and dressed for the day and then went downstairs. The breakfast table was already set; she always set it for herself and Brent before going to bed. She put the kettle on then looked around the house, checking the lounge and utility room, then her modest back garden just in case he was sitting outside on the bench. He might have thought the doors would be locked overnight but they hadn't been, she left them open all the time while she was in the house, so that he could return any time without disturbing her, if that's what he wanted.

When the kettle boiled she made a pot of tea, enough for two, and then settled down to a lonely breakfast of corn flakes, a piece of toast with marmalade and a nice cup of tea. As she sat staring at the walls and fittings of her kitchen over her lonely breakfast, she wondered how she was going to occupy herself today, being a Sunday. She could go out and buy a newspaper, she supposed, or she could even pop into the leisure centre's cafeteria and have a snack there while asking if they had heard from

Brent. An alternative was to walk around the town to see if he was sleeping rough for any reason.

Lots of young men slept rough in alleys and doorways. There were beggars too, who scuttled away and vanished like rats if a police officer appeared. Many of them looked like foreigners and she wondered if they were illegal immigrants: she hoped Brent would never be reduced to such a thing. She did wonder if he might have taken to sleeping rough through being frightened of the accusations that had been made against him, although she knew he would never hurt a child. But if people thought he had assaulted a child, they could be nasty to him, they could attack him, which might explain why he hadn't come home. They might find him here, just like those people who invited him to the shooting party; they had known where he lived. Some people could do awful things to men who assaulted little girls and boys, she'd read about some dreadful attacks in the paper. There was that man in the south who'd been shot dead because he had interfered with some children . . . Her Brent would never do that, never hurt children, but she also knew that once a person had been tainted with that kind of reputation, it was difficult to prove their innocence. But surely people would not believe Brent would do such a thing, would they? He was such a nice boy, so nice and kind to others, especially those less fortunate than himself.

Even so, the words of the man at the leisure centre had bothered her all night . . . should she have told the police about that? About what Brent was supposed to have done to the children? Would it have made any difference to how they dealt with her? Or looked for him? Maybe she could check once more at the hospital to see if he had been hurt in an accident of some kind, an attack even.

Yes, she decided, there was plenty to do. And she might even go to church. Brent went to church, being an Anglican; he'd been in the choir but had said he didn't want to go any more, that was just before the choirmaster had been asked to leave. She'd never really believed all those rumours about the choirmaster but now she wasn't so sure. Was that why Brent had stopped going to choir practice and stopped going to church? Had something happened between them? Brent had not said anything about it. So, yes, she would go to church this morning and pray for Brent, and then carry out all those visits. Those – and lunch – would occupy her for most of the day.

Detective Chief Inspector Sanders was in the office early because he had to prepare for the visit of Detective Inspector Pluke from North Yorkshire. There was a lot to do in a short time and he was anxious to discover whether Pluke, as an officer from another force, would agree to help set a trap for the suspect assassins. He required someone totally unknown to the local population and hoped the Yorkshire detective was up to the task he was about to propose.

That same Sunday morning, Detective Inspector Montague Pluke rose from the depths of his bed, looked underneath as he always did in case something nasty was lurking there, stepped out of bed on the right side while making sure he began his day's activities with his right foot first, and then went about his morning ablutions.

After several minutes' frantic activity with his razor, toothbrush, face cloth and comb, he dressed for work and went downstairs. Millicent was in the kitchen and Montague's breakfast place was set at the table. Millicent, as always, made sure that his knife was not crossed with any other knife, fork or spoon because that heralded a forthcoming quarrel and she had no wish to quarrel with him, or to have him quarrel with anyone at work. It had taken Millicent many years to get Montague's permission to set the breakfast table before going to bed because he believed a knife left on the table overnight heralded bad fortune of some kind. Millicent, however, had succeeded in persuading him that the belief only applied to Lincolnshire and that it related only to the death of a farm animal before morning. As the Plukes did not live in Lincolnshire and did not keep farm animals, she was convinced the superstition did not apply to them. And in time, Montague had accepted that logic.

His shoes were waiting near the back door and she had made sure there were no knots in the laces as that was a sign of impending bad fortune. She had arranged them in the form of a letter T with the soles uppermost, a wonderful means of keeping away cramp, rheumatism and nightmares during the night hours.

And so it was that Montague Pluke prepared for his day's work of finding a savage killer or killers. Just after eight thirty, he confirmed he had his mobile telephone and could use it, then bade farewell to Millicent, saying he would walk to the police station where Detective Sergeant Wain and the others would be expecting him.

He had his lucky rabbit's foot in his pocket and he started the journey from the house with his right foot while making sure he did not stumble because that was a sign of bad luck, but in fact he sneezed just before leaving the house. Fortunately, he managed to direct his blast to the right to ensure very good luck throughout the day. To sneeze to the left was most unfortunate but he had managed to avert that disaster.

As he walked through the small town of Crickledale the church bells were ringing, one of the finest methods of driving away bad fortune, but Pluke was never quite sure whether it was true that a church bell would sound if someone committed a crime nearby. Certainly, the bells of Crickledale Parish Church had never sounded of their own accord but, he supposed, that could be because no crimes had been committed within their range. This morning the town was quiet. None of the shops was open and so he did not meet any of the people he regularly encountered on his way to the office although he did raise his hat to greet several churchgoing ladies and gentlemen. There were people walking dogs too, which meant he raised his distinctive hat many times during that short journey.

Fortunately none of the dogs was howling, which was a good omen, and he felt particularly pleased that one of them was a black-and-white terrier. It was extremely auspicious to meet a black-and-white dog while on the way to an important business appointment, as indeed Montague Pluke now was. In Lincolnshire, of course, it was unlucky to meet a white dog but the misfortune could be averted by keeping silent until one met a white horse. Montague Pluke was glad he did not live in Lincolnshire. Living there meant he would have a troublesome time if he met any white dogs or set his breakfast table the previous night. He was pleased, however, when a black cat ran across his path even though he was not able to stroke it three times. He couldn't even stroke it once because it leapt on to a wall and vanished into someone's garden before he could reach it.

Upon arrival at the police station, he entered with his right foot first, poked his head around the door of the Control Room to alert Sergeant Cockfield pronounced Cofield to his arrival, then climbed the stairs to the Conference Room which was now being used as the Incident Room. It was very noisy, he noted as he approached, but of course it was full of detectives awaiting a stimulating address from their esteemed leader before embarking on their day's detecting duties. Inspector Horsley was in position at his desk, Detective Sergeant Wain could be seen chatting to him and the gathered officers were enjoying their first cup of tea or coffee, prepared by the ever-willing team of three young female computer operators. Once, they would have been typists who would have prepared all the statements collected during the investigation; now it was all done on computers.

That was a wonderful improvement because, instead of a person having to read all the statements to filter them for names, the computers would now do that. You just had to ask the computer to find a particular name or car or other thing and bingo! It would do so in a matter of seconds. Quite magical, thought Pluke as he fought his way through the mass of humanity to hail Horsley.

'Good morning, Inspector Horsley, good morning, Detective Sergeant Wain. I trust both of you had a restful night because I sense we are to have a busy and successful day. The omens are good, the weather is fine and I saw a black cat on my way to the office.'

'Then the devil can do his worst!' said Horsley. 'You can't beat a black cat for bringing a spot of luck to a murder enquiry on a bad day.'

'Many a true word spoken in jest, Inspector,' beamed Pluke. 'Now, have there been any relevant developments overnight?'

'None,' confirmed Horsley. 'Things are very quiet, but of course it's the weekend and the murder is not yet in the wider public domain. Once it is in the news, I would expect calls and sightings of suspects from members of the public as far away as John o' Groats and Land's End, but to date all is quiet. How about you? Did you speak to Detective Chief Inspector Sanders in Manchester?'

'Yes, I rang him yesterday evening and we decided the only way forward was to meet and exchange information. He can see me today and is preparing a file. As there is much of a confidential nature, he will prepare a floppy disk although a discussion is vital due to the type of crime. We have arranged it for eleven today, midway between here and Manchester, at the Leeds/Bradford airport which is in the West Yorkshire Police area. It is exactly halfway on neutral ground between our locations and Detective Chief Inspector Sanders will obtain permission to use one of the offices of the Airport Security Service. So that is where we are going, Wayne, you and I. With you driving. First, though, I must address the teams of detectives.'

Horsley hammered his desk to indicate he wanted silence, and then said, 'All right, everyone. Time for work. Detective Inspector Pluke will now address you.'

The assembled multitude fell into silence as Pluke clambered on to a chair to make his speech. He started with fulsome praise for their work yesterday and an appreciation of what they were going to achieve today, then told them there had been an important development.

'This is not for general release, not for the public and most certainly not for the press,' he emphasized. 'The deceased is a twenty-eight-year-old man from Manchester called Brent Fowler. His mother and perhaps other family members are not yet aware of his death so we must be very careful in the way we conduct our enquiry in these early stages. His mother will be told today and will have to come here to make the formal identification; in any case, she will wish to see her son. More importantly, you should know that Fowler was a known paedophile and suspect child murderer, albeit without any convictions. He worked in a leisure centre in Manchester, formerly as a swimming pool attendant and latterly in the kitchen of the cafeteria. His close attention to very young girls resulted in him being relocated to the kitchen, but at this stage I do not know much more about him. I shall be speaking to a member of Manchester CID later this morning when I hope to gain more information about Fowler. You should also be aware that Manchester Police believe he was executed because of his paedophilia. The weapon was a .22 calibre firearm – pistol or a rifle – and you all know he was found on the swidden yesterday. I suspect he was killed there or nearby but to date we have not found the murder weapon nor any spent cartridges from it. It is almost certain he was seen alive at the Cockatrice Inn on the moors above Hurnehow a week last Friday. The time was from around seven to eight o'clockish and he shared a meal with six other men, believed to be from the Manchester area. They arrived in a silver-grey people carrier, like a Ford Galaxy, and all were wearing white T-shirts except their leader who had a white sweater. They shouldn't be difficult to recognize. Perhaps a witness saw them and thought they were a sports team of some kind?

110

Clearly, we are anxious to learn more about those men and that vehicle – where they went, whom they talked to, what time they left the area – anything that will be relevant. If we find that vehicle, it will be a bonus, it might yield a lot of scientific evidence and some DNA, so enquire at garages especially those with CCTV cameras. It might have called for petrol. Also highly confidential is the fact that Manchester Police believe Brent Fowler is not the first man to disappear in such circumstances. At this stage, their information is very scant and no bodies have been found but I should learn more when I speak to Manchester CID. Those are the foundations upon which you need to work. Inspector Horsley will allocate your specific actions for today and I wish you all the best with your work. Now, any questions?'

There were some questions about the descriptions of the men seen in the Cockatrice but Pluke was deliberately vague because he wanted his officers to trace any likely suspects and obtain their descriptions, then to ascertain if they matched those of the men in the pub. It would be a wonderful bonus if their movements in that locality could be traced.

He told the teams he expected to return to Crickledale before five thirty when he required them to regroup in this room for the final conference of the day. He said he could be contacted on his mobile telephone through Inspector Horsley and closed the meeting. The teams finished their teas and coffees, were issued with their actions and details of their areas of operation, and left.

'Who's going to tell Fowler's mother, Montague?' asked Horsley.

'That is something I shall discuss with DCI Sanders. I expect it will fall upon a sensitive member of Manchester Police. We need to speak to Mrs Fowler, though, to find out more about her son. That sort of thing is never easy.'

'We don't have much about him on file, and what about the other enquiries in Manchester, Montague? Who'll be

111

doing those? It's not within our force area and we're not familiar with the town, its people or its underworld.'

'That's another point I shall raise with DCI Sanders, rest assured I will deal with all those points, but I would like to conduct some enquiries there myself. I need to absorb the atmosphere of Fowler's home, his place of work, contacts and so forth. To solve a murder, one must become closely acquainted with the victim's background and lifestyle.'

'Right, well, I can cope here. So you're off to Leeds/Bradford airport now?'

'As soon as Detective Sergeant Wain is ready. It is a good hour and a half's drive from here.'

They arrived at the airport to find a very busy, noisy and confusing traffic system because major construction work was in progress. Pluke thought there would not be many horse troughs in this complex. Wayne remained calm at the wheel, however, and managed to weave his way through the cones and barriers, between huge cranes and JCBs, until he arrived at the offices of Airport Security. He parked outside and was permitted entry upon showing his warrant card, with Pluke doing likewise; they were eventually admitted to a waiting area. DCI Sanders had paved the way and was known to the official on duty; the airport had lots of dealings with Greater Manchester Police. Pluke and Wayne were shown into another small but comfortable room, given a tray containing a vacuum jug of coffee, cups, milk and a chocolate biscuit each with a selection of Sunday newspapers to read. All very civilized, thought Pluke, much more welcoming than the average police office. There were easy chairs with coffee tables before them and a larger dining-room size table surrounded by chairs if they wished to use them.

Coffee in hand, Pluke settled for an easy chair and Wayne did likewise. They did not discuss the murder at this stage, as they were not very certain whether or not the room was secure, so instead they settled down to read the papers and supplements. Twenty minutes later, the door opened and a scruffy individual with long hair and several days' growth of beard came in. In his early thirties, he was dressed in a pair of ripped jeans, trainers and a sweater with holes in the elbows.

'Good morning,' he smiled. 'I'm Paul Sanders,' and he flourished his warrant card for Pluke's benefit. 'I'm told by reception that you are DI Pluke and DS Wain? So, where's the coffee?'

Wayne wasn't sure who looked less like a police officer, Sanders or Pluke. Wayne was very much out of place in his smart dark suit and clean shoes. Sanders said no more as he helped himself to a cup of coffee then sat down as Pluke identified himself by his full name, then Wayne.

'This room is secure, gentlemen,' said Sanders. 'That's why we use it.'

He did not seem at all surprised by Pluke's odd appearance with his massive greatcoat, panama hat, pink socks and spats as he sipped at the coffee, discussing the traffic situation on the M62 this morning and the hectic activity on his drive to the airport.

'Right, Mr Pluke, down to business. I am Paul Sanders, Detective Chief Inspector by rank, and I am a member of SIOUX.' He pronounced it 'Sue'.

'Sue?' queried Pluke.

'Special Intelligence and Operations Unit, group ten. X is for ten. SIOUX.'

'Oh.' Pluke thrust out his chest and said he was in charge of Crickledale Sub-Divisional Criminal Investigation Department, with Wayne as his deputy.

'Ah,' said Sanders. 'Got you! You're the boss then?'

'I am indeed,' thundered Pluke.

'I'm not,' admitted Sanders. 'I've loads of top brass above me, but our unit specializes in undercover work, criminal intelligence, subversive activities, espionage, secret operations, asylum seekers who are dodgy, illegal immigrants, that sort of thing, as well as major crime, both national and international, provided there are links with Greater Manchester. Drugs, art thefts, blackmail, sabotage,

113

you name it, we look into it, all the big stuff, criminal families, armed gangs and so on. Much of our work is covert and intelligence-led, and we have many operatives who are not known even to me. All very hush-hush, but necessary. Not many of Manchester's own officers know us or what we do. It's due to our undercover work, and the intelligence we gather by means fair and foul, that we are interested in your murder. Officially, I'm just a member of the CID. So tell me more, Montague.'

In considerable detail now they were face to face, Pluke explained the finding of Brent Fowler's body and the presence of the men at the Cockatrice Inn, adding that in his view there was an added factor because it seemed the victim had been deliberately orientated with the head to the north with the body lying on its belly.

'It means the body had not simply been dumped,' Pluke asserted. 'It had been positioned there. One can see when a corpse has been thrown out of a vehicle or allowed to fall to rest. This body was carefully arranged. I consider that to be important.'

'Why?' puzzled Sanders.

'It suggests it was done by someone who knows about such things. The head to the north indicates utter contempt for the deceased, and placing him face down means he was not looking up to heaven, he is eternally looking down to hell. And furthermore, a small cairn of stones had been built near the body. A dozen or so stones, potato-sized, piled into a pointed heap. That means that whoever placed the body on the moor did not want its ghost to haunt him. That is the purpose of that cairn.'

'You mean folks do that in England? Are we talking ethnic killers here?'

'Possibly, but they could be very English with ancient roots,' said Pluke. 'I think the killer, or those who placed the body there, is involved in bygone British religions and culture. On the lines of the Celts perhaps. Some ancient races, the Celts included, always burnt the bodies of murderers, rapists and thieves. Another form of contempt.

There was a fire after this man's death – at this point, I do not know whether that was a coincidence or planned, but he was a suspected murderer, not merely a paedophile. The fire could be relevant. There is much in this man's death that is not normal in a case of murder.'

'You're telling me! You know about these things?'

Pluke then explained his interest in folklore, ancient customs and horse troughs and asked Sanders whether any of the other supposed victims of the killing group had been treated in an unusual manner.

'I dunno, I must be honest, it's something I've never thought about but we'll have to bear it in mind, won't we?'

'I was wondering whether there are groups of such people operating or meeting in your police area?' Pluke asked. 'Say Celtic, someone following an ancient faith.'

'Yes, there's a group called the Church of the White Kelts led by a character called Jacob Hampson. We're targeting him right now. And he does own a silver-grey people carrier. We've no firm evidence of him being involved in criminal activities and it might be a legitimate church. But he has come to our notice and he works part time at the leisure centre where Brent was employed. We are very interested in him.'

'Fake religions can sometimes be used as a cover for illegal activities,' said Pluke. 'It's fairly easy to persuade zealots to do wrong in the name of religion.'

'Right, we realize that. The truth is we've thousands of other weird and nutty people in clubs and organizations in our part of the world, Montague, some at the leisure centre where Brent worked and taking part in all sorts of weird rituals. All of them believe they are absolutely right and sensible in what they do but I'd hesitate to consider them potential killers or vigilantes. Most are utterly harmless, not even a nuisance in most cases. But in this instance, we're talking vigilantes. The snag with your killers is we've no idea who they are. They're clever and very organized.'

'So what can you tell me about other missing men?' asked Pluke.

'You'll know as well as me that across the UK hundreds of people go missing every day, most of them simply because they want to. They leave home for whatever reason takes their fancy, and most are no concern of ours. However, in the Greater Manchester area alone, over the past two years or so, we've had eight men of special interest to us vanish without a trace. Special interest means they are known to the police or suspected of crime, but in these cases, all were paedophiles, either known, convicted or merely suspected. That's why we're interested. They've not been kidnapped or taken out by our known vigilantes, we're confident about that. They could have merely gone away of their own accord, but they've vanished so we can't ask them. Because these men are all paedophiles or suspected paedophiles, we think some other group, so far unidentified, is actively removing them.

'We've had snippets of gen filter down to us, always without concrete evidence. That silver people carrier was one example although it's made us focus on Hampson. I can tell you we pick up a lot of stuff from our bugging devices, not to mention street gossip, informers, undercover operators and places where druggies gather or where large numbers of people assemble, clubs and so on. Most of it's a load of gibberish, but now and again a gem of information shines through. Of those eight missing paedophiles, the body on your moors is the first that's been found, Montague. You can see why we consider it very important. We've not found the bodies of any of the others, although we believe we know where two were disposed of and a silver people carrier was seen in the vicinity on both occasions at the material time. One problem is that both cases are outside our jurisdiction, like yours.'

'So you think the fire in our case was supposed to dispose of the remains?'

'That wouldn't surprise me. Obviously, they don't want

116

their handiwork to be found, so you need to make more enquiries into that aspect. Now, the two we know about. We are sure one was weighted down and sunk in Lake Wastwater, and we think another was thrown down a disused lead mine shaft in Derbyshire. Both paedophiles, both from Manchester. Before they vanished, both told relatives they had won prizes which enabled them to travel to those places but none of the relatives knew whether they'd bought tickets or submitted their names.'

'That's got all the hallmarks of Brent Fowler's disappearance,' said Pluke.

'Yes, Mrs Fowler told us that Brent had received a letter saying he'd won the prize of a shooting party weekend on a country estate.'

'It would seem a pattern or technique is emerging,' agreed Pluke.

'Exactly, but it's all circumstantial evidence, and with no bodies in the other cases we've no real evidence. What it boils down to is this, Montague. I'm hoping you can help us find this killer or killers. We'll help you – and the intelligence we've gathered so far is on this disk,' and Sanders dug into his pocket to produce an envelope. 'There are even photographs of that scene in Derbyshire, and the shores of Lake Wastwater.'

'If we had a laptop, we could look at that disk,' chipped in Wayne Wain.

'I'd like to see if there are cairns at either place,' said Pluke.

'Say no more!' With that, Sanders went to the phone on the window ledge in the corner and asked, 'Hi, Ben, do we have a laptop? I've a disk I'd like my friends to see.'

And then he replaced the phone. 'On its way,' he said.

When the laptop arrived, Sanders quickly brought it to life, slid the disk into its slot and began his search. He knew where to look for each item and within seconds, the screen was showing the shores of Wastwater.

'This is where we believe the body was put into the water,' said Sanders. 'That's only because it's one of the

117

few places you can get a vehicle close to the lakeside without it being seen and they'd need a vehicle to transport the body. Someone came forward to tell us about some odd activity here, that's why we are interested.'

'There is a road along one side of Wastwater and a footpath at the other, under the screes,' said Pluke. 'I've walked the area, seeking horse troughs.'

'This is off the road, near where Lingmell Gill enters the lake,' said Sanders. 'We found tracks . . .'

'And,' said Pluke, pointing to the picture, 'a small cairn of stones, see? On the left of the picture. Made from stones by the lakeside . . .'

'Good God, yes! We missed that . . . or didn't appreciate its significance.'

'I doubt it will be there now,' said Pluke. 'Weather, wind and water may have demolished it. Now, what about the Derbyshire scene?'

'It's near Wirksworth,' said Sanders. 'The place is known for its extinct lead mines and some are now caves, but a lot are mere fissures in the rock, inaccessible even to skilled cavers. One of our experts suggests the body of a vanished man was thrown deep down one of those mines, well out of sight and reach . . . ah, here we go.'

This time they were presented with a rocky scene in a moorland setting, albeit with no heather but with lots of exposed limestone. Sanders took them through the rugged landscape until they came to a dark hole in the ground – but Pluke spotted the cairn on a rock above.

'There's the cairn, Mr Sanders,' he said. 'I suggest that fissure contains your body, and that you'll probably never get it out or even see it. But I think, in fact I am sure, we have a pattern here. The same people are involved in these crimes, and ours.'

'Right,' said Sanders. 'Thanks for your contribution. That cairn seems to provide just the sort of confirmation we need. It's something new to us and it means the killers are leaving their signature at each crime scene, probably thinking no one will know what it is. I'll pass your information on to my boss and he'll relay it to the teams who are looking into these killings. Now, I'm authorized to say you may conduct any enquiries within our force area, Montague, provided you keep us informed of your presence and the outcome. We will do likewise. If our officers turn up anything extra, particularly in view of your contribution about the cairns, then we will notify you. I'm even more convinced one team is responsible even if we have very little data about its members. What we do know is that each time a man vanishes, a people carrier is stolen and later burnt out; we've recently found one burnt out in Oldham. From your crime perhaps? Forensics are examining it now. I should tell you that the leisure centre may be a factor too – all the vanished men had links with it, but so do thousands of other people, including Hampson, so it may or may not be relevant. However, that disk is worth very careful study. It's yours to keep.'

'This is all very useful,' said Pluke. 'So what now, Mr Sanders? Will your officers be notifying Mrs Fowler about the death of her son?'

'We felt that was your job, Montague, as the crime was committed in your area. In view of what you have told me about your findings, you'll need to talk to Mrs Fowler about her son, and find out whether he was involved in any of those weird groups. You have her address?'

'It's in my files,' said Pluke.

'What about publicity, Montague? Do the press know of your murder?'

'They do, but they don't know the identity of the victim nor of any links with Manchester. I have not released that information because his relations are unaware of his death.'

'In view of what we now suspect, can I ask you to keep the Manchester aspect of the enquiry out of the press? I don't want our killers to know this body has been found. At the moment they have no idea we are on to them. What we need to do, Montague, is to set a trap for them, to maintain the element of surprise on our side, possibly with

119

a covert operation of some kind. We need to draw them into a carefully planned trap. If we take that route, we might want your help because you are unknown to the Manchester villains.'

'Yes, of course, I shall be pleased to help.'

'Good. Leave it with me, Montague, I'll be in touch again soon.'

'Might I raise one concern. If I inform Mrs Fowler of her son's death, the killers could be alerted to the fact we have found the body.'

'We'll have to keep the news from them. You could ask her to be silent and of course, there'll be nothing in our local papers and no funeral until the coroner releases the body. In a murder case, that can take months. What about her going away somewhere? Have you any safe houses in your force area?'

'We do, yes. She could use one of those.'

'Our force would pay the costs. Put it to her, Montague. She might like a week or two on your moors, and she might like to be close to her son at the same time. Just a thought. Keep in touch. So you'll go and see Mrs Fowler today?'

Pluke looked at his watch.

'How long does it take to get to Manchester from here?'

'An hour or so.'

'Then that is my next call,' said Montague Pluke.

Chapter Eight

Mrs Fowler had been to church. After a succession of sleepless nights, she'd had great difficulty keeping awake, particularly during the homily. Afterwards, she had walked around the city looking at young men, including those begging in shop doorways and sleeping rough, in the hope she might catch sight of Brent. Although it was a Sunday, the streets were surprisingly busy with people just walking up and down, window-shopping or admiring the architecture, with youngsters already visiting the city centre bars and pubs. Beggars were around too, sitting in shop doorways or squatting hopefully near busy places such as pedestrian crossings and bus stations.

By quarter to one, she was hungry. Most of the places she liked to eat at were closed today, so she decided to go home and make a bowl of soup, perhaps followed by some baked beans on toast. She had considered the cafeteria in the leisure centre where Brent worked but decided against that; it would probably be very busy and besides, it was quite a walk from the city centre. After lunch, she would decide what to do with herself during the afternoon. She felt very lonely because Brent spent most Sundays with her. He had no close friends either, so Sundays were very boring unless they arranged an outing. Sometimes Brent would arrange a coach tour in the countryside and they would visit big houses like Gawthorpe Hall, Lyme Park, Rufford Old Hall or Tatton Park. Otherwise, he'd stay at home and work on his computer. He always said he'd love to live in a big house in the countryside, with the open moors around him and lots of visitors and shooting parties to keep him entertained.

It was an impossible dream, of course, but it cost nothing to dream. As a young woman she'd had dreams too, dreams of marrying a rich man, of going on holidays overseas, of flying in an aircraft . . . but she had been to London once, on a bus trip to Buckingham Palace, and she'd also been to Edinburgh on the train for a long weekend. That had been a special treat by Brent for her fiftieth birthday. She couldn't afford to go far now, not with just her pension from the factory, although Brent was good with money and helped with household expenses, like council tax and electricity. If something had happened to him, her life would be dreadful, so lonely and pointless. It would be so empty with even less money to spend.

She walked back to her terrace house in a cul-de-sac just off Gould Street and as she approached, a small car eased to a stop outside the front door. Brent? Was he coming home? Had someone brought him back? She didn't recognize the car but knew he'd been given a lift to that shooting party in Yorkshire and so she increased her speed because she didn't want the car to leave, not until she'd had a chance to speak to the passengers. The house was locked now, she didn't like leaving the door unlocked when she was out. She saw two men clamber out and go to the front door. One was young, tall and very handsome, a bit like that Pete Sampras who used to play tennis, and he was smartly dressed in a dark suit. His friend was a bit odd, though, in an old black and yellow patterned coat with a shoulder cape, a panama hat with a blue band, spats and brown shoes. He had glasses with thick black frames and his hair seemed to be sticking out in all directions under his hat.

'Hello,' she shouted as she grew nearer. 'Hello, I'm here.'

Following his chat with Detective Inspector Pluke, DCI Sanders realized Pluke would be the ideal person to act as bait for his trap to catch the killers. For one thing he was a police officer with all the necessary training and skills of his profession, so essential if the necessary evidence was to be gathered, but he was also one of the least likely-looking detectives Sanders had ever seen. And he was not known in Manchester. It would be easy to spread word around the leisure centre that another suspected paedophile was active in town. Many in the town and its public facilities were already alert to such things. Because of Brent's links with the centre, Pluke was sure to make enquiries there and so it would be easy to spread a rumour that a peculiar-looking paedophile was lurking around the swimming-pool area. Once suspicion and fear were present in a community, rumours could easily be spread. Sanders could make sure Pluke had reason to hang around the place, and a little research into Pluke's background plus some strategically created rumours would add authenticity to the scheme. Sanders wanted the killers to send Pluke one of those prizewinning invitations. He called his boss and arranged to meet him so that his plans would receive official approval, with all the necessary back-up. The question was whether to acquaint Pluke with the whole plan or just part of it . . .

'Mrs Fowler?' asked Pluke as the plump, short, grey-haired and rather untidy woman hurried towards him with her hands waving.

'Hello, hello, I'm here, don't go away,' and she hurried breathlessly towards them, wondering who they were. There were alone, there was no one else in the car. No Brent. Maybe they were Jehovah's Witnesses? Or someone selling double-glazing? She was panting now, with a combination of exertion and hope.

'Mrs Fowler?' repeated Pluke when she drew to a halt beside them.

'Yes, that's me. I've been out, to church and for a walk . . . I hope you've not been waiting long?'

123

'No, we've just arrived,' said Pluke. 'But you are Mrs Fowler? Emily Fowler?'

'Yes.' Her heart was pounding because she sensed they might have news about Brent.

The man in the funny clothes looked up and down the street and said, 'I think we had better go inside, if you don't mind.'

'Yes, yes, of course, so rude of me. Yes, do come in.' She unlocked her green door with a Yale key and went in ahead of them. A dark passage led past a front room and into the middle room, the one between the kitchen and that front room. It had a large window which overlooked a back yard, and although some might use this as the dining room, it was Mrs Fowler's lounge with a cheap but clean neutral-coloured three-piece suite, an equally cheap but clean neutral-coloured carpet and an open fire, ready laid but not burning. Pluke's immediate response was that the room lacked colour, there was not even a vase of flowers or a picture on the wall.

'I'll put a match to the fire – I've been out, you see . . .'

'No need,' said Pluke. 'Don't light it on our account, we won't be staying long . . . Now, we are police officers, from the CID. I am Detective Inspector Pluke and this is Detective Sergeant Wain. We are not from your local force but from North Yorkshire.' They waved their warrant cards before her but she took scant notice. She asked them to be seated and they occupied each of the armchairs while she sat on the front edge of the settee with her hands clasped in her lap. She hadn't even taken her coat off at this stage, but neither had Pluke.

'North Yorkshire?' She frowned. 'I've never been there . . . is it about Brent?'

Her instincts told her that they had come about Brent, and that it was not good news. She knew that by the way they were sitting, by the expressions on their faces and because they had come all the way from North Yorkshire. That's where Brent had gone for his shooting party – the letter had mentioned a big house there, a manor of some kind. Was he in trouble in Yorkshire? With more little girls?

'I'm afraid it is about Brent,' said Pluke. 'I'm sorry, Mrs Fowler, very sorry indeed to have to come to you like this but it is not good news.'

'Something's happened? I knew it, I knew something was wrong, he's not been in touch, you see, and he always keeps in touch . . . So what is it, Inspector? What's happened to him?'

'I'm afraid he is dead, Mrs Fowler.'

She went very pale. 'Dead? He can't be, not my Brent, he's so young . . .'

'I'm dreadfully sorry to have to break this news to you, Mrs Fowler, but it's worse. He was shot, I must tell you this, but he did not commit suicide and I'm afraid it was no accident either. Your son was murdered, Mrs Fowler, and we are so dreadfully sorry to bring you this news.'

She did not respond for a long time, her only reaction being the tears which were welling up in her eyes and the quivering of her bottom lip as she tried so hard to hide or control her feelings. In her heart of hearts, she had feared something like this, she knew something terrible had happened because Brent had not been in touch – but murder? Who'd want to murder such a nice young man as her Brent?

'Where did it happen?' she asked after a long pause. 'Am I allowed to know?'

'We will tell you all we can.' Pluke tried to appear as sympathetic as possible. 'He was found on the North York Moors, in fact I found him, Mrs Fowler, by chance. If it's any consolation, his death would have been swift. But there is worse. The moor had been set on fire, as part of the annual controlled burning, but unfortunately your son's body was in the path of the flames. He has been badly burned, Mrs Fowler.'

The repeated shocks numbed her temporarily as she tried so hard to absorb each piece of news. It was bad enough knowing he was dead, but to be murdered and then to have a fire harm him . . . it was almost too much.

Pluke tried to ease her feelings by adding, 'The fire did not cause his death, Mrs Fowler. He was dead before the fire reached him.'

'Oh my God, this is dreadful . . . my poor poor boy . . . can I see him, Mr Pluke? I must see him. They can't stop me seeing him, can they?'

'No, of course not. You can see him, in fact we need you to see him, to make the formal identification, and that will mean going to North Yorkshire. I have to remind you that he has been burned but not too severely.'

'I don't know where to go, Mr Pluke, I've never been far in my whole life, you see, not on my own. I haven't a car and don't drive.'

'Have you family? Someone who could come with you?'

'No, there's just me and Brent, well, just me now. I have no other family and I don't get out much, just into town for my shopping and things, and bus trips with Brent, he was so very good to me, you know, I don't know how I'll manage now, really I don't. I don't know what to do . . .'

Pluke recalled Detective Chief Inspector Sanders' suggestion that a safe house might provide temporary accommodation for Mrs Fowler, and that it would be a good idea to get her away from Manchester, especially if they wished the killers to remain unaware of the discovery of Brent's body.

'Mrs Fowler,' said Pluke, 'before I deal with anything else, can you tell me why Brent was in North Yorkshire?'

'Oh, yes, Mr Pluke, it was that shooting party. He won a prize to go on a shooting party at some big country house, a manor of some sort. He was so pleased because he has a passion for country houses and big estates, he's always fancied owning one, you see, and living the life of a country gentleman . . .'

'Shooting party? I don't understand, shooting parties don't go out at this time of year. Where was it?'

'I can't remember, Mr Pluke, it was a manor in York-shire. He got a letter, you see, very nice and hand-delivered, saying he'd won and he had to decide whether to go or not and they would ring up and check . . .'

'They?'

'Well, whoever sent the letter.'

'And who was that?'

'I don't know, there was no address or telephone num-ber on it. The letter said somebody would ring Brent in a day or two to check whether he was going, and he had to go to the Arndale Centre car park on the Friday at half-past three, when he would be taken to the shooting party, a free lift. He had to take suitable clothes and it would run from the Friday evening to Sunday lunchtime, all expenses paid. He was one of six from this area who'd won, the letter said. He was so delighted, Mr Pluke, it was a dream come true. So naturally, he said he would go and got time off work.'

'Work? Where did he work?'

'At the swimming pool. He got a job as an attendant but some people said he'd been interfering with little girls and so they made him work in the kitchen, washing up. At the leisure centre that is, in the cafeteria. He never told me that, Mr Pluke, I think he didn't want to upset me because he'd never do a thing like that anyway, not my Brent, he was such a nice boy, so decent and caring. That's typical of him, so sensitive, so caring to his mum.'

As Pluke paused to try and digest or make sense of all this, Wayne spoke.

'Did those people ring Brent, Mrs Fowler?'

'Yes, they did, a few days after the letter came. Just to check he was going and to answer any questions about the trip.'

'Did they leave a contact number? Give their names or anything?'

'No, nothing, there were no names – not that I know of, that is – so Brent said he would go and they'd see him at half-past three that Friday in the Arndale Centre car park.

Their bus or car or maybe a people carrier would have red stickers in the windows with the name of the big house on them. That's how he'd know it.'

'And so he went, eh? But didn't come back on the Sunday? Did he contact you at all, in the meantime?'

'No, that's what was so puzzling, that's why I began to think something was wrong because the letter said that some successful candidates might have a chance to stay on a bit longer, a further five days. So even though he didn't send me a postcard or ring up, I wasn't too worried when he didn't come back that Sunday. I just thought he must have done very well at the weekend and wanted to take full advantage of everything that was on offer, after all it was all free.'

'So what did you do while you were waiting?'

'Not a lot really, there's not a lot I could have done, but I did check at the pool and cafeteria to see if he'd been in touch with them, and the library, and such places, just to see if they'd had a postcard or phone call, but they hadn't. So yesterday, when I'd heard nothing, I thought I'd better tell the police but they said a grown man can leave home any time he wants and so they weren't too bothered but a nice sergeant heard me and must have seen I was very upset so he said he would do what he could. I was going to tell the National Missing Persons Helpline but thought I'd wait until this weekend was over . . . and then you came. I mean, it's all so awful, Mr Pluke, so unbelievable . . . I don't know what to do . . .'

'This is a very strange story, Mrs Fowler. What else can you tell me about the letter? It is important.'

'Nothing, Mr Pluke. It didn't come through the post, it was pushed through our letterbox without a stamp on. It was on very colourful paper and, yes, now I remember, it had a number on the top corner, on the right.'

'Number?'

'It was Brent's identification number, he had to use it to prove who he was.'

'Can you remember the number?'

'No, it was a very long one.'

'So where is the letter now?'

'Brent took it with him, it said he had to keep it with him at all times, in case he had to prove who he was. It was how he had to identify himself if anyone asked.'

'So is there anything else in the house that came from these people?'

'No, nothing.' She shook her head.

'And have you any idea who they were?'

'No!' She was weeping now. 'No, no idea at all. It was just a smart letter, like those you get from *Reader's Digest* offering big prizes. Do you think the killer sent him that, Mr Pluke? I mean, why go to all that bother . . . playing tricks on people like that? You don't think there was a shooting party at all, then?'

'It seems there was, Mrs Fowler, but not the sort Brent envisaged. It's possible several people were involved in his death, which brings me to the next point. I think we need to get you away from here, at least for a while. For your safety. You see, we believe the men tried to hide Brent's body, they wanted to conceal his murder so no one would know what had happened to him. If they know he's been found, they might try to stop people talking to the police. So can I suggest you go away from here?'

'Away? But where can I go, Mr Pluke? I have no savings, no family, no friends, there was just my Brent.'

'We need you to identify his body, Mrs Fowler, which means you must travel across to North Yorkshire, and we have a house you can use, it's called a safe house and Greater Manchester Police would pay the costs. You could stay there for as long as necessary. We have several such houses and if you are in agreement, I will ring my office to prepare things for your arrival, at a house close to where Brent died.'

'So I could see him?'

'Yes, I would make sure of that.'

'Well, if you think that's all right . . .'

'I do,' said Pluke. 'I think it's important too. And, Mrs

129

Fowler, I don't want you to tell anyone in Manchester that Brent has been found, not even the people he worked with. If you are away from here, then that will make things much easier to keep a secret. So, let me call my office.'

And, with a show of confidence, he produced his mobile phone from the depths of his clothing, managed to find the right buttons to press and was soon speaking to Inspector Horsley.

'Ah, Inspector Horsley, Detective Inspector Pluke speaking from Manchester. I need to make use of one of our safe houses, for a witness in the Hurnehow murder case. Mrs Fowler, the deceased's mother. I intend to bring her from Manchester today, she is with me and Detective Sergeant Wain at this minute. Can you make the necessary arrangements to prepare one of the houses for her?'

'The one in Crickledale is empty at the moment, Montague. A discreet two-bedroomed cottage in a quiet position, with all mod cons.'

'That will be ideal, then help will always be on hand for her through my officers at Crickledale. Please go ahead. Now listen, we are with Mrs Fowler at this moment and there is much more we need to ask about her son's life and movements, but I think it would be prudent for us to leave her for the moment. She needs to come to terms with her loss, to cast her memory back over recent events and then to pack for her trip. There are other people I wish to interview in this area, guests from the birthday party, so Detective Sergeant Wain and I will carry out those enquiries, return to collect Mrs Fowler and then come back to base.'

'Sounds fine by me, Montague.'

Pluke felt that giving Mrs Fowler the task of packing for an indeterminate period away from home would take her mind off Brent, at least for the time being. She said she was very happy for them to leave her alone for a couple of hours or so. In spite of the shock, she assured them she would come to terms with these dramatic developments and managed a smile, adding that she would be ready when they returned for her.

As they left, Wain said he would interview Mr and Mrs Sharpe in Stockport, while Pluke went to Salford to talk to Alison Wharram and Mark Newbury. Neither detective would give any indication that the body of a Mancunian had been found; so far as the witnesses were concerned, the body had not been identified. Pluke felt it would not be too difficult to keep the Manchester element of the murder secret from the local people and out of the local papers.

Wain would make his way to Stockport in the official car while Pluke would head for Salford by public transport.

Pluke took a taxi from the railway station and quickly reached the address given for Mark Newbury and Alison Wharram. It was a large detached house in a neat suburban street with a topiary bird near the front door and several neatly trimmed conifers along the dividing fence. A silver Mercedes was parked in the drive and he could see the couple were busy in the garden, clearing away the debris of last winter. He dismissed the taxi but not before noting its telephone number so that he could ring for it when it was time to return.

'Good afternoon,' called Pluke as he entered the tidy front garden. Both the woman and the man stopped work and stared at the apparition which had materialized upon their premises.

'I'm sorry, old chap,' said the man, a stocky person in his early thirties. 'We don't want to buy anything, we never deal with door-to-door salesmen. Now, it's no good arguing and trying to be persuasive because we shall ignore you and if you persist in remaining on my property, I shall call the police.'

The fellow stepped forward a few paces with a pair of hedge shears in his hand as if to confront the trespasser while the woman, probably in her late twenties, moved to

131

stand at his side. They might be a formidable couple, thought Pluke.

'I am the police.' Pluke produced his warrant card, and stood still so they would have to approach him to check it. 'Detective Inspector Pluke from North Yorkshire, the officer in charge of Crickledale Sub-Divisional Criminal Investigation Department.'

'You don't look like a police officer!' snapped the man.

'I am a detective, I am not supposed to look like a police officer,' responded Pluke, enjoying this banter. 'Are you Mark Newbury, and is this lady Alison Wharram?'

'Yes, we are, but look here, I don't want to conduct my private business in front of the neighbours, whatever is the reason you are here, so you'd better come in, er, Inspector.'

'Detective Inspector, actually,' said Pluke, following them into their spacious and well-furnished drawing room.

'Sorry about that reception out there, Detective Inspector, but one is not accustomed to having unexpected visitors on a Sunday afternoon, and one has to be so careful about whom one allows on one's premises. You took me by surprise. From North Yorkshire, you say? So what can I do for you?'

'I believe you were guests recently at Hurnehow Hall, a fine country house on the North York Moors?'

'We were. It was Jonathan Hurne's twenty-first birthday party, as I am sure you know.'

'Might I ask what time you arrived and left the party?'

'Look, what is this about, Detective Inspector? It might be helpful if we knew the purpose of your questions.'

'I would prefer you to answer that question first,' said Pluke.

'Well, we arrived – what time, Alison? Mid-afternoon?'

'Four o'clockish, I'd say,' the woman responded. 'Maybe quarter-past. The revels started at five thirty, so we had ample time to get freshened up after our drive. There were facilities at the house.'

'And your time of departure?'

'We left early, we didn't stay till the bitter end because Alison had a swimming competition on the Sunday, she wanted to get back in good time for that. We left about ten thirty, didn't we, darling? And we didn't drink alcohol nor did we break any speed limits on the return home. We were the essence of good behaviour! Does that satisfy you, Detective Inspector?'

'I know the party was in a marquee in the grounds of Hurnehow Hall but did you leave the party for any reason? For a walk on the moor perhaps?'

'No, not likely, we were in party gear, hardly the right sort of thing to be tramping across the moors in. Look, Detective Inspector Pluke, why are you asking all these questions?'

'The body of a young man was found on the moors not far from Hurnehow Hall, Mr Newbury. I found it personally. I am checking first to see whether the deceased person could have been one of the guests, and also to determine whether or not the guests noticed anything unusual that evening. The Tuesday that was, or in the early hours of Wednesday morning.'

'A body?' The woman put her hand to her mouth. 'Oh, my God . . . who is it?'

'We don't know, Miss Wharram.' Pluke told a necessary white lie. 'That is why we are checking every male guest to see if he is alive. Checking in person, that is. My colleague is elsewhere in the Manchester area at this very moment, speaking to another couple who were also guests. A Mr and Mrs Sharpe from Stockport. We also want to be sure the deceased is not Mr Sharpe. Do you know them?'

'No, sorry, we didn't know many of the guests.'

'Might I ask how you are associated with Lord Hurne and his family? How you came to be invited to Jonathan's birthday party?' Pluke asked that question because the couple seemed older than Jonathan.

'Sure, Alison was at university with Dominic, Jonny's older brother. They became friends and she spent a lot of time as a guest at the Hall, weekends, summer breaks and parties, long before we married. We are married by the way, although Alison uses her maiden name for professional reasons. There was never any romance between her and Dominic, it was just a nice platonic friendship. We've maintained those links ever since, haven't we, darling?'

'Yes, we get Christmas cards from Lord and Lady Hurne and we are invited for various events, they always hold a New Year party, for example, and they did a wonderful Millennium celebration complete with fireworks.'

'Clearly you are on good terms with the family?'

'Yes, with all of them,' she smiled.

Pluke had never heard of Dominic, his name was not on the guest list but he did not let them know of this omission; that was another interview to complete, wherever Dominic was now. Why wasn't his name on the guest list? He must speak to Lord or Lady Hurne about that. So was Dominic the heir? Heir to a noble family one of whose ancestors had reputedly killed the cockatrice, or at least saved the local people from a great evil. Pluke found that an interesting thought.

'And which university was that, might I ask?'

'Manchester,' said Alison. 'I did a science degree, I'm a lecturer at UMIST. Fashion and Textile Retailing.'

'Ah,' smiled Pluke. 'Now, did you see or hear anything out of the ordinary while the party was in progress? On the moors or about the house?'

'Sorry, Detective Inspector,' and both shook their heads. 'Sorry, no, we never noticed anything out of the ordinary. We're not being much help, are we?'

'At least I know you, sir, are not the victim, that is my main purpose in talking to you,' said Pluke. 'The fact that you are alive is a great relief to me. Thank you for your time. Now I must go, I have more interviews before I return to Yorkshire.'

'You haven't walked, have you?' smiled Alison. 'I didn't see a car when you arrived.'

'My colleague has taken our car to Stockport,' said

Pluke. 'I used the train and a taxi. Now, I will recall my taxi, and thank you for your time.'

And he left. Recalling the taxi would be another test of his skill with the mobile phone.

Wayne Wain had a similar story to tell. Mr James Sharpe was a man in his late twenties, a former colleague of Jonathan Hurne at Leeds University, and they were good friends. Sharpe was slightly older than Jonathan and married, but he had read law after a period in work as a surveyor. He and his wife had stayed at a bed-and-breakfast place near Hurnchow village on the night of the party but had not seen or heard any unusual occurrences that night. They had no idea who the victim might be and admitted they did not know many people at the party, other than members of the Hurne family. They had not gone for a walk on the moors while the party was in progress and, apart from walking to and from the Hall from their digs, they had spent the entire evening in the marquee, or very close to it.

They had popped out on occasions, for a breath of fresh air around the grounds, but had never ventured more than a few yards from the marquee, nor had they seen or heard anything on the nearby moors. Like Pluke, Wayne had not revealed the identity or home locality of the victim, merely saying he was checking that it was not Sharpe. Wayne had no reason to be suspicious of this man and felt he could be ticked off the list of guests.

Both Pluke and Wayne returned to Mrs Fowler's house, arriving within a few minutes of each other, by which time she had her suitcase packed. She assured them she had no pets to worry about, she knew how to turn off the water and had done so but decided to leave the landing light burning to suggest someone was at home, and she had cancelled the milk. There were no papers to cancel because she went out each day to buy one from the newsagent.

'Just one more thing before we go,' said Pluke. 'Can we

135

look in Brent's room? He might have left some evidence which will lead us to his murderer. It might be necessary, of course, for our scenes of crime experts to examine his room on a more scientific basis but a quick glance might help us to find the person responsible.'

'Yes, yes, of course, whatever you feel is necessary. He hasn't much upstairs except for his computer and the magazines he buys.'

'Magazines?' asked Wayne Wain with evident interest.

'*Country Life*, *The Field*, *Shooting Times*, that sort of thing.'

'Oh,' said Wayne. 'So what does he do – did he do – with his computer?'

'I don't know,' she admitted. 'It's a mystery to me, I never touch it.'

'I think we should take it away with us, sir,' advised Wayne Wain. 'Brent might have kept a diary or something which will help us. Do you mind, Mrs Fowler?'

'Not at all, I'll be glad to see the back of that thing, he spent all his spare time in that room, playing with it. There were times I wished he had a girlfriend.'

'Didn't he ever bring girls home?' asked Wayne, who could not understand why healthy young men did not chase healthy young girls.

'No, he would make friends with them at work, there were some nice ones there, he once told me, but usually he was wrapped up with his computer and his love of country life, a funny combination but at least he was no trouble to me, not getting into fights, breaking into houses or taking drugs, I suppose I have a lot to be thankful for.'

'There is good in all of us but I think we need to talk a lot more about Brent,' said Wayne Wain. 'We can do that when you are settled in the safe house. Right, sir, it's just a case of unplugging it and making sure we have all the software. It will all go in the boot. When we can get back to Yorkshire, Mrs Fowler, our experts will examine the computer to see if it can help us find Brent's killer.'

And so the deed was done. Wayne unplugged all Brent's

computer equipment, including the scanner and printer, and carried it down to the car.

'Well, Yorkshire here we come,' he said as he settled in the driving seat. 'You've never been across the Pennines before, Mrs Fowler?'

'No, I must admit I haven't. I've heard of Scarborough and Whitby, and the dales and moors, but I've never been. I've seen pictures on the telly, though.'

'I'm sure you are going to have your horizons broadened,' said Pluke. 'Right, Wayne, off we go. We have a good deal more to do before we conclude today's investigations.'

'I do wish Brent was coming with me,' said Mrs Fowler.

Chapter Nine

During the journey across the Pennines, Mrs Fowler alternated between long silences and spasms of rapid chatter about the passing sights and scenery. The silences were for remembering Brent, his days growing up, his time at school, his worries about finding a suitable job and his lack of interest in Manchester United or girls. Then there were his other activities which she knew little about. She didn't understand computers, for example, and he'd never tried to explain them to her. She never knew why he spent so much time in the library either. He hadn't spoken much about his work, she now realized, and found herself admitting that perhaps he might have made friends with little girls rather than mature ones. But there was nothing wrong in that, was there? Some adults were very good with children.

Then she would chatter excitedly for a time about the old mills which they passed as they began to climb towards the roof of England; she wondered about the farmhouse isolated between the east and west lanes of the M62 and was surprised by the sheer volume and speed of motorway traffic. She loved the views down into Yorkshire at the other side of this backbone of England, the sheer emptiness of the moors in some places, the reservoirs and wind turbines on the skyline. Pluke had to tell her that these moors were not the North York Moors where Brent had been found even though they were in Yorkshire. This side of Yorkshire was the Dales. When they stopped at a motorway service station, she was beguiled by the con-

138

tents of the shop, the gambling and amusement machines, the photo-booth, the noise in the cafeteria and the stream of cars, vans, heavy lorries and buses roaring past non-stop. She wondered where they were all going, and why. And why was everyone in such a hurry? At the cafeteria Wayne, charming as ever, bought her a cup of tea and a cake. She did not mention Brent during the journey or during that stop and the two detectives did not attempt to quiz her about him, not at this early and delicate stage. It was sensible, from their point of view, to allow her time to reflect so that her mind could range over his life before they settled down to the tough but vital task of asking searching questions. During the trip, she might recall incidents in his life, people he'd met, contacts or enemies he'd made, problems he'd faced at work or at home, or some other matter of value to their enquiry.

As they descended from the lofty Pennines into the Vale of York, leaving behind the roar of traffic for green hedge-rows and quiet villages, Pluke began to tell her a little about this part of Yorkshire, explaining what could be seen from the car such as the White Horse of Kilburn, enlightening her upon some aspects of history ancient and modern, and pointing out how the North York Moors, which bordered the coast and included a huge area of open heather, differed so greatly from the Yorkshire Dales and the Wolds. And then they were approaching Crickledale.

'Crickledale is a small market town,' he began to explain. 'It's very small compared with a city the size of Manchester, in fact you might think it is only a village but it has all the necessary amenities, some nice shops and cafés, a church, a busy social scene and yet it is not plagued by tourists. There is a small market place which is cobbled and we have a market there every Friday, you can get things like fish, fruit and vegetables, or even household articles. You'll like that.'

Then he launched into what was almost a tourist guide's explanation of the delights and history of his home town, even making reference to the unique horse trough outside

Crickledale town hall. He told her that his office was in the town, not far from the church, and that she could pop in at any time to see him or any of his officers for a chat. He added that his secretary, Mrs Plumpton, would provide any help or advice she required, and she was in her office every weekday, from eight thirty until around five. Mrs Fowler could either phone her or call in; she'd be there tomorrow, said Pluke, and he would give Mrs Plumpton a full account of this arrangement. After all, Mrs Plumpton was well versed in dealing with highly confidential matters.

'We've allocated a nice cottage for you,' he went on. 'It's in a quiet alley just off the market place with the lounge window looking over the town centre, and the local people think it is a holiday cottage. People come and go quite regularly, you see, just like holidaymakers, and the local public seldom get to know them, which is what we want. You don't have to make conversation with the neighbours if you don't want, you can keep yourself to yourself, and yet you are handy for the shops and buses and you can watch the passing show because the cottage overlooks the market square. It's got lace curtains, too, for privacy.'

'It will be just like my house in Manchester, except I don't look on to a market square, just the street,' she said. 'But I like to keep myself to myself, Mr Pluke, I'm not one for having people in for cups of tea and a chat.'

'I'm sure you will be happy here,' he said. 'We will take you there straightaway, show you the house and the town, and then leave you to settle in. There will be a welcome pack for you, with enough food for tonight and tomorrow, and a list of where things are and how to contact me or my officers, with a list of telephone numbers. You may use the telephone as often as you wish, all the costs will be met from official funds.'

'I'm not a spendthrift, Mr Pluke, and I don't think I'll be making many telephone calls. But there will be Brent's funeral to think about . . .'

'I'm afraid that will not happen for some time yet,' and

140

he explained that in cases of murder, the victim's funeral was often delayed for some weeks. 'But we will keep in touch. I will ask my wife to pop in tomorrow, to see if you are all right, and if anyone does ask who you are, you can always say you are an old school friend of Millicent Pluke, and you are staying in the area for a while. But don't talk about Brent, we don't want the press finding out who he is or what's happened to him just yet. And then tomorrow, I myself or one of my officers will take you to see Brent, to formally identify him.'

Both Pluke and Wayne Wain provided her with as much detail as they could about what she might expect while living in Crickledale. She assured them she would be fine and seemed surprisingly cheerful about the whole idea. She even said it would be like a holiday, a real holiday away from home, if it hadn't been for the awful news about Brent. She had some money with her, she had her cheque book and had always coped alone, she told them, so things would be no different now.

And so it was that Mrs Fowler was delivered to No. 2, Lime Lane, Market Place, Crickledale, a two-bedroomed cottage tucked away down a narrow alley close to the King's Head Inn. It had gas central heating and gas fires, a gas oven, nice furniture, a double bed and a single bed in separate rooms upstairs, plus a bathroom with a shower and separate toilet, and there was even a small back yard with a shed large enough to accommodate a pair of pedal cycles. There was a telephone, a television set, a radio in the kitchen as well as a microwave oven and plenty of crockery, kitchen utensils, towels and bed linen. Everything she wanted, in fact.

'Oooh, it's lovely,' she said. 'Really, it is, and so clean. Thank you, Mr Pluke, but I really think I should pay something towards this.'

'No, that is not necessary,' he assured her. 'You are here because you are a valuable witness, therefore you are our responsibility. So shall we leave you to settle in? Either of us may call later, and I am sure my wife will pop in.'

141

And so, somewhat bewildered by this sudden and fast-moving turn of events, Mrs Fowler became a temporary resident of Crickledale. Her first job was to find that photo of Brent in her luggage and put it on the mantelpiece.

DCI Sanders' superiors thought his idea of setting a trap for the paedophile killer or killers was excellent, particularly as it appeared a sound means – perhaps the only one – of acquiring the necessary evidence against them. Because at least eight paedophiles had unaccountably vanished with the possibility of more becoming targets, and with the likely capture of serial assassins, the costs could be justified. It would be expensive if all the support services were mustered in what could be a major exercise and Sanders was told to formulate his plan in draft form, to come up with an estimate of the expenses likely to be incurred and submit his plan for official approval.

Once that had been done, Detective Inspector Pluke would be contacted.

Back in the Incident Room, after notifying Sergeant Cockfield pronounced Cofield of their return and handing Brent's computer to Horsley so that an expert examination could be arranged, Pluke and Wayne Wain brought him up to date with their adventures in Manchester. The two sets of birthday party guests were ticked off the list because the menfolk were seen to be alive and neither was suspected as the killer.

For Horsley's ears alone, Pluke provided an account of his meeting with Detective Chief Inspector Sanders, referring to the likelihood of an undercover operation to trap the killers, although at this stage he had no idea what such an operation might entail. He stressed Sanders' insistence that news of Brent Fowler's death and the discovery of his body should not be made known in the Manchester area because Sanders felt it better if the killer or killers

142

remained blissfully unaware that Pluke and his team were hot on their trail. The idea was to lull them into a false sense of security. They confirmed to Horsley that Mrs Fowler was now in residence at the safe house in Crickledale, having been given suitable advice about not revealing the reason for her presence, and that tomorrow she would be taken to identify the body of her son. They said the Fowler home had not been forensically examined, their only act being to seize Brent's computer.

'So we've had a busy and fruitful day, Inspector Horsley. What developments have there been in this section of the investigation?'

Horsley admitted nothing much had happened. The routine moorland search was continuing with nothing of evidential value being yet found and house-to-house enquiries had not produced anything positive. Scores of local people had been eliminated from the enquiries with not a single suspect being found among them. Checks of the party guest list were going well too, with forces ringing in to say the men in question were alive, and that they and their partners had neither seen nor heard anything suspicious or unusual that evening. Of some concern was the fact that they had not yet found anyone who had seen the silver people carrier with its load of white-clad passengers, apart from the staff of the Cockatrice Inn.

'What about Lord and Lady Hurne? Have they been formally interviewed?'

'Not by the house-to-house teams, no. Why? I thought you or Wayne had talked to them?'

'We did, but it was rather informal. I think we need to talk to them at greater length, Jonathan too, and they also have an elder son called Dominic. He almost got through our net. I'd not heard of Dominic until I interviewed a party guest in Manchester and the family's never mentioned him. We must speak to him, and check him like all the others. We can't treat that family any differently from other witnesses.'

'The family names are not on the guest list,' pointed out

143

Horsley. 'We're going through that at the moment, along with all villagers on the Electoral Register.'

'We must be sure all guests are checked and interviewed and Mrs Fowler must be taken to identify her son after morning conference. I shall do that. My presence will ensure continuity of evidence, so necessary in these cases. Then I shall revisit the Hurne family at the Hall, with Detective Sergeant Wain as my driver.'

'Fair enough. So what about further enquiries in Manchester? Won't you want to visit the victim's place of work, his haunts, his friends, neighbours and so on? And do our SOCO need to search the victim's house, or will that be done by Manchester Police? It's not going to be easy, having two police forces working on the same case.'

'All those matters will be dealt with once I have spoken to Dominic Hurne,' said Pluke. 'What I can say is that there is a very good spirit of co-operation between our two forces at the moment, and I see no reason why it should not continue. So what reaction have we had from the press today?'

'Very little,' said Horsley. 'Sundays are usually quiet press days. I had a call from that local freelance and he didn't pursue things when I said the body had not been identified, and that we had no idea where the victim had come from. I said we were no further forward with the investigation and that no one had been arrested. He said he would stress the need for people to provide possible names for the deceased, and any sightings of likely suspects. We must keep that angle running for the time being.'

'It can remain the official line until I countermand that order,' said Pluke. 'I would expect a little more press interest tomorrow, from the local weeklies, the evening papers and radio stations.'

'That's no problem, Montague, you know what you're doing.'

'Well, it is almost time for the final conference of today.

My goodness, how time has flown, it has been a busy day.'

'And you have returned safely from enemy territory!'

'So I have, my luck must have been with me,' smiled Pluke as the first of the house-to-house teams arrived to file the statements they had taken during the day. When all the teams were assembled, Pluke gave an edited account of his sojourn in Manchester, stressing that the identity of the deceased must not be made known to the public and most certainly not to the press, but he did not mention that Mrs Fowler was now living in Crickledale. That fact was known only to a select few police officers; it would be revealed to key operators in Crickledale Police Station in case they had to deal with her in any way, but that information was not for general release. In return, the teams could add nothing positive after their day on the moors and around the villages, except to eliminate more local people from suspicion. It seemed the killer or killers had zoomed in, done their foul deed and departed without anyone being aware of their presence – except staff at the Cockatrice Inn.

And so Pluke dismissed them with his thanks and asked them to report back in the morning for the first conference at nine o'clock. It was now time for him to go home to Millicent.

'I've made a nice Sunday dinner of roast beef, Yorkshire pudding, mashed potato and two veg,' announced Millicent as Montague divested himself of his huge coat, panama hat and spats. 'And with rice pudding to follow.'

'There is nothing I would like more,' he said. 'I have been in Manchester all day upon enquiries, and a good helping of Yorkshire pudding will just put me right.'

Millicent knew better than quiz her husband about police matters which were invariably confidential, murder enquiries being especially sensitive, and so she told him about her day, relating how she and Mrs Dunwoody had

had to step in at the last minute to arrange the flowers in church because the listed arrangers had both been taken ill with some kind of virus. Then, of course, there was the coffee to organize after the service, a sherry party at the vicarage to attend and the forthcoming Spring Flower Festival to discuss this afternoon. Millicent had had a very busy day and she felt that both should have a sherry. And so they did. As they enjoyed the meal, Pluke felt it was time to explain about Mrs Fowler. Normally he did not discuss police matters but Millicent could be trusted implicitly and would never divulge the real reason for Mrs Fowler's presence in No. 2, Lime Lane, nor of course would she even hint that the cottage was really a safe house for people who needed security and even round-the-clock police protection.

'Millicent,' he began after completing his sweet course, 'I have a matter of some importance and sensitivity to discuss with you.'

'It's not that itch again, is it? The one in a rather embar-rassing place?'

'No, it's not that, and in fact that embarrassing itch has never returned. No, this is police work.'

'Ah, then I am all ears.' She loved it when he spoke about the incredible things he had dealt with during his police work. He led such an amazing life, did Montague, far more exciting than having coffee with Mrs Dunwoody or coping with a flower-arranging crisis at short notice. Millicent realized that Montague rarely spoke about his work to her because he did not wish to place her in the difficult position of having to keep secret or confidential information; he trusted her, of course, but to impose such pressures upon her was unfair, he thought. Clearly, this was an exceptional case.

'I must insist that what I tell you does not go beyond these four walls,' he began.

'Of course, Montague. I know that when you trust me with highly confidential information, it is a matter of the gravest importance. Normally, you never discuss police trivia with me.'

'Quite so,' he said. 'Now, this is the situation. There is a safe house at No. 2, Lime Lane just off the market place and we use it on occasions to accommodate vital witnesses, to protect them against interference or worse. Well, Millicent, we have a witness there right now. I installed her only a short time ago. She is a very ordinary lady called Mrs Emily Fowler who lives in Manchester. She is the mother of our murder victim; his name is Brent Fowler and he was twenty-eight. His name and place of origin are not for public consumption yet, nor for the press. Mrs Fowler is there because we do not want the name of her son, or the fact that he has died, or the fact that his body has been found, to become known in the Manchester area. Nor, of course, do we want his killers to harm or influence her.'

'Ah,' she said, not fully understanding what he was really talking about. 'So she is all alone?'

'Absolutely, Millicent. She has no one, no family, no friends so she says, and now no son. She is entirely alone and it would seem this has always been the case, except for having a son. I know nothing about her marital status, I must confess, for I have not yet formally interviewed her. She has the awful task of identifying her son tomorrow, and that is not going to be easy, but afterwards there will be nothing to look forward to, the funeral could be some weeks away and she will be in Lime Lane for an indeterminate period. I shall interview her during her stay, perhaps in stages. She is retired, by the way, and I think she is probably between fifty-five and sixty. She has a small company pension, I believe, so is not without money.'

'Ah,' she said again, still not sure why she should have to know this.

'I was wondering, Millicent, if you could find it within your generosity to pop in to see her from time to time, just to show that we Yorkshire folk are as friendly as people believe, especially so far as Lancastrians are concerned. I do not expect you to encourage Mrs Fowler to join your

Ladies' Circle or the Women's Institute or Local History Society, or anything else, or even ask her to meet you and your friends for coffee or tea in town, but I think we should do a little to make her feel welcome, to reassure her that there is someone to whom she can turn if necessary.'

'Well, I'm sure I can pop in to see her, Montague. Is she expecting me to make a call?'

'She is. I thought it best that I pave the way for this, with her being such a stranger. She is not a sophisticated lady, I ought to add, and has not travelled very far. I believe this is the first time she has been to Yorkshire.'

'What sheltered lives some poor people must endure!' she said. 'Now, Montague, you hinted at some kind of mystery surrounding this, keeping secrets from the Manchester people, you said. Do I have to know what that is all about?'

'I think that would be wise,' he mused. 'Yes indeed, it would be very wise.' And he launched into the story of the murder, the cause of death, the effect of the swidden burning and the belief by Manchester Police that Brent had been assassinated due to his molestation of little girls during his work at the swimming pool. He then outlined, briefly, how Manchester's specialist squad felt that some subterfuge and perhaps an undercover operation might be the only way to trap the killers and gain the necessary evidence of their activities. Exactly what form that secret exercise would take was not yet known. Or rather, it wasn't known to Pluke but he guessed its purpose would be to trap them into breaking their cover, revealing their *modus operandi*, providing names of the participants and producing sufficient evidence for a conviction. What was important was that Mrs Fowler was removed from a possible source of danger, and she must not be allowed, however unwittingly, to alert Manchester's criminal fraternity to the fact that Brent's body had been found and that the renowned Detective Inspector Pluke was hot on their trail.

As he spoke so calmly and in such a matter-of-fact way

148

without any show of fear or emotion, Millicent wondered just how many secrets her husband really knew, and how many dangers he fearlessly faced every working day. She felt a few tremors in her stomach: she began to wish she'd never had that rice pudding and thought another sherry might not be a bad idea.

But all the time she was saying, 'Oh, that poor Mrs Fowler . . . oh, how awful, oh what dreadful people there are about . . . oh dear me . . . yes, of course I must go and see the poor woman.'

Millicent assured Montague that she would be a good neighbour and would call and see Mrs Fowler after she had been taken to identify Brent. Montague said that tonight he would celebrate Millicent's wonderful co-operation with a nice mug of cocoa.

On Monday mornings, the good people of Crickledale expected to see the distinctive figure of Detective Inspector Montague Pluke as he strode to work at the police station. He was a familiar, regular and reassuring sight and on this Monday they were not disappointed. Some would argue they could set their clocks and watches as he progressed through the streets, passing the same shops, offices, pillar boxes, bus stops and lamp posts at precisely the same time each day. He always bade a respectful good morning to everyone he encountered and raised his distinctive panama with its blue band to each person, irrespective of his or her status in Crickledale society. He had even been known to pat dogs and coo to babies in prams.

This morning, therefore, the burghers of Crickledale were well aware that the town was in safe hands – but Montague Pluke sprung a surprise upon them. Instead of walking past the King's Head as was his daily practice, he turned up the narrow alley which was called Lime Lane. Those who regularly observed Detective Inspector Pluke's magnificent and unimpeded progress through town were somewhat surprised by this diversion and it must be said

that one or two had seen a woman, who was not Mrs
Pluke, popping into the cottage near the entrance to that
lane. She had emerged not long ago to hurry down to the
Co-op. Or had she been seeking the elusive Montague
Pluke? Surely Mr Pluke was not deceiving his wife of
many years?

It did become known that Mr Pluke had knocked on the
door and been admitted, even before arriving at his office,
and so it did not seem this was any part of his police duty.
It was also known that the cottage was used by holidaymakers and other visitors so it must be said that
Montague's unexpected behaviour that morning caused
something of a minor sensation in town. It was so unchar-
acteristic and undoubtedly there would be mutterings over
coffee that morning, even though Mr Pluke's visit was of
very short duration. Pluke, of course, was engaged upon a
police duty mission because he wanted Mrs Fowler to
view the body of her son.

'Did you have a good night's sleep?' asked Pluke when
he was admitted.

'Better than expected,' smiled Mrs Fowler. 'The bed is
very comfortable but everything was so quiet. I'm not used
to the quiet, you see, where I live you can hear buses and
trains, cars and lorries, people talking but here there was
nothing. I slept a little, but thoughts of Brent kept me
awake quite a lot.'

'Silence is something we pride ourselves upon in
Crickledale,' said Pluke. 'Noise is one form of pollution we
can do without and I am sure you will sleep well in the
fullness of time. Now, Mrs Fowler, I must fix a time for you
see your son. I repeat it will not be a pleasant experience
and you must be very strong, but it is essential.'

'I've been thinking about it all night,' she said. 'I must
see him, it might be the last time, so yes, Mr Pluke, I am
ready when you are.'

'Good. Well, I am on my way to the office now and have
some formalities to attend to, including a conference of

detectives, so if I come back here at, say, ten thirty, to collect you? Is that suitable?'

'Yes, very. That would be fine by me,' she said. 'Yes, I have no other commitments. That will give me time to get ready, I'll put my nice black dress on and I have a nice hat.'

And so it was that Montague Pluke left Mrs Fowler minutes later and returned to the morning life of Crickledale. As he made his way to the police station near the church, the town was already buzzing with gossip about the mysterious new lady in Mr Pluke's life but, of course, he was totally unaware of the sensation he had created. Upon arrival at Crickledale Sub-Divisional Headquarters he entered with his right foot first, as always, and poked his head around the door of the tiny Control Room where Sergeant Cockfield pronounced Cofield was in charge.

'Good morning, Sergeant. Any major incidents or serious crimes overnight?'

'Apart from a lady locking herself out of her house, sir, nothing. We managed to open a window and get inside, the key was inside too, sir, it was one of those self-locking locks. Otherwise all quiet, sir.'

'Just as it should be, Sergeant. Well, I have a conference of detectives this morning, I have to take the mother of the murder victim to view his body, and then I shall be interviewing the Hurne family at Hurne Hall. Afterwards, I may have to enter further discussions with Manchester Police. But you should know about the lady in Lime Lane, Sergeant, a Mrs Fowler, mother of the deceased,' and so Pluke explained the situation, stressing its high degree of confidentiality and reminding Sergeant Cockfield pronounced Cofield that Mrs Fowler might come to the police station if she needed help or advice. The vastly experienced sergeant said he would cope.

Pluke ascended the stairs to his office and already, Mrs Plumpton, his amply rounded secretary, was at work. Aware of his slightly delayed arrival, she had made a mug of coffee and upon hearing his approaching footsteps, had

151

already placed it on his desk. She hovered nearby, the gossamer-like fabric of her dress quivering and floating as it executed yet another superb example of well-designed containment, holding in and up all those ample fleshy pieces at which he must not stare. On frequent occasions, he wondered what lay beneath those tantalizing layers of frothy clothing but never dared express the slightest interest.

'Ah, coffee,' he said. 'How thoughtful of you, Mrs Plumpton. Is there anything of note in the post?'

'Nothing of importance,' she said. 'I shall deal with the routine correspondence as always and prepare it for your signature.'

'I fear we have a major crime to concern us today and for the foreseeable future,' he told her, moving his blotter just a shade to the right, shifting his plastic trough-shaped paper-clip container to the rear of his desk and placing the paperweight (a hagstone) closer to his in-tray. 'It is a murder, perhaps you have heard?'

'A murder? Good heavens, Mr Pluke! No, I had no idea, I have been away for the weekend, to Scotland. And you are in charge?' She gazed at him with undisguised admiration.

'I am indeed, Mrs Plumpton, and already the case is proving to be complex. I guessed we might have a murder because I spotted an apple hanging on a tree last week, and an apple remaining on the tree throughout the winter into the spring is always a sign of sudden death or even murder.' He sat down behind his desk, indicating she should be seated on her chair while he told her all about it. He mentioned Mrs Fowler, and Mrs Pluke's generous offer of companionship, then the possibility of Mrs Fowler calling in for advice or assistance. Mrs Plumpton assured him she would, if necessary, offer the hand of friendship towards the bereaved mother.

'So there we are, Mrs Plumpton, you are up to date, and I fear we are in for a busy time.'

'I do like being busy!' She beamed at him.

'Well, I now have to address a conference of detectives in the Incident Room, then I shall take Mrs Fowler to identify her son. Can you ring the mortuary in advance and ask for the body to be placed in the Chapel of Rest for Mrs Fowler's visit? Much better than being on a slab in the operating theatre. And following that, I will head for Hurnehow to interview the family at the Hall.'

'I'll ring immediately and I'm sure you will find the murderer,' oozed Mrs Plumpton, standing up then bending over to collect his coffee mug. He was aware of oceans of female flesh being thrust in his direction with their external covering of fabric barely being a covering at all. It was very difficult to concentrate upon the murder.

'I shall be in the Incident Room if you want me,' he said, rising from his chair.

She wondered if he really meant what he had just said, but he always seemed to be very busy doing something. She sighed.

Chapter Ten

Mrs Fowler rather liked Crickledale. It was a friendly place, she decided: the lady in front of her at the Co-op check-out had smiled and said, 'Good morning,' and a man in a car had stopped to allow her to cross the street with her bags, even though there was no pedestrian crossing or traffic lights. She had managed to get to the Co-op supermarket and the flower shop before Detective Inspector Pluke had called and now she busied herself getting ready to see Brent.

She knew she must be strong and brave. It would not be easy, looking at him in death, and if what Mr Pluke had said about him being burnt was true, then it would be worse than normal. She must control her emotions in the presence of important people like Mr Pluke. The consolation was that her Brent was a real nice boy, a decent young man who would never do anyone any harm, no matter what people said about him, and so he would be in heaven now. That knowledge made all this heartache so much easier to bear and so, as she changed into her black dress and black hat, with a black coat to keep her warm and black matching gloves, she shed no tears.

She knew Brent would be happy wherever he was and in whatever form his spirit now existed, but his sudden enforced absence from her life did make her very unhappy. For her, that was the hard bit, the unhappiness, the sense of loss, of emptiness, of not having a future together. He might be happy in heaven, but she was not happy and was far from being in heaven. Put on a strong front, be firm and in control of herself, that's what she must do. She must bravely learn how to cope in his absence . . . and at that point, tears did well in the corner of each eye just above her nose but she brushed them away with her handkerchief, not wanting her eyes to appear red or her face to reveal the fact she'd been crying. Not when she was going to be driven to see her son, probably the last time she would see him.

Smartly dressed, therefore, she sat on the front edge of the armchair in the lounge to wait for Mr Pluke. The flowers she bought, daffodils, were in a glass vase on the dining-room table. Brent liked daffodils. She was ready very early, Mr Pluke wasn't expected for some time yet but she could sit and watch the market place until he got here. She would be able to see his approach and be ready to leave the moment he arrived. Or should she offer him a cup of tea?

'No, thank you,' said Detective Inspector Pluke when Mrs Fowler offered him the tea. 'We must be getting along for I have other duty commitments and besides, I breakfasted not long ago. Now, is everything to your satisfaction? You have found everything you need in the house?'

'It's wonderful, Mr Pluke, truly wonderful. Yes, I've found everything, it is so well equipped. I do wish Brent was here to see how I am being looked after, he would be so pleased, but I am sure he is up there looking down. And I have found the Co-op, it opens at half-past eight, you know, so I got there early and did a bit more shopping before you came . . . Everything is so handy here, just a short walk, and the people are so nice.'

'Good, well, Mrs Pluke will come to see you later in the day so if there is anything you need or want to know, just ask her. Or call at the police station and ask for my secretary, Mrs Plumpton.'

'Thank you, Mr Pluke, for everything.'

'Now we must leave. My car is outside with Detective

Sergeant Wain at the wheel, we have completed our morning conference and I must tell you there have been no developments in the hunt for your son's killer. But I have more than thirty very skilled detectives working on the case and I am confident we shall produce a good result. Before I take you in to see Brent, I must remind you that it will not be easy, Mrs Fowler, for reasons I explained earlier. The fire especially. All I need from you is for you to look at him and confirm whether or not he is your son. If you wish to remain with him for a while, then that will be quite in order, but, from my point of view, this is a most important part of the investigation. Formal identification of the victim is essential. Now, the drive will take about half an hour. Are you ready?'

'Yes, I am.' She took a deep breath as she prepared to leave. 'I got him some flowers, Mr Pluke. Daffodils. Am I allowed to take them to him?'

Pluke did a swift mental recap of the rules governing flowers; he knew one must never take red and white flowers into a hospital, the official reason being that they might upset the patients. He knew, however, that if mixed bunches of red and white flowers were taken into a ward, it heralded the death of one of the patients, but yellow flowers, or to be precise flowers with yellow corollas, were ideal as a protection against evil. In the past, yellow flowers had been used to create protective charms. Pluke had already had the foresight to have Brent taken into the Chapel of Rest. He was not sure how flowers would be received in the mortuary's operating theatre. They might contaminate the atmosphere with pollen or insects, so he felt that was not a very sensible idea.

'He will be in the Chapel of Rest,' nodded Pluke with some satisfaction. 'And you are taking daffodils? I see no problem. In fact, it is a very nice idea. Daffodils are ideal for this purpose,' he added, thinking of their yellow corollas.

'Thank you,' she said and followed him out to the car clutching the precious bunch. She, Pluke and Wayne Wain spoke very little during the journey, with Pluke's mind on the difficult and complex enquiry in which he was now embroiled with some of Manchester's elite undercover squad – although Brent Fowler was his sole concern, not the other deaths in Manchester and district. His mind was ranging over the likely scenarios as he sat beside Wayne, while Wayne's mind was on that lovely blonde called Fiona from the Council's accounts department he'd been out with last night and Mrs Fowler was still wondering whether all that had happened to her was real or just a bad dream.

Wayne knew where to park and drove confidently through the complex of brick buildings which formed the hospital; the mortuary and Chapel of Rest were behind the main block, each with its own car park, and so he gently guided the unmarked police car into a convenient space, climbed out and opened the door for Mrs Fowler.

Smiling, with her face now very pale and looking even more so due to her black clothing, she climbed out, straightened her coat and hat, and prepared to follow the two policemen. She was very nervous and hoped it did not show, but she did reach out and take Wayne's arm for support. He smiled at her and she gripped him tightly as Pluke said, 'This way, Mrs Fowler.'

Gently, he led her into the Chapel of Rest where a woman attendant waited in the foyer; she smiled and took the daffodils from Mrs Fowler, saying she would get a vase, and then she opened the silent doors and the little party entered the calm, quiet and chapel-like place. Brent was lying on a plinth, his body covered with a clean white sheet except for his face. Most of his burning injuries were out of sight but his face looked very brown and his hair was frizzled; the tiny bullet hole was almost invisible and Pluke felt she might not notice it. He led her towards the plinth as she clung to Wayne's arm and she merely stood and gazed down upon her son.

She said nothing for a long, long time and neither Pluke nor Wayne Wain tried to hurry her; she stroked his face as

157

she gazed upon him, ran her hand across his hair then stopped and kissed his cold forehead. Then the tears came.

She turned as if to leave, still clinging to Wayne, and so the little party went outside where the lady attendant asked if Mrs Fowler would like a cup of tea. The daffodils were now in a vase on the table in Reception.

'No, thank you,' she said. 'It's very kind, but no, thank you.'

'I'll take your flowers in now.' The woman disappeared inside with the vase.

'You're so very kind,' said Mrs Fowler.

Before returning to the car, Pluke said, 'Mrs Fowler, I must ask this official question. The person in the Chapel of Rest, is that your son, Brent Fowler?'

'Yes, yes it is, Mr Pluke. That is Brent, and I thought he looked very peaceful and at rest.'

'I shall need a short signed statement from you to that effect,' he said. 'I have the form in my car. Perhaps when we return to your house?'

'Yes, yes, that will be all right, I know you have your duty to perform.'

'There is another matter, Mrs Fowler. You will remember I asked you not to reveal to strangers the reason for your presence here. Obviously, you can discuss things with my staff and indeed with Mrs Pluke, but we do not want you to reveal to anyone else, certainly not the newspapers and radio people, the fact that Brent has been found, or that we know who he is.'

'Yes, I remember you telling me that, Mr Pluke. I shall pretend I am on holiday as a friend of you and Mrs Pluke. I shall enjoy helping you like this.'

'During our enquiries, we will pretend that Brent has not been identified, we need to exercise a little subterfuge if we are to catch his killers. Manchester Police have asked for that and although this is unusual, I have agreed because I believe it is necessary. We do not want the killers to know his body has been found, and so we shall not tell the press. So far as anyone is concerned, we are still trying to identify the murder victim.'

'Oh, I understand that, Mr Pluke, I do read quite a lot of detective novels and I know you have to be as clever or cleverer than the killers. Which reminds me, is there a library in Crickledale?'

'Indeed there is, Mrs Fowler, and it is a particularly good one. You'll find it just behind the town hall.' He wondered whether he should mention his own books on the history of horse troughs which were proving so popular with borrowers, but decided against it. After all, one should not be boastful to a lady in a situation of this kind; she would have other things on her mind.

'Thank you, Mr Pluke.'

'There is one other matter, Mrs Fowler, which can wait a while. We need to ask you a lot of deep questions about Brent, his friends, the way he lived, whether he had any enemies, that sort of thing. Perhaps you could be thinking about that? Then we can take a formal statement from you. As soon as possible.'

'Yes, I've been doing a lot of thinking, Mr Pluke, and you are welcome at any time. Now, if you like.'

'I have other commitments this morning, Mrs Fowler, such as a visit to Lord Hurne, but I may be free this afternoon.'

'Thank you, yes, that will be fine, and you know I will help all I can. Call any time you like. Now, perhaps you will both have a cup of tea with me?'

'Yes, I think on this occasion we might,' said Montague Pluke, thinking Mrs Fowler was remarkably composed and at ease with herself, bearing in mind her recent ordeal. She might reveal a little more about her late son's lifestyle and contacts when they spoke and there was also the question of searching her home to see whether any evidence lay in Brent's belongings. And even after all this, more time might help her to recall all those tiny but important facets of Brent's life.

Over tea, Mrs Fowler prattled on about how good a son Brent had been, how thoughtful, how good-natured and kind and how quiet he was about the house, especially when he went into his computer room. In spite of her chatterings, however, the two detectives gained very little additional information about him but steadfastly refrained from pressing her to answer any questions. After the tea, they took their leave with Pluke saying Mrs Pluke – Millicent – would call very soon, while he and Wayne would endeavour to visit her later this afternoon.

'So off we go to Hurne Hall,' said Wayne when they returned to the car. 'What's our strategy there, sir?'

'Strategy, Wayne?'

'Well, yes, don't we have a strategy?'

'We are going to ask a few questions, that's all, Wayne. We have to establish whether Dominic is alive and whether we regard him as a suspect, and we have to question the rest of the household about their movements and likely sightings on the Friday in question.'

'Ah, so we are ignoring the birthday party? That was on the Tuesday following his death.'

'No, we are not ignoring it, Wayne, not if we are pretending we do not know the identity of the deceased. We know Brent Fowler died on the Friday, and we know who he is, but if we are pretending that we do not know who he is or when he died, then we cannot ignore the party. We must let people think the party is critical if we are to confound the killers. One never knows who is involved in this death, Wayne, it may be someone from that household. We shall ask our questions in a way which helps us to determine who killed Brent Fowler. We shall be using subterfuge, Wayne. I shall begin by establishing whether Dominic Hurne is alive and, if so, his whereabouts at the time of the murder. That is my subterfuge.'

160

'So that is your strategy, sir? To maintain a certain level of subterfuge?'

'If that is how you see it, Wayne, then yes.'

As they approached Hurne Hall, they could see a string of plain-clothes policemen in overalls still searching the moorland around the swidden with their vehicles using the roadside within the grounds of the Hall.

'Do they still need to do that?' asked Pluke. 'I thought they'd finished the search?'

'It's been scaled down,' Wain reminded him. 'But they still need to find the shell of the .22 bullet which killed Brent, sir; now we know he was killed somewhere nearby on that Friday, Inspector Horsley will want to be completely sure the shell is not anywhere near the scene of his death.'

'It is like searching for a particular grain of sand on a beach,' said Pluke. 'Ah, here we are. The estate office once again. We'll start with Lord Hurne.'

When Pluke introduced himself and Wayne to the secretary, she smiled a welcome and said, 'I think His Lordship has been expecting you, Detective Inspector Pluke. He asked me to let him know if you arrived.'

'We did promise to return for more in-depth questioning, but before I see him, might I ask if you were at Jonathan's birthday party?'

'Yes, all the staff were there.' Smartly dressed in a dark skirt and white blouse, she was in her thirties, a stoutish young woman with rimless spectacles and neat black hair cut short. Pluke saw she was wearing a wedding ring.

'And did you notice anything out of the ordinary around the time of the party? Gate-crashers perhaps? Arguments? Fights even, either in the marquee and grounds, or on the moor?'

'No, nothing. We've been asking ourselves those questions, Mr Pluke, it's all so puzzling. We just can't believe this has happened here and we can't think why. Have you checked all the guests yet? In case any of them are missing?'

161

'Not yet, that is an ongoing process by almost every police force in Britain, but so far everyone can be accounted for. Were you alone at the party?'

'No, my husband was invited, although he doesn't work here. We've had some of your detectives around to our house, Mr Pluke, checking to see if he was safe. And he was. They asked us if we'd seen anything.'

'Ah, then I need not trouble you any more. And your name?'

'Bentham. Alicia Bentham, my husband is Steven, we live in the village.'

'Make a note of those names, Wayne, and then we can check with the teams, to make sure Mr and Mrs Bentham are accounted for on our lists. Well, thank you, Mrs Bentham.'

'I'll check with His Lordship.' She pressed an intercom button before saying, 'Detective Inspector Pluke and Detective Sergeant Wain are here, Your Lordship, asking if you can spare a little time to see them.' After a pause, she said, 'Yes, I'll show them in.'

'Follow me,' she invited, heading outside and turning towards the big house.

Minutes later they were being shown into a large book-lined study with oak panelling on the walls and an array of leather chairs before a blazing log fire. Lord Hurne rose from one of the chairs, placed a file of papers on a side table and beamed a welcome.

'Ah, Detective Inspector Pluke and Detective Sergeant Wain, nice to see you again. Can I get you a drink apiece? Coffee? Something stronger?'

'Not for me, thank you,' said Pluke who never accepted possible bribes from those who might be suspects. Wayne took his lead from the boss and also declined.

'So, what's the news?' asked His Lordship.

'We haven't made much progress,' Pluke began his subterfuge, and then explained how his teams were checking names on the guest list, so far with everyone accounted for; he said no useful evidence had been found during the searches of the swidden and its environs but he did say that a vehicle containing seven men had been sighted at the Cockatrice Inn on the moors, although at this stage there was no evidence to link it to the deceased. He mentioned this because he had already discussed it with the landlord of the inn and he knew how word would spread, and probably become exaggerated, among the people in this small community. He also told His Lordship that he was anxious to learn of any incidents on the moor or perhaps within the vicinity of Hurne Hall in the week preceding Jonathan's party.

'We've talked about nothing else since your last visit, Detective Inspector. My wife and I, and my staff, we've racked our brains but I have to say we can't recall anything out of the ordinary. Everything's been as dead as a dodo but you will appreciate we can't see the whole moor from this house. I've had a long chat with my keeper and he's had words with those of his acquaintances who regularly cross the moor, but there's been nothing, Mr Pluke. I just cannot see how a fellow can end up shot dead on my moor without anyone knowing, and lie there for God knows how long without being found. Had it not been for that fire, he might never have been found.'

'Precisely, My Lord, and that is an important factor, but we have already discussed the fire and which people knew that the burning was imminent. Now, there is another matter.'

'Then ask me, I promised all the help I could give.'

'When we checked the guest list more closely,' said Pluke, 'I noticed that neither you nor your wife nor Jonathan were listed.'

'Well, no, of course not. That would have been a waste of time. It was a foregone conclusion we would be there.'

'In that case, might I ask which other guests were absent from the list? We need to trace absolutely everyone who was there, to check that they are alive and for elimination purposes. If the list was incomplete, I need to know.'

'There was no one else, Mr Pluke. Just the family.'

'I believe you have another son, My Lord. Dominic.'

'Yes, of course I have, my eldest. My heir in fact. But he could not be here, he's in Australia.'

'Oh,' said Pluke.

'Working on a sheep station, Mr Pluke, to gain experience before he takes over the reins from me. That will not be for some time yet, I trust. Since leaving university, he's been working here for a time, with the gamekeeper and our shepherds, he's also done a spell in the office to see how the accounts system, stock-taking and admin procedures work and now he's in Australia, on a cousin's spread over there, studying large-scale sheep farming. If you really need to check that he's alive, I can give you my cousin's phone number and you can call him.'

'I don't think that will be necessary at this stage,' said Pluke, thinking he would rather ask the Australian police to check Dominic's whereabouts. Then he added, 'And which university did he attend?'

'Manchester. He did a course on agricultural science.'

'And is he married?'

'Not him, Mr Pluke, he's too busy sowing his wild oats. But he has had girlfriends, lots of them, all shapes, sizes, colours and backgrounds. He gets on well with everyone, he has no hang-ups about class, race or culture. He's a good chap, Pluke.'

'Did he bring his friends home?'

'You bet he did! Lots of them, male and female, or both. I think he liked to show city types and townies how well we live in the countryside.'

'Can you recall any of them? Names? Addresses?'

'No, sorry. They just used first names like Chloe or Jasper and when we were given word he was inviting someone for the weekend, we told the housekeeper and she did the rest. Sometimes we hardly saw them – it's a big house, Mr Pluke, designed for entertaining guests and allowing us to keep out of their way if we wish! Of course, it was all a long time ago, he left university at twenty-one.

164

Four years ago. He didn't take a gap year after school, wanted to get busy right away. That's Dominic.'

'I understand some of those friends of Dominic's continue to receive Christmas cards from you,' said Pluke, as if to dismiss His Lordship's statement of not knowing their names.

'Do they really? Well, that will be due to the efficiency of the girl in our estate office. Alicia. Have a word with her, she might have their names and addresses. My wife and I always sign a mighty big pile of them each year but I can't say I remember any of those youngsters particularly, although they did eat and drink as if the world was about to end and they made rather a lot of damned noise too.'

'May I take a copy of your Christmas card list?' asked Pluke.

'What on earth do you want with that? If it's of any possible use to help you get to the bottom of all this nonsense, then get Alicia to print one for you.'

Pluke realized, of course, that Dominic's friends at university were probably now spread far and wide around the globe, without Manchester addresses, and there would probably be no means of identifying them from the whole guest list. But each name could be checked if he felt it necessary. The Christmas card list might be the only means of ascertaining who had stayed or visited the Hall in addition to the birthday guests. He thought, however, that he should provide His Lordship with some reason for wanting this apparently odd information.

'I need to trace anyone who might be familiar with this district,' said Pluke. 'For the purposes of elimination.'

'Well, some of my Christmas card list people have never been near the place, Pluke, they don't even know where Yorkshire is let alone this house! Others know the area well, so yes, do what you will. I hope it's of some use!'

'I am sure it will be,' said Pluke. 'Well, I think that is all for the time being. I will leave you and call in to speak to Mrs Bentham. I don't think I need trouble your wife at this stage and I am sure Mrs Bentham will give me all the information I need.'

Pluke and Wayne took their leave, returning to the estate office for another word with Alicia Bentham. Pluke informed her that Lord Hurne had authorized them to be given a copy of the estate's official Christmas card list and she said she could print one for them within minutes. And so she did.

'Is that all?' asked Mrs Bentham. 'It's just that Lord Hurne said I should give the police every assistance in this enquiry.'

'That's all for the moment,' said Pluke, picking up several pages of print-out material. 'We will study this in our Incident Room, but before we leave, can you tell me if you know any of the people on this list?'

'Not all of them!' she said. 'I might know most of the locals and staff, tradespeople, bankers and so on, but there's all sorts on that list, Mr Pluke. People from all over the world, abroad as well, Australia, America, France and more. And family, friends, business acquaintances, visitors, bank managers, accountants, other local estate owners, local business people, our suppliers, newspaper editors, politicians . . . It's a very long list, Mr Pluke.'

'Ah, so you could not identify the names of those who had been at university with Dominic? Those who'd been guests here?'

'Oh yes,' she beamed. 'I think I could. I got the job of compiling the list and then maintaining it. I thought it might be sensible to categorize people. You know, put them in groups. With the computer it's easy to make sub-lists. Like lists of those people dealing with money, accountants, bank managers, financial advisers, share brokers and so on. And local tradesmen. Neighbouring estate owners. Residential visitors to the house. So yes, Dominic's old friends will be in a separate list. The house-keeper always made a point of remembering the name and address of everyone who was a guest, and she included things like special diets and so on.'

'All very efficient,' praised Pluke. 'I am sure this will be of great help to us.'

'I do hope so, Mr Pluke, although I must confess I can't see how the Christmas card list could relate to the poor man on the moor.'

And so it was that Montague Pluke was handed a print-out of all those recipients of Hurne estate Christmas cards, although he was more closely interested in those who had been at university with Dominic. Those who had been residential guests at Hurne Hall were marked with an asterisk.

'I am most grateful, Mrs Bentham,' he said. 'Most grateful indeed. Well, Detective Sergeant Wain, I think we can return to the Incident Room now to continue our enquiries.'

'Really, sir?'

'Yes, really, Wayne. Good day to you, Mrs Bentham.'

And so it was that Montague Pluke was driven back to the Incident Room bearing a fistful of the names of Hurne estate's Christmas card recipients.

'Sir,' said Wayne Wain as he drove back to Crickledale, 'why on earth did you ask for that list? I can't see how people receiving Christmas cards from Lord and Lady Hurne are of interest to us. So far as I know, Brent Fowler had nothing to do with this place.'

'It's all to do with names, Wayne, names. They are the raw material of any murder investigation. Names to check, people to interview. I can understand Lord and Lady Hurne not knowing the full names or addresses of Dominic's university friends if they came and went during a weekend, but fortunately his staff are more efficient. That is not in the least unusual, Wayne, in such households. Not at all unusual. Getting guests to sign the visitors' book, then keeping lists of those names for Christmas cards.'

'Forgive me repeating myself, sir, but why do we need all these extra names?'

'Dominic was at Manchester University, Wayne. He met

friends there, they came to stay at Hurne Hall. If they came regularly, they would soon become familiar with the land-scape, life in the big house, layout of the Hall and its environs.'

'I can understand that, they'd go for long walks with dogs or guns or something.'

'Or they might just want a bit of fresh moorland air, Wayne. But remember this. Our enquiry is strongly linked to Manchester. And somebody has known precisely where to dump the body of Brent Fowler. We are sure it is linked to Manchester, even to somebody who has been to Hurne Hall, dare I suggest? Probably on more than one occasion? Someone on that list of Christmas card recipients perhaps?'

'Right, sir, got you! So we check all those people on that list, to see where they were at the material time?'

'That's the starting point, Wayne, merely the starting point. Nonetheless, it will enliven the enquiry and I do appreciate that most of the addresses on this list will not be in Manchester, people will have moved on since their time at university and some will not have updated their addresses. But we must examine the list in great detail, Wayne. For elimination purposes.'

'So now we have a database, sir? Another one. To check against the known times of our murder? And a long list of other suspects?'

'Yes, Wayne, we do. And it could be very important. The killer might be among those people, or the list might contain the name of someone who knows the killer. So let's return to the Incident Room and get these names pro-grammed into the system, shall we? And then we can ensure our teams check each person's whereabouts last Friday, not forgetting to see if any have a criminal record or have been suspected of crimes.'

'Yes, sir,' smiled Wayne Wain.

'And have you looked at that disk Manchester gave us?'

'No, sir, I thought you'd be doing that.'

'I do not understand such modern contraptions, Wayne, so perhaps if you've a moment, you would, er, access it on your computer? Is that the right term?'

'Yes, sir, I'll do it as soon as possible.'

Chapter Eleven

Mrs Fowler had just changed out of her smart black clothes when there was a knock on the door. She hurried to answer it, thinking it might be those policemen returning to ask more questions, but instead there was a neat and rather slender little woman on the doorstep. She had greying hair and was dressed in a smart tan overcoat with a red hat and red shoes. She carried a red handbag too.

'Mrs Fowler?' asked the lady.

'Yes?'

'I am Mrs Pluke, I believe my husband has mentioned me.'

'Ah, yes, how lovely, yes, do come in.'

After taking off her hat and coat, Mrs Pluke was invited to sit down in the lounge where a realistic log fire was burning with gas, and then Mrs Fowler joined her. She wiped her eyes, red-rimmed with crying in her loneliness.

'Montague thought you might need some company, being new to the town,' began Millicent. 'I've called to see if you need anything or want to go anywhere.'

'He is such a kind man, your husband. So gentle and considerate. But I am finding my way around the town and got to the Co-op and the flower shop this morning before Mr Pluke arrived. I was thinking about getting something for my lunch. Would you like to join me, Mrs Pluke? It will be nothing grand, just a sandwich. I bought some tinned tuna and salad from the Co-op and it would be so nice to have someone to share it with and talk to.'

'We can go into town if you like, there are some nice

cafés and tearooms, but if we're going to talk about your son, it might be best if we did it here,' smiled Millicent. 'Yes, I would love to have lunch with you. Montague will be getting his meal at work, they have a mobile canteen when there's a big enquiry going on. Perhaps afterwards we might have a walk around the town when I can show you where things are.'

'Mr Pluke said I must not talk about Brent outside, or tell people why I am here, but he said it's all right to talk to you.'

'Yes, he's a very clever detective, is my Montague.'

'Look, why don't you come into the kitchen while I'm making the sandwiches, and we can talk in there. We have to appear to be friends, Mrs Pluke, so I am Emily and he said your name is Millicent.'

Millicent followed her into the neat little kitchen. Emily was a short woman, somewhat stout in build and dressed in rather cheap clothes with an unflattering hairstyle. She seemed very pleasant and appeared to be coping admirably with the loss of her son. Millicent settled herself at the kitchen table to help prepare the lettuce and tomatoes as Emily busied herself with the rest of lunch. As they chatted the two ladies decided to become friends while concocting a cover story that Emily was someone from Millicent's schooldays, someone she'd not seen or been in touch with for many years. The story would be that they were now getting to know one another all over again after Emily had moved to Manchester. That was the tale they would develop if they met any of Millicent's friends in town.

Emily, through her background of reading detective stories, found all this subterfuge quite thrilling and was sure it would help Mr Pluke find Brent's killer. Millicent was also able to make a useful contribution thanks to her knowledge of Montague's important work. And so the two ladies quickly forged a friendship which both were sure would help to identify Brent's killer.

As they got to know one another, Emily spoke a lot about Brent while Millicent listened politely. It seemed

Brent had always been a quiet boy, even from his earliest childhood, and he'd never been anxious to play football or take part in other rough games. He hadn't shone at school although she felt he was highly intelligent and this had revealed itself in later life when he'd shown an interest in computers. He'd saved up for one through his work at the swimming pool and she knew he enjoyed some of the clever games he could play on it, he could chat to people on the internet too although she had no idea what that really meant. He could do research into all sorts of subjects, he'd told her as he'd tried to explain it all to his mother, but she never understood. The whole machine looked like a cross between a television set and a typewriter which she found quite bewildering.

She told Millicent that her main concern about Brent's transition from child into young man was that he had never found himself a nice girlfriend. He liked girls, she assured Millicent, there was nothing homosexual about him, and he'd often talked about a girl at the pool called Ali. From what Brent had said, Ali was always willing to talk and they would have a coffee and a chat whenever he had a break at work, but he'd never brought her home.

That was a pity, Emily would have loved to meet her. Then there was Brent's interest in the camera club and computer club, though she had no idea where those clubs were or who he met there. He also went to the library. He'd always been a good lad, she said, never in trouble with the police or getting involved with drugs or heavy drinking, and he'd never been bothered with motor bikes or fast cars. She did say, however, that he tended to be very secretive even at home, and got very cross if he thought she was snooping among his belongings. He never left anything personal lying around in his bedroom or in his dressing table or wardrobe; all his deepest secrets were in his computer but she had no idea how to operate it. Not that she wanted to, she told Millicent, but she had once, very accidentally, read a letter which had fallen out of his trouser pocket and he was very cross, even if she'd never

172

understood what it meant. It was using some sort of funny language about sexual activities which meant nothing to her, but Brent had become very agitated and upset at the intrusion into his privacy.

Millicent noticed, however, that apart from saying she'd once worked at a clothing factory housed in an old mill, Emily revealed very little about herself and nothing about Brent's father. Millicent did not like to pry into her private life, but from the conversation she discovered Emily had no other children or family, and that her entire world was focused on Brent. Or had been. Now she was utterly alone.

When they had finished their meal, Millicent said, 'I'll take you to see our library where I am sure there are some good detective novels, and then we'll look around the church and maybe have a cup of tea in a nice little tearoom I know.'

'I would like that,' said Emily.

'I'm sure you will meet other people while you are here, Emily, and I am also sure Montague will do his best to find Brent's killer.'

'Yes, that would be nice. But not a word about Brent once we leave this house!'

'Not a word,' promised Millicent.

'I'd like your teams to check some names on this list,' said Pluke as he presented the Christmas card list to Inspector Horsley in the Incident Room. 'I am interested in people who have been guests at Hurne Hall at times other than the birthday party and this is probably the only source available to us, taken from the visitors' book. You'll see the secretary has categorized everyone on the list and I am interested in those who were friends of Dominic. Now, Detective Sergeant Wain and myself have already interviewed some people on the list. They are Alison Wharram and Mark Newbury, and a Mr and Mrs Sharpe, all from the Manchester area, and all of whom were also guests at Jonathan's birthday party. Both pairs were friends of Lord

Hurne's sons while they were at university, one at Leeds and the other at Manchester. I want all the others interviewed and eliminated from our enquiries, Inspector Horsley.'

'Why? I thought we'd put the birthday party guests on low priority now we know Brent Fowler's identity and the fact he was murdered on the Friday, some days before the party?'

'Subterfuge, Inspector,' smiled Pluke with more than a hint of mystery in his voice. 'All I want to do is trace the whereabouts of those residential guests on the Friday in question and, if possible, obtain the dates they were at Hurne Hall. Some might have been there a considerable time ago, four years even, and then only on one occasion. But I do need to know when any of them came to the Hall, and who with. I need to know who were guests *prior* to the body being found, even if their visit was several years earlier.'

'Well, you know what you're doing, Montague. So this list supersedes the party guest list?'

'It runs parallel to it, Inspector. We need to trace, interview and eliminate everyone on both lists. There will, of course, be some names who are on both – and they are important; certainly they are very interesting to me.'

'Fair enough, you're the boss. Now, I've some news for you too. Fowler's computer. We've carried out an initial examination and he's been using it to visit child pornography websites and to download material. It's clear he used it for games and contacting people by email too, and visiting other websites, but child porn appears to have been his chief interest, an obsession almost. Our boffins don't think he was part of any computer-linked group, he seems to have been a lone operator, contacting others for chats about things like country life, art, photography and so on. A complex character judging by the variety of his interests. He ran up some hefty phone bills through using his computer and we've been able to source those calls.'

'Does it contain addresses of his local clubs, societies,

friends? I would imagine he was the sort of man who entered his life story into his computer,' asked Wayne.

'Yes, it's crammed with personal stuff. Birthday dates of colleagues at work, their addresses and phone numbers, club addresses, the names of the girls in the library, the names of some old school friends, all the usual trivia you'd expect anyone to keep at home. I'll make sure they're all interviewed. From what our boffins have learned so far, it seems he used it for hours each day, putting everything into it, using it for all manner of things. They're still digging, of course, there's a lot more deep work to do but they felt you might like to know their initial discoveries. We've nothing new from house-to-house enquiries by the way, or from the scene.'

'Thank you, this helps a lot,' said Pluke. 'It makes me wonder whether we need to search his home in Manchester. If we could be sure all his personal records and data are stored in his computer, we might not need any further searches. It would be interesting to see if there's any reference to the people who took him to the Cockatrice Inn, and to Jake in particular. Can you ask the experts to look for that name in Brent's computer? Jake and five other men, all from Manchester. And there might be something about that letter he received, and the silver Galaxy. He might have recorded details of the letter. In any case, we might learn more when we talk to his mother but I think the enquiry is moving nicely forward.'

'Jake's name is already in the system from the Cockatrice sighting, so can we consider him to be in the frame? A real suspect?'

'Indeed we can, Inspector Horsley. Jake and five other men, all wearing white according to the landlord of the Cockatrice. I am confident Jake is none other than the Jacob Hampson currently being targeted by Manchester Police. He's head of a church called the Church of the White Kelts, which excites my interest in him.'

'Do you want me to contact Manchester Police about Jake and his friends?'

'Not at this stage,' said Pluke. 'They are formulating plans to obtain evidence and these might include Jake. I'll be discussing my strategy with Manchester Police very soon. I don't want to disturb any arrangements they might have made. Well, Wayne, it's lunchtime, and this afternoon we must brace ourselves for an in-depth interview of Mrs Fowler. We know so very little about Brent so we must press her for more details. It won't be easy.'

'I'm not sure she knows much about him herself,' said Wayne Wain. 'But yes, lunch calls. I wonder what culinary delights the canteen has for us today? Bangers and mash, I wouldn't be surprised.'

Before visiting Mrs Fowler, Pluke and Wayne paid another visit to the swidden where a handful of devoted detectives were still searching for the elusive spent bullet case. Detective Sergeant Tabler confirmed it had not yet been found.

'So what is the general opinion of your teams, Sergeant?' asked Pluke.

'We know with reasonable certainty that Fowler was alive at the Cockatrice Inn that Friday evening for his last supper and then driven out here. He wouldn't be executed in the vehicle, sir, that would be too risky for all sorts of reasons, so we think he was driven out to this part of the moor, still alive. The vehicle, the silver Ford Galaxy, was probably parked on a verge near the murder scene. We've found nothing to suggest otherwise and there is no evidence of a vehicle being driven through the heather. We all know how difficult it is to carry a dead body by hand so we think Fowler was brought out of the people carrier and marched across the moor at gunpoint. Marched to his death in fact. It was dark, we know that from the time they finished their meal, so any light would come either from torches or the vehicle lights. We've had no reports of lights being seen, though that's not surprising; it's a very remote place, hidden from the road and from any local houses, including the Hall. We think he was shot very close to

176

where he was found, sir, with the body being neatly laid out as you have told us.

'We also think the killer or killers were clever enough to remove all evidence of their crime, even taking the spent bullet shell away with them and removing anything from the body which might have led to an identification. From all that, sir, we believe it is the work of professional or very experienced killers. Assassins in other words. A team of five led by a sixth called Jake.'

'That scenario confirms the generally accepted theory, Sergeant. Well done.'

'So how long do you want to us to keep looking? We've searched from where the body was found back to the road, several yards on either side of the most direct route. If the bullet shell had been ejected, its most likely resting place would be somewhere in that patch of moor. It isn't there, sir, we can guarantee that.'

'In that case, I suggest you stand down. I'll visit the Incident Room and tell Inspector Horsley. Like you, I think the killers have removed every scrap of evidence, and that smacks of professionalism.'

And so Pluke returned to the Incident Room, suggested to Horsley that the moorland search be halted and thanked him for being so doggedly determined to find every snippet of evidence. The bullet itself had been recovered from the corpse and would provide its own useful evidence. Pluke announced his next interview was to be with Mrs Fowler. He didn't require Detective Sergeant Wain to drive him there because Lime Lane was a short walk from the police station, but he wanted Wain to join him for the interview. The walk would do him good. Wayne Wain had winning ways with women. There was no response to their knocking at the safe house and after peering through the windows Pluke decided that Mrs Fowler was not at home.

'She will be with Mrs Pluke, I am sure,' he pronounced. 'Now, if I know my wife, she will be showing Mrs Fowler those parts of Crickledale which will be of particular interest to her. Mrs Fowler is a keen fan of crime novels and, judging by her appearance, is not sufficiently well off to purchase her own copies, so I imagine Mrs Pluke will be showing her the library. And I would also imagine the tearooms will feature in her itinerary. Mrs Pluke does like to talk over a nice cup of tea. Let us therefore perambulate around the town seeking Mrs Pluke; it will also provide a few minutes of our own deep thinking time. We need to rethink this murder case, Wayne, we are not making much progress. It is a good thing that Manchester Police are intent on staging some kind of trap, their work will surely help us.'

As Pluke had deduced with his Sherlock Holmes type of insight, Millicent was in the library with Mrs Fowler. She was reading a fashion magazine at a table while Mrs Fowler was studying detective story titles on the shelves. Montague, with Wayne at his heels, crept inside in keeping with the tradition of silence and attracted Millicent's attention.

'Montague! What's happened?' The unexpected appearance of her husband resulted in a look of horror on Millicent's face. She feared something awful must have happened.

'My earlier enquiries have concluded rather more swiftly than I anticipated,' he hissed. 'As I must interview Mrs Fowler, I thought the sooner I speak to her the better it will be for all concerned.'

'Oh, is that all! I'll go and get her.'

Millicent left them as Pluke, Wayne and Mrs Fowler returned to her little cottage where she settled them down in the lounge for a long chat. They declined her offer of a cup of tea because they wanted to concentrate upon the task in hand and, after asking Mrs Fowler if she felt able to cope with an in-depth interview about Brent's life (to which she agreed), they started their questions. This was not the interrogation of a suspect, they explained to her, but an official witness statement in which it was hoped that hitherto unknown facets of the life of the murder victim would be revealed.

However, as they gently led her through the highlights of his life from his birth and early childhood up to his time in secondary school, then his work and hobbies while not forgetting his home life, they realized she knew very little about her son. She had no real idea how he spent his leisure time, for example, other than that he messed about with computers and sometimes went to a computer club or a camera club, but she knew none of the precise details they needed – she had no idea of the addresses of his clubs, or their names and phone numbers, or when they met and who else went there.

She confirmed, however, that Brent was an only child and that she had never married the father; he was a married man who had denied paternity and she had no idea how to deal with that, except she knew she must work to rear her son. She had worked in a clothing factory, she told them, but for much of the time after reaching school age, Brent was alone. He would come home from school, let himself into the house and read a lot, seldom going out to play with other boys and never staying late at school to play football or cricket, or join the drama group or anything. He was very much a homebird, she told them, but she did not mind because he was company for her in the evenings and at weekends when he would accompany her on bus trips to stately homes and other attractions.

'He was so good with me,' she sighed with tears forming. 'So gentle and considerate, never going off to watch Manchester United at home or away, always making sure he was with me, especially at weekends. He was so good to me, Mr Pluke, so very good. I shall miss him.' Her eyes grew moist.

After letting her get this aspect of his life out of her system, Pluke, with Wayne sitting patiently at his side, decided it was now time to ask the more difficult questions.

'Mrs Fowler, I must ask some difficult questions now.

179

I shall not be offended if you feel we are being too intrusive, but it is vital that we ascertain whether Brent had any enemies, whether he was ever attacked at work or in the street, whether he got anonymous letters and so forth. Sometimes, when men get that kind of treatment, they remain indoors, out of the public eye, as a form of security. I wondered if Brent had shown any signs of that? Of having an enemy or enemies?'

'Good heavens, no, Mr Pluke. Everyone liked Brent, he was such a lovely boy . . .'

'Which pool did he work at?'

'The one in Dean Road, it's part of the leisure centre.'

'There were problems at the swimming pool, something involving Brent. You told us you knew nothing about it until this case arose.'

'Brent wouldn't tell me about it because it would upset me, it doesn't mean he was guilty of anything. I don't believe Brent would harm children, boys or girls, he was so gentle, such a lovely gentle boy with never an ounce of wickedness in him.'

'But something must have happened because there were complaints and he was transferred from the poolside into the kitchen.'

'Well, all I can think is that people told lies about him.'

'Does the name Jake mean anything to you? Jake, a man with five friends, all men? Men who wear white T-shirts, with Jake in a white sweater?'

'No, Mr Pluke, I've ever heard him mention Jake or the others.'

'So apart from that incident in his life, there was never any reason for you to think he might be subjected to harsh treatment by others? Attacks? Verbal abuse?'

'Good heavens, no, Mr Pluke. Everyone loved him.'

'Did he bring friends home?'

'No, never. I was at work, you see, when he was little so there was no one there to look after other children and he didn't do so when he got older. No, he's never brought friends home.'

'Girlfriends?' asked Wayne Wain. 'Did he ever have girlfriends?'

'Not real girlfriends. There was his friend at the pool, Ali, who used to talk to him, so he told me, but I never met her.'

'Who was Ali?'

'I don't know, he never brought her home and always called her Ali. They would talk at break time, he said he liked her. He could talk to her. She was often at the pool but didn't work there.'

'Was he a homosexual?' asked Wayne.

'No, I'm sure he wasn't, he had no men friends. He was just a gentle, nice young man who kept himself to himself.'

'Mrs Fowler, we have to establish a motive for his death, a reason for someone to kill him. From what you tell me, you are not aware of a reason?'

'Well, no, Mr Wain, there isn't. That's what I'm trying to tell you, there is no reason why anyone would want to hurt my Brent which is why all this is so puzzling and horrible.'

The tears came now. The two men left her to weep silently for a while, then Wayne moved to her side and put an arm around her shoulders, probably totally contravening whatever politically-correct rules governed such actions, but it helped her to regain her composure. After a while, she apologized for her lapse and they continued.

Pluke took up the questioning. 'Did he receive threatening telephone calls or letters? People coming to the door? Scrawling graffiti, sending hate mail, that kind of thing?'

'No, never,' she said. 'Or if they did, I never knew about it.'

'Do you think he would have told you if that kind of thing had happened to him?'

'I don't think so, Mr Pluke, he was very secretive about things. He seldom told me anything about his life, other than what I noticed at home.'

181

'This makes it difficult for us to learn things which might lead to his killer. We haven't searched his bedroom either, that often gives a clue to a victim's lifestyle. What can you tell us about his room, Mrs Fowler? Or the room he used for his computer?'

'Well, it was just an ordinary room, Mr Pluke, a single bed, a double wardrobe, chest of drawers, nice rug on a nice carpet . . . quiet.'

'I mean, Mrs Fowler, did you ever come across anything which suggested he was keeping things secret from you? Was he involved in a deeply secret way of life which he wanted to hide from you?'

'Well, like I said, he was secretive, Mr Pluke, very secretive indeed, and I think he had things he never wanted me to see, but I never searched his room and never found anything except a letter I did not understand, something to do with sex but if you ask me what it meant, I can't remember the words and I did not know what it was supposed to mean anyway but at the time I thought it was nothing out of the ordinary for a lad of his age. I mean, Mr Pluke, young lads do read dirty magazines and look at pictures of women with no clothes on, I bet you did, didn't you?'

Wayne smiled as Pluke withered under her onslaught and blushed at her belief that he might have sneaked a look at such a picture. He'd not even seen Millicent without any clothes on, let alone any strange woman in life or in pictures. Pluke now decided he must shock Mrs Fowler.

'Mrs Fowler, I don't like to tell you this but we have examined Brent's computer, the one we removed from your house. Our experts are still examining it but preliminary searches reveal he was visiting pornographic websites and indulging in child pornography searches. In my view, this fits his profile as a child molester at the swimming pool and supports our belief that he was engaged in that kind of abuse. In other words, Mrs Fowler – and I hate to say this – there is clear evidence, not mere speculation, that your Brent was a paedophile, even if he was never convicted by a court.'

He expected some kind of outburst from her, some protestation of his innocence, but it did not come. She just sat there, unmoved. He ploughed on.

'He was arrested on several occasions and nothing was ever proved against him but there was no doubt about his activities. Sadly, the reliable testimony of children is notoriously difficult to obtain, Mrs Fowler.'

'I don't believe any of it, Mr Pluke, and I am shocked to hear you make such a suggestion. My Brent was a lovely, lovely boy.' Here was the expected defence by a mother of her son.

'What I am saying, Mrs Fowler, is that his paedophilia provides a motive for his murder. Even suspected paedophilia would do that. That is why I must question you like this. What I must investigate is whether you are aware of the names of anyone who might have been sufficiently incensed by Brent's activities, or even rumours, to want to kill him. Are you sure he has never received threats or abuse?'

'Well, no, of course not. If I knew anyone who had threatened him or wanted to kill him, I would have told you. I want his killer caught, Mr Pluke, just as you do.'

'I am very sorry that this means facing some unpleasant truths about your son, Mrs Fowler. Truly I detest having to speak to you in these terms, but it is important. I must be realisitic, I must base my enquiries on what we already know and I must carry out my enquiries based on the available evidence, however distasteful that might be.'

She hung her head with the tears now rolling down her cheeks and then, after a very long silence, said, 'Mr Pluke, you are right, of course. I am defending him as any mother would but I had no idea what he kept on his computer, believe me. I did find things in his room, when I was cleaning or getting his washing ready, but I thought it was nothing more than teenage male lust. Then a neighbour complained about what Brent had done to his daughter, that was years ago, Mr Pluke, when Brent was only fifteen but that man had moved away, he went to live in New Zealand. It's the only time anyone has come to the house to complain about him, but Brent did tell me he had never hurt a girl and never would . . . and I did know he'd been arrested once or twice, the police came to the house rather than go to his place of work, but I thought they were false accusations because he never went to court. He would never hurt a little girl, never. He loved children, in the nicest possible way.'

'Thank you for being so honest,' said Pluke. 'That takes courage.'

'I've been silly, shielding myself from the truth, but if any good has to come out of this, then it has woken me up. But that's no excuse for killing him, is it?'

'No, it's not,' said Pluke. 'Which is why we need to tackle this together. You and my officers. Now, I think you realize the seriousness of the allegations against Brent – I don't have a full list of the complaints, that is with Manchester Police, but I must now search his room. If there is material there, it might contain the name of the killer, or at least some lead-in to him. Or her.'

'I would not prevent that,' she whispered. 'When would you want to do it?'

'I am thinking of tomorrow, Mrs Fowler. If you would give us the key, we would let ourselves in after driving across the Pennines. You can come with us if you wish, I would not wish to abuse your hospitality, but it is important that we make the search.'

'I think it is perhaps time for me to go home, Mr Pluke, to face things. All this has been such a shock, I'm not really sure what I'm doing, so if you want to go to my house tomorrow to search it, could I come with you? You can leave me there, I will not tell anyone about Brent, I assure you . . . there is no one I can tell. No one talks to me these days, I think Brent was responsible for that. If anyone asks, I will simply say he has gone away, looking for work. I can do that, I can be strong.'

'If you don't want to stay here willingly, there's no way I can compel you,' said Pluke. 'Shall we leave it overnight for you to consider? I'll call again tomorrow morning, just after half-past eight, for your decision?'

'Yes, all right.'

'And if you want to return to Manchester, I will have to inform Manchester Police. I also need to speak to people at the leisure centre and make enquiries at other places Brent visited. We must trace his movements in town, the places he visited, the people he knew, contacts he made, that is vital.'

'You are so kind, Mr Pluke. So kind to me.'

'Until tomorrow morning then? Will you be safe here tonight?'

'Yes, of course. No one knows I am here. And I shall lock my doors.'

And so they left.

As they walked away, Pluke said to Wayne, 'I don't think she is in any danger, is she? Either here or in Manchester? It's just a case of keeping secret the fact her son's body has been found and identified.'

'I still think she's holding out, sir, concealing something. I think she knows more than she's admitting about her son.'

'A mother's protective instinct, Wayne.'

'Fair enough, sir, she's having a tough time. Let's see what tomorrow brings,' said Wayne Wain.

Chapter Twelve

When Mr Pluke and the sergeant had gone, Mrs Fowler sat down and had a really good cry. She had cried before, many times, as Brent's behaviour had become increasingly transparent and although she had pleaded with him to refrain from touching little girls, he had not given up. He had tried, she knew that; he'd said it was like other people trying to give up smoking or to come off drugs. He couldn't help himself and always maintained he'd never hurt any of his little friends. Then there was that awful business about the little girl who was found dead in the canal. She'd been sexually assaulted. Quite viciously. Viciously enough to kill her. The last time she was seen alive was when she had been in the swimming pool talking to Brent. He'd been questioned by the police but released and the killer had never been found. Brent told her it wasn't him.

She had asked Brent if he knew who'd done it but he'd only shaken his head and said he had no idea, although he had admitted going for a walk along the canal that same evening. And he had been late home that night. He'd told her he'd had a difficult day at work without explaining what the difficulty had been, and said he'd wanted some fresh air. She thought, at the time, he was being his usual secretive self because he hadn't said much about whatever was troubling him and had gone straight up for a bath. His behaviour was odd that night, and the following days; he wasn't his usual self for some time afterwards. She did worry he might have been responsible but he'd always denied any involvement, sometimes losing his temper when she mentioned it.

Mr Pluke hadn't mentioned the girl's death so perhaps he had no idea Brent had been suspected. Unless some other person was now the real suspect. She wondered if she should have told Mr Pluke but she had always tried to block out those memories, those thoughts. Now it was all coming back, but that couldn't have any bearing on Brent's death, could it? Surely not now, not after all this time? And would that little girl's family know he had been questioned? Her mum, for example. No dad had been mentioned in the papers.

Alone with her thoughts, she wondered if she really ought to go back to Manchester. She'd told Mr Pluke she'd like to, but after thinking about it she wasn't sure. Even now, people hadn't forgotten that little girl, Amy was her name. That's why people had stopped talking to her. Neighbours and friends had known Brent had been taken in for questioning, not just once but several times, and they knew he'd been with the girl at the swimming pool not long before her body was found in the canal. He'd been seen with her. All the neighbours had shunned her and Brent, they'd wanted nothing to do with him after that . . . or her. But he had not been to court and had always denied harming her. Always.

And as she sat alone, her mind ranged over the past years with Brent, her loneliness with him and now without him. She had to decide if she really should return to Manchester. Or stay here a little longer. She liked it here, people were so friendly and nice. But then, they didn't know about Brent, did they? Mr Pluke and Sergeant Wain were so gentle with her too, in spite of their very difficult work. Mrs Pluke was nice too. She'd said she might take Emily to meet some of her friends.

That was far better than always being alone; it was so lonely, so very lonely, living in Manchester. But with Brent gone, would people change their minds? Talk to her again? Be more friendly and understanding? Really, she began to think, it was all his fault; her loneliness was Brent's fault, she realized quite suddenly. And now he was gone, maybe it was time to start a new life? Here in Crickledale? She sat very still for a very long time, then decided to make a cup of tea and have it with a scone and some strawberry jam. Then she might watch television as she tried to make up her mind about the future. Without the shadow of Brent.

Instead of returning immediately to the Incident Room, Pluke and Wayne Wain retreated to Pluke's office.

'I found time to look at that disk, sir, the one we were given by Manchester,' said Wayne. 'Now I know what Mrs Fowler's been covering up. Brent was suspected of killing a little girl, sir. He was questioned but there was not enough evidence to justify a prosecution.'

'Now things are making sense . . . he was worse than we thought.'

'There's more, sir, the dead girl was Jacob Hampson's daughter. The mother lived alone, they weren't married or living together. Hampson never appeared in the publicity following the murder, but thanks to a good informant, SIOUX learned of his paternity during their enquiries. He's unaware of their knowledge, I might add.'

'That does alter things! Well done.'

At that moment, the fulsome Mrs Plumpton came into the office and displayed her considerable charms before the two most important men in her life (apart from Mr Plumpton).

'I heard you return, Mr Pluke, and wondered if you wanted me for anything?'

'Of course, Mrs Plumpton, you know what I like.'

Not knowing what he really liked, she organized a cup of tea for them, along with some jam tarts she had made herself. She knew that Mr Pluke loved a jam tart in times of stress, and she guessed that this murder enquiry, with its lack of progress, was causing him a good deal of anxiety.

'Mrs Plumpton,' said Pluke in that stern manner he could sometimes adopt, 'can you bring your shorthand notebook and take some notes? Detective Sergeant Wain and I have been to interview the mother of the deceased, and we must make a written record of the experience.'

And off she went to do his bidding with her chiffon dress wafting like gossamer in the breeze as she moved. He averted his eyes, and then she was gone. A hint of perfume lingered.

'Mrs Fowler did not say a great deal, Wayne, and I got the impression she was being rather coy about her late son. She has not told us much about herself, or her family life, either past or present. Perhaps with good reason.'

'We need more from Manchester Police,' suggested Wayne. 'They must have more on Brent than is on that disk, clearly he's been in their sights for some time, and there might be something on his mother. We know nothing about her either. I was watching her as you were talking and I'm sure she's hiding something. She did reveal she knew rather more about Brent's behaviour than she had first admitted, but only after some considerable time. How much more does she know, I wonder? And what is she hiding? And more importantly, why? What else has Brent done? Why hide the truth now he's dead? Surely she wants us to find his killer?'

'A woman's thought processes can be very complex, Wayne, and sometimes they defy logic and explanation. She has probably been shielding him for such a long time that's it's second nature to her. It's just what one would expect a loving mother to do while blotting out the worst memories. Perhaps she's now coming to terms with his behaviour. We know he was a murder suspect and I fear she is blocking that fact from her memory. He's not here to dominate her either, that could be a factor and now she's free from his influence, we may talk to her again. I hope she decides to remain in Crickledale, it would do her a power of good, give her a new lease of life, a complete break from the past. I must admit I felt she was rather cool or even cold when making the formal identification though.'

'Now you're speaking like a counsellor, sir!'

'Or someone with common sense, Wayne. Ah, Mrs Plumpton. You've found a notebook.' She was now hovering like a purple-winged dragon with her mighty bosoms only inches from Pluke's face. 'Sit down, please, and we shall begin.'

Munching jam tarts and sipping tea, Pluke dictated an account of his personal impressions of their talk with Mrs Fowler, asking Wayne for his input on occasions. In this way, their joint interpretation was recorded for inclusion in the murder case files. It was then time to return to the Incident Room; Mrs Plumpton would bring her work along when she had finished. There, Pluke told Inspector Horsley that his visit to Mrs Fowler had been distinctly unpromising because she professed to know next to nothing about the activities of her late son.

'So what's next, Montague?' asked Horsley. 'We're getting nowhere. We've no witnesses except those folks at the Cockatrice, no real evidence, no recovered bullet case, all the people we've checked on the guest list and Christmas card list so far are accounted for and can't be considered suspects. Where do we go from here?'

'Manchester,' said Pluke. 'I need to ask questions over there, from people who knew Brent. The staff of the swimming pool, for example, and the leisure centre cafeteria. The local police too. I need to know what additional intelligence those undercover operators have found. I fear I have not been told everything and I am now wondering if Brent's killers knew he was once suspected of murder.'

'Was he, by Jove?'

And Pluke explained about Jacob Hampson's murdered daughter, adding, 'Taking everything into account, I believe it's highly likely his killers knew he'd been suspected of murder.'

'What makes you so sure?'

'The cairn of stones, it's part of an ancient Celtic ritual.

190

But so is burning the body of a murderer. Brent's body was burnt, remember.'

'But we're not sure whether the fire was a coincidence, are we?'

'Exactly. In view of what I have just learned, it could have been quite deliberate – putting the body in what would become the path of the flames. Tomorrow I shall head across the Pennines, once more to enter Lancashire. Foreign territory.'

'We really do need a breakthrough,' said Horsley. 'Something for the teams to get their teeth into. It's all boringly routine just now, with no results, not in the least stimulating. The teams need stimulation if their commitment is to be maintained.'

'Perhaps Brent's computer will spark off something else? A new line of enquiry?' offered Wayne Wain.

'Let's hope so,' said Horsley.

'Our teams have worked very hard for so little return,' admitted Pluke, checking his watch. 'Look, I know it's not yet finishing time but there is so little happening that they should be allowed to end early. A refreshment of spirit is sometimes of great value. So recall them all, Inspector, I shall not conduct a conference this afternoon or this evening, give them the rest of the afternoon off but ask them to report for duty as usual in the morning. I shall address them briefly tomorrow before going to Manchester with Detective Sergeant Wain, and I trust our visit will provide the breakthrough we so desperately need.'

'Well done, Montague! A real man of action!'

'Do we need to notify Manchester Police of our intended visit tomorrow?' asked Wayne Wain.

'I think we should inform DCI Sanders,' said Pluke. 'We must not disrupt or compromise any undercover operation currently being planned by Manchester Police. I will ring him now to acquaint him of my plans.'

It was during that call that Sanders asked Pluke if he was willing to take part in a sting operation to catch the killers, even if it involved elements of danger, and Pluke agreed. After discussing the entire case along with their knowledge of the crime world in Manchester, plus a useful contribution from Pluke including some biographical details of his interests and authorship, Sanders suggested types of subterfuge at the leisure centre to which Pluke added his consent. He felt it was all very exciting.

And so it was that Montague Pluke went home early for his cocoa while Sanders began to circulate scurrilous rumours about the same Montague Pluke.

Sanders was delighted that Pluke was returning to Manchester and that he had agreed to be the bait for the killers. Now he could put his plans into action. Pluke knew some of those plans, but not all. It was best he did not know everything.

Next morning, Tuesday, did not produce a very auspicious start for Montague Pluke. Even though he climbed out of bed on the right side, he dropped the soap in the bathroom and that was a sign of bad luck. To have a sign of bad luck during such an early part of the day was rather worrying. Then, when he approached the breakfast table in the kitchen, he found his knives crossed. The knife set out for his bacon and eggs had somehow spun on the table overnight to cross its blade with that of his toast and marmalade knife. That was a very clear sign that he must take great care during the day and so he uncrossed them immediately. The rest of his preparation for work was not sullied by ill omens and he had his rabbit's foot in his pocket which was always a good sign, and so, as promised, he called upon Mrs Fowler at half-past eight to receive her decision and she met him smiling and almost radiant.

'I have decided not to return to Manchester with you, Mr Pluke, not today and perhaps never. I have decided I need to break away from my former life, to start something new, and this might be the very place. I shall not

192

burden you with my problems, though; today and in the days that follow, I shall look for a nice little cottage to rent and will then make arrangements for my things to be brought over from Manchester. When the coroner releases his body, I will have Brent cremated here, I am sure that can be arranged and so my life will be completely new. In view of all that has happened, I want to make a complete new start. Does that make sense to you?'

'It makes great sense, Mrs Fowler. Very great sense indeed.'

'Then you can search Brent's rooms without me being there. I have finished with that house as from today, Mr Pluke. I will get rid of all Brent's things too, he dominated my life far too much in the past and I shall not allow it to happen in the future. So here's the key. And look, I admit Brent was not very nice towards those little girls, I am sorry for being rather obstructive but I've had a good think about it and now he's dead, he can't do any more harm. That must be a good thing, Mr Pluke, good for children, I mean. Did you know he was once suspected of murder?'

'That fact has been brought to my attention, Mrs Fowler.'

'Oh dear, I must look silly and deceitful. I should have told you, I was foolish, protecting him as I did. So am I being callous towards my own child now he can't answer back? I think not, he had his chances, I've defended him for years and years and now I have no need to do so. With his death, Mr Pluke, my new life begins . . . Am I making sense?'

'I think you are, Mrs Fowler,' and he accepted the key from her. 'I will bring this back when we have finished. Later today perhaps, or certainly tomorrow.'

'I won't be far away,' she smiled. 'I am going to an estate agent's this morning to start looking for my new home.'

'I am going to Manchester today, Mrs Fowler. With Detective Sergeant Wain and perhaps one of our scenes of crime officers. I'll visit your house and I want to talk to people at the swimming pool and cafeteria, all those who knew Brent at the leisure centre in fact, and then, depending on what we find in Brent's things, I may call at other places like his camera club or computer club or wherever we find it necessary. We shall have to be very careful, however, while asking our questions, not to reveal that his body has been found or that he was murdered; we shall continue to treat this as if he was a missing person, with the police showing concern for him.'

'Yes, I understand, Mr Pluke.'

And so Pluke left a transformed Mrs Fowler, wondering if her sudden change of heart was genuine or whether she would have second thoughts, but it was surely a very good sign for her future happiness. He walked through the town towards his office, raising his panama to those he met and wishing them all good morning as was his daily custom, but he was concentrating so hard upon greeting that delicious Miss Fanshaw that he walked under a ladder. He did not notice until he had passed completely beneath it but the moment he realized his error, he crossed his fingers and spat on the ground. But then he noticed a single magpie on the roof of the church and did his best to frustrate its prognostication of impending bad luck by raising his hat to the bird and saying 'Good morning, sir' in the politest of tones.

He hoped that that would ensure he had a good day ahead, so important if he was to cross the majesty of the Pennines into Lancashire, but in his heart of hearts, he knew this day was not going to be a good one. He had experienced far too many signs of impending bad fortune in such a short time, even if he had tried to contradict them. Doing his best to ensure an improvement in his fortunes, he entered the police station with his right foot first as he always did, popped his head into the Control Room to ask Sergeant Cockfield pronounced Cofield whether there had been any serious crimes, incidents, strikes, aircraft crashes, new murders, Acts of God or other things of interest overnight, and upon receiving a negative response made for his office. The well-upholstered Mrs

Plumpton was already installed with yet another dress of gossamer-like fabric which floated around her like a haze of spiders' webs while somehow revealing a good deal of her ample bosom.

As always, she had made sure the kettle was boiling. Even before he had hung his hat on the hat peg and his coat on the coat peg, she was heading towards his desk with a mug of tea in her hand as he moved his paper-clip tray, his paperweight and his pen rack to their rightful and very precise places.

'Good morning, Detective Inspector Pluke,' she oozed, stooping low to set the mug in exactly the right place while managing to position her ample cleavage directly before his eyes. 'A very nice morning.'

'I am not so sure about that, Mrs Plumpton,' he said. 'I saw a single magpie on the church roof during my walk to work, inadvertently I walked under a ladder, my breakfast knives were crossed and I dropped the soap, but I think my responses were fast enough to cope with any ill fortune that might follow. I have my rabbit's foot and so I hope the day augurs well. I have to travel into Lancashire to make further enquiries into the death of Brent Fowler, and so I will need all the luck I can get.'

'But you will be holding your usual morning conference of detectives before you leave?'

'Indeed I shall, that will be at nine o'clock, and then I shall dictate any letters that are necessary, check with the Incident Room to ensure nothing requires my urgent attention and then head for Manchester with Detective Sergeant Wain and a specially selected scenes of crime officer.'

He told her what he planned to do in Manchester, adding that DCI Sanders there was aware of his proposed itinerary, and then went to the Incident Room where his teams of detectives were gathered. He reminded them that their only suspects were the man called Jake and five others from Manchester in a silver people carrier and that any further sightings in or near Hurnehow would be important. Pluke said he would return that evening and would provide a full account of his work at the next morning's conference. He expressed a hope that the day would result in the necessary breakthrough and gave Inspector Horsley permission to stand down any officers who may have completed their enquiries rather earlier than expected.

He then asked Detective Sergeant Tabler to select a scenes of crime officer to accompany him to Manchester to make a search of Brent Fowler's room. Tabler chose an efficient young detective constable called Ed Livesey. Before leaving, Pluke issued a statement for the press saying that enquiries were still ongoing in an effort to identify the victim but that there had been no significant developments in the investigation; house-to-house en- quiries were continuing and a search was still under way to find the murder weapon. All good, regular and routine information of the sort needed for public consumption.

And then it was time to once again leave Crickledale for the urban throb of Manchester.

When Millicent Pluke went upstairs to make the bed and tidy the bathroom, she discovered Montague had left his wallet behind. He'd also forgotten to take his mobile phone. He carried the wallet in the hip pocket of his trousers but somehow it had slipped out and was lying on the floor near the foot of the bed. It had been hidden by the covers after he had turned them back to get out of bed which explained why he had not noticed it. She didn't think he would need it today because he was on duty and busy with his murder enquiry, and he always had enough loose cash in his pockets for his daily needs. She knew she must let him know she had found it; if he missed it, he might think it had been stolen or lost and she wanted him to know it was safe at home. She rang Crickledale Police Station and asked for him, but was put through to Mrs Plumpton.

'Montague has left for work without his wallet and

mobile phone,' she told Montague's secretary. 'Can you tell him they're at home, in case he wonders where they are. He might not miss his wallet, he always carries loose cash and I don't think he'll need his credit card today or his phone if he's in the Incident Room.'

'He's not, he's gone to Manchester,' said Mrs Plumpton. 'With Detective Sergeant Wain and Detective Constable Livesey, so he won't be alone. I know he will cope or be taken care of. But if he rings in, I'll tell him.'

'Thank you. It's funny really – before he left for work he said today had not started very auspiciously. I hope nothing more serious happens!'

'Whatever does happen, Mr Pluke will cope,' said Mrs Plumpton with a certain pride and lots of confidence.

It was almost noon when they arrived in Manchester: Wayne had had no difficulty finding his way across the Pennines and into the city centre. Pluke suggested that Wayne drop him at the Dean Road Leisure Centre where he could conduct his enquiries at the swimming pool and cafeteria, while Wayne and DC Livesey searched Mrs Fowler's terrace house. Wayne knew where to find it, and so that was agreed. They agreed to rendezvous in the reception area of 'A' Division Headquarters of Greater Manchester Police. Whoever was first to arrive would make contact with either Sergeant Russell or Detective Chief Inspector Sanders, the latter being aware of their presence in the city.

From either of those officers, Pluke or Wayne would request a copy of the official CID file on Brent Fowler and if time permitted they would visit any places whose names appeared during the search of Brent's rooms. Pluke reminded his team that, when speaking to non-police personnel during their enquiries, they must continue to treat Brent as a missing person; they must not reveal that he was dead or that he had been found and identified. Pluke also said that, when making his enquiries at the swimming pool and

197

cafeteria, he would pretend to be an uncle of Brent who had been asked to look into the absence of his nephew. He would adopt his guise as an expert in folklore and superstitions while ignoring his trough expertise. If anyone researched his background, they might discover his books, and that might reveal his true role as a detective. He did not want that to happen.

And so it was that, in line with his earlier telephone conversation with DCI Sanders, Mr Montague Pluke arrived outside the Dean Road Leisure Centre. In his voluminous old coat, panama hat with its blue band, big black-rimmed spectacles, long straggly hair, crumpled trousers, spats and brown brogue shoes, he looked as if he had escaped from an institution of some kind. He made his way through the car park to the large entrance with its glass sliding doors; they opened automatically to admit him and he found himself in a massive and well-lit foyer with a reception desk on the left, a barrier just beyond it with a turnstile bearing a sign saying *Members Entrance*, lots of seats around the extremities and doors which were always closed but which must lead to somewhere important.

Some were marked *Staff Only*, although there were toilets for ladies, gents and people in wheelchairs. There was another small gate, closed but bearing a sign saying *Authorized Visitors*. As he stood in the centre of this massive space, he watched people arriving – they pressed what looked like a credit card into a machine close to the members' turnstile whereupon it revolved to admit them. Others, he noted, used the *Authorized Visitors* entrance and it seemed that that gate was opened by the receptionist pressing a button beneath her counter. It was a busy place, even though it was a mid-week day near lunchtime, and people in sports clothes, some accompanying parties of schoolchildren, were hurrying in and out with never a glance in his direction.

Beyond the turnstile and visitors' gate was a wide corridor which seemed to extend into infinity and which, according to the signs, led to all parts of the complex, including the swimming pool, gymnasium, indoor tennis courts, badminton and squash courts, weight-training room, cafeteria and all other areas, both on the first floor and at ground level. Behind the complex were outdoor pitches for games like cricket, football, hockey and tennis, and a children's playground with climbing apparatus and a sand pit. As he walked around the foyer, Pluke could see, through open doors, that there was a library full of sports literature, a television room, a games room with snooker and billiards, another with games machines and a quiet room with settees and machines dispensing cool drinks and water. There were lots of other rooms too. They were used for small meetings, club gatherings and minor conferences. There were people in them all; the complex was buzzing with activity.

Its patrons were young and old, children and pensioners, male and female. It was quite a wonderful place, Pluke thought and, having gained a brief appreciation of the layout, he decided it was time to make his move. Remembering that he must not give any hint of his true identity as a police officer, he approached the young female receptionist in her smart green uniform and she smiled a welcome. 'Can I help you?'

'I would like to talk to either the person in charge of your catering or the human resources manager.' He used the modern term for 'personnel manager'.

'Do you have an appointment?'

'No. I have unexpectedly found myself in Manchester and wanted to make the most of the opportunity.'

'So what is it in connection with?'

'It concerns my nephew.' Pluke uttered his first piece of necessary deception. 'He used to work here. He has disappeared and I am trying to trace him. I thought his employer might be able to help me. It is very distressing for his family, not knowing where he is – his mother is distraught.'

'Ah, which department did he work in?'

'The cafeteria,' said Pluke.

'Then you need to talk to Eileen Bilton, she's our catering manager. I am sure she will do her best to help you. And your name, sir?'

'Pluke,' he said. 'Mr Pluke.'

'Just a moment, Mr Pluke,' and she lifted an intercom telephone. 'Eileen, I have a Mr Pluke in reception, he'd like to discuss a personal matter with you.'

Pluke did not hear Eileen's response but the receptionist replaced her handset and said, 'Eileen said to send you through, Mr Pluke. If you make for the swimming pool entrance, you'll see some benches outside. If you sit there, Eileen will come to collect you but she has someone else with her just now, so she might be ten or fifteen minutes.'

'That will be fine,' he agreed. 'I can wait.'

'Well, if you would just enter your name, address and phone number in the guest book, Mr Pluke, and the purpose of your visit, I will let you in.'

She pushed a large volume across to him in which he entered M. Pluke but, bearing in mind his secret mission and the desire of Sanders for Pluke to attract one of those prizewinning letters, he did not enter his home address. Instead, he put his publisher's, knowing they would forward any letters which might arrive, and so his entry read, *M. Pluke, 3 Church Lane, Upper Thongford, Huddersfield, West Yorkshire, HD1 4ET*, although, again on the advice of Sanders, he added his own private telephone number. It comprised a series of numbers with no mention of Crickledale. He gave the reason for his visit as *Family matter*. The girl smiled her acceptance and pressed a button whereupon the visitors' gate opened and he walked through. It closed after him. He followed the signs towards the swimming pool, the shouts of children being confirmation that he was upon the right route.

Directly outside the pool, along the wall of the corridor but overlooking the pool through large windows, were several benches, some bearing towels and bathing hats, and so he settled down to wait for Eileen Bilton. He would entertain himself by watching the antics of the children, some of whom were receiving tuition while others leapt off diving boards, jumped in from the side or simply splashed and had fun in the shallow end. As he waited and watched, small boys and girls in swimming costumes were running up and down the corridors, adults were in attendance along the sides of the pool and the entire scenario seemed to be controlled – clearly, this was time for the schools to bring youngsters for tuition.

Eileen never came. Pluke waited. He checked his watch. Quarter of an hour had passed. The receptionist said it might be ten or fifteen minutes before she attended Pluke and he knew these things often took longer. And so he settled down to wait a little longer, the antics of the children keeping him well entertained. Another fifteen minutes passed without her arrival. He did not like to leave this bench to go looking for her office in case she turned up when he'd gone, and so he had no option but to wait. That half-hour grew into three-quarters. And then a man came to sit at his side. He was heavily built with fair hair; in his mid-thirties, he wore a smart dark suit.

'Would you mind if we had a word, please, sir,' said the newcomer. 'In that office over there.'

'I'm waiting for the catering manager, Eileen Bilton,' said Pluke. 'I don't want to leave here in case she comes and finds I have gone. It's very important, she knows I am here, I don't want to miss her.'

'She's gone for lunch,' said the other. 'She won't be back for another hour.'

'But the receptionist told her I wanted to see her, I was told to wait here.'

'And just what is your purpose?' asked the other.

'It is private,' said Pluke, remembering he was not supposed to be a police officer.

'Then I suggest you come quietly with me, sir, for a little chat. Come along, Miss Bilton won't see you for at least an

hour and I would like a quiet word or two with you. In
private.'

'And who are you?'

'Detective Sergeant Howell, Child Protection Squad,'
and he showed his warrant card to Montague Pluke, then
seized Pluke's arm in a powerful grip to raise him from the
benches and steer him away from the swimming pool.

Chapter Thirteen

Mrs Fowler could not afford to rent a very grand house and it was absolutely impossible even to think about buying one, but she felt able to cope with something small like her present house in Manchester. Something with one or perhaps two bedrooms. Nothing bigger. A garden wasn't important but perhaps a back yard would be nice, somewhere to sit outside when it was sunny or to put plant pots. She would even consider a flat if it was nice and airy with good views, but it would have to be quiet. She did not want to listen to the neighbours having rows or playing loud music. There must be something suitable, even in a small town like Crickledale, and she would enjoy looking. There was no rush to find somewhere to live, the police said she could use their house for as long as she felt necessary.

Feeling bouyed by her new sense of freedom, she put on her smart coat, not the black one she'd used to identify Brent, but a nice blue one which fitted her well, and she had a hat to match. Smiling at the joy of the fresh and rather chilly morning, she walked out of the house and into the cobbled market place of Crickledale. There were a few people about but no one took any notice of her. With the town hall at one end, the market place was surrounded by lots of shops, banks, building societies and estate agents; there was a stationer's too, a butcher, a fruit and vegetable shop, a chemist, several pubs, one or two cafés, an electrical supplier, a delicatessen, the Co-op of course, and even a ladies' clothes shop.

This little town would easily cope with her modest needs, and so today she would get a local paper to see if it contained notices of any houses or flats to rent and she would buy herself a cup of coffee and a bun while she read it. Then she would call at one or two estate agents and that would fill her morning very nicely. It was a good start to her day, a nice beginning to her new life. She hoped Mr Pluke and Sergeant Wain would have an equally good day in Manchester.

In the stationer's, she bought a copy of a local paper and took it across to Sally's Coffee Shop, bought herself a mug of milky coffee and settled down to study the adverts. When she opened the paper, the story of Brent dominated the front page. It told how the unidentified body of a young man had been found on burnt moorland last Saturday by the famous local policeman, Detective Inspector Montague Pluke. The account confirmed that the police were treating the case as murder because the man had died from gunshot wounds, but at this stage, according to the report, the man had not been identified and no one had been arrested. It told how teams of detectives were searching the scene and conducting house-to-house enquiries, with Mr Pluke expressing his confidence that the killer would soon be traced.

As she studied the words, she realized she knew a great deal more than the newspaper was revealing, just like some of the detective stories she read, but she knew she must not say anything to anyone about Brent. Except Mrs Pluke, of course. Even if the story did produce a small tear or two in her eyes, she bravely turned the page and began to study the adverts for places to let.

Detective Sergeant Wain and DC Livesey eased their unmarked police car to a halt outside Mrs Fowler's terrace house in Manchester, checked the street for signs of vandals lurking, vandals who might kick their car doors or rip off the aerials and external mirrors, and, with the street apparently deserted, let themselves in. They closed the door and switched on the hall light, then stood very still for a few minutes to observe the scene before them. This was not a search of the kind they would make of a suspect's house but even so it must be treated with the same degree of professionalism. They did not really know what they were looking for but they would recognize it when they found it; all they knew was that it would be something associated with Brent's life, something which might provide a clue to his killer or an indication of some secret lifestyle. Names, places and contacts were needed.

'It's like my granny's place,' said Livesey. 'These terraces of small town houses are all the same, brick-built, good and warm, solid, plain and practical. Lounge to the left, dining room next to it also on the left, kitchen at the far end of the entrance hall and stairs leading up from here. Two bedrooms, perhaps a box room and a bathroom and toilet combined. All with cupboards, lots of cupboards. Back yard with an outside loo and maybe a coal house and wash house. And a loft. We mustn't forget the loft, Sarge.'

'You're the expert at this sort of thing, Ed,' said Wayne. 'Lead on.'

'His bedroom will be the real treasure trove, bedrooms always are,' said Livesey. 'But we'll be methodical, starting down here with the lounge.'

A search of the downstairs rooms and kitchen revealed nothing of interest to their enquiry although it did show the house contained very little of anything. Although everything was clean and tidy, the furniture was cheap and there was very little of it, just the essentials like a small three-piece suite along with an old TV set in the lounge. All the walls were rather bare and covered with wallpaper that looked as if it had been there since the 1970s. There were very few pictures, photographs or mirrors on the walls or mantelpieces; there were no books, no newspaper racks or signs of an external interest or hobby for Mrs Fowler. The dining room had a table which folded against the wall and four chairs with a sideboard bearing an empty vase while the kitchen, also with a small table against the bare wall, was functional, clean and bare with a small gas cooker but no dishwasher or washing machine. Wain felt there was a distinct lack of warmth and colour; the whole place seemed functional rather than comfortable. It was clearly the home of a family with little money and apparently no homely interests, rather like a holiday cottage; indeed, some holiday cottages were better equipped and far more stylish.

Mrs Fowler's bedroom, with a single bed, was likewise very plain. The wardrobe, dressing table and drawers held very little but the detectives felt obliged to search her private belongings, including her underwear drawer, the pockets of two overcoats and the contents of two handbags, just in case something of evidential value had been hidden there, probably by Brent. But there was nothing, not even any letters from friends and family, nor albums of photographs. Nothing. She seemed to possess nothing but the very basic essentials.

'I don't think I've ever come across a house with so little stuff in it,' observed Livesey. 'You'd almost think it wasn't a family home, it's more like a holiday cottage with the barest of essentials.'

'She's never talked about her family, except Brent,' said Wayne.

'Maybe her entire life was centred around him,' said Ed. 'But most people have someone else who contacts them or is a family member or friend, but there's nothing here. Nothing about her own family, or from them, no album of photos, no wedding pictures, no letters waiting for an answer, not even a postcard from somebody on holiday, or a Christmas card list, no book of addresses or phone numbers, nothing.'

'She's the sort of person who could die in her home and no one would miss her. She could lie undiscovered for months. Sad, isn't it? She's not the only person like that but at least she had Brent to care for and now he's gone.

She's alone in the world . . .' Wayne Wain could hardly imagine living in such a vacuum; how could people live so totally alone?

The small box room was where Brent had installed his computer and now that it had been removed by the police, there was little else except the desk which had borne it, an empty waste bin and a pile of computer magazines tidily arranged on the floor in a corner. In another corner were back copies of his countryside magazines like *Country Life*, *The Field*, *Horse and Hound* and so forth. The two detectives searched the drawers of his desk and flicked through the pages of the magazines to check whether anything was hidden between them. They searched every nook and cranny, but found nothing. It was almost as if the room – or the entire house – had been thoroughly cleaned before their arrival.

'He's like his mother, eh? Or was like her, I should say,' said Livesey. 'Doesn't want unnecessary stuff cluttering the place.'

'Unless his mother cleaned up after him,' said Wayne. 'Mothers do that. If she's an obsessive tidier, she'd never want litter around. Even his waste bin's empty.'

Brent's bedroom was equally tidy, clean and neat. His dressing table and chest of drawers contained nothing but his range of clothes, including underwear and socks. There were no papers or other items such as CDs or DVDs, none of the usual things that young men collect or hang on to such as souvenirs of holidays, photographs of girlfriends, memorabilia and trivia of all kinds. His shirts and T-shirts were all clean and ironed, and arranged in neat piles on the wardrobe shelves or in drawers. In his small cheap wardrobe were his other clothes, some clearly for use at work and others for leisure, jeans, light trousers, a few sweaters, a fleece or two. From his drawers, dressing table and wardrobe, they took out everything and opened the lot, searching the pockets and even checking for things hidden up sleeves or inside linings, but there was nothing.

The bathroom and separate toilet revealed nothing of

interest, except that there were no toothbrushes to be seen, and the loft was a similar desert. Apart from an old enamel wash basin which might have been used years ago to catch water from a leaking roof, it was empty. The two detectives went into the tiny back yard where there was an external toilet and a coal house, but found nothing of interest.

'So what so you make of this, Sarge?' asked Ed Livesey.

'I don't think I've ever seen such a clean and empty house,' said Wayne. 'You'd hardly believe people lived here.'

'She must have tidied Brent's things while he was away. She hasn't deliberately gone through it, has she? To dispose of anything she didn't want us to find?'

'Why would she do that?' asked Wayne. 'Surely she'd want us to find Brent's killer?'

'But she might not want us to find out just what sort of unpleasant character her son really was. She must have known what he was like.'

'You could be right, Ed, but there's another way of considering this,' Wayne suggested. 'If Mrs Fowler was obsessive about keeping her house like this, with next to nothing in it, Brent would never be able to hang on to the things he cherished, would he? She'd throw them out while cleaning his room, while he was out of the house. That might explain his interest in big country houses.'

'I don't follow.'

'Well, Ted, big country houses are full of stuff. The walls are dripping with pictures, paintings, mirrors, family portraits and much more while the furniture is rich and varied, and lots of it, and there are heirlooms galore, lots of rugs and carpets, thick curtains, walls lined with books . . . I'm no psychiatrist but it wouldn't surprise me if Brent had longed for a house of his own where he could keep his things around him like those aristrocrats did, and still do. If his mother got rid of all his stuff, he'd think a country house full of old and interesting things was a piece of heaven.'

'My, Sarge, we are being theoretical! But you could be

right. So if he has nowhere to keep his private things, what would he do?'

'He'd buy a computer and store things there,' said Wayne. 'I'll bet his computer was his life . . . he could keep his letters there, his diary, use it for his hobbies, search for information, go into country house websites. His computer would be his world when away from work.'

'And he could delve into child porn!'

'Which is where we started, and which might have started Brent on this slippery slope. So, Ed, I think we've done here. I think it's the first house I've searched where we've produce a nil result!'

'So what next?'

'The libraries, I think. Brent was a regular user of libraries. Let's see if we can find out which ones he visited, and if they knew anything about him. We'll start with the Central and go on from there.'

'Right, Sarge. I wonder how DI Pluke's getting on at the leisure centre?'

The man calling himself Detective Sergeant Howell steered Montague Pluke towards a small office not far from the swimming pool entrance. The door was marked *Staff Only* but the man opened it and almost thrust Montague inside. The sudden push and subsequent tumble almost knocked Pluke's hat off.

'Over there,' said the man, pointing to a chair at the far side of a stout wooden table.

'Now look here –'

'Sit down,' spat the detective. 'Now.'

Pluke sat. He must remember he was pretending not to be a detective but perhaps, in these somewhat unusual circumstances, it would be wise to reveal his true identity?

'Your name is M. Pluke and you live near Huddersfield, if your particulars in the guest book are correct,' the man began.

'Yes, that is true.'

'So what are you doing here?'

'I have come to see Eileen Bilton on a private matter,' said Pluke.

'But you have been here a long time, Mr Pluke, watching those children . . . Ms Bilton has gone for lunch and I am sure that if I ask her if she knows you, she will say she does not. She was in her office earlier, I spoke to her, and she has not come to talk to you. All of which makes me wonder what you are really doing here.'

'I might ask you the same question,' ventured Pluke.

'I was called here, Mr Pluke, by a member of staff who reported a suspicious character hanging around the swimming pool watching the children. Waiting for what? You have been here almost an hour, Mr Pluke, always on the same seat, always watching. I am from the Child Protection Squad which makes me very interested in your real purpose for being here.'

Pluke decided it was time to tell the truth.

'Detective Sergeant Howell, I am not a paedophile –'

'You have no convictions,' interrupted Howell. 'I put your name through our computer. But you are recorded as being of interest to the police so far as this kind of activity is concerned. Our computer lists you as a long-term suspect from Yorkshire. It means I am very interested in the reason for your presence here.'

Pluke began to perspire. He knew Sanders had prepared the background to this but nonetheless, the seriousness of his situation began to dawn upon him. He thought his purpose was to draw the murder suspect from cover, not get himself arrested. Clearly something had gone wrong. In spite of his innocence, he began to see his cover story would not be sound enough to convince this man of his true purpose. His task was to remain in the leisure centre to expose Jake's real purpose, but something had gone awry and it was now time to reveal his true identity.

'All right, Sergeant. I am sorry you have pushed me into revealing the truth of my visit, but I am Detective Inspector Montague Pluke, the head of Crickledale Sub-

Divisional Criminal Investigation Department in North Yorkshire, and I am here upon a very delicate murder enquiry.'

Howell stared at the apparition before him. A smallish man with a panama hat bearing a blue ribbon, a huge ancient coat almost down to his knees and coloured like something from a child's drawing book, crumpled trousers of the same colour, spats and brogue shoes. And long black hair poking from beneath that hat like that of a scarecrow. He looked like an off-duty clown.

'A detective, you say?'

'I am indeed.'

'From North Yorkshire? Crickledale, you said.'

'Yes.'

'I've never heard of it. Is it anywhere near Huddersfield?'

'Huddersfield? Good heavens no, that's in West Yorkshire, Crickledale is in North Yorkshire, miles away.'

'So you have entered a false address in the visitors' book?'

'It is my publisher's address, it was done for a particular purpose.'

'Publisher? I thought you said you were a police officer, a senior detective?'

'Yes, I am Detective Inspector Pluke, I write books in my spare time. About horse troughs.'

'Really?'

'Yes.'

'Then let me see your warrant card.'

Pluke stood up and lifted the voluminous tails of his coat to thrust his hand deep inside the deep rear pocket of his trousers. That's where he kept his wallet and in it was his warrant card. But it was gone. Surely not? He didn't believe this . . . He dug and delved and ferreted around in his pocket, but it was empty apart from his comb. He dug into his side pockets, fishing around his handkerchief and loose change, finding his rabbit's foot and a pair of dual hazel nuts which he'd had for years . . . good luck omens.

'It's here somewhere,' he muttered as the detective stood and watched his performance.

The man before Howell lifted up his skirts, dug into every pocket in his jacket and trousers, and then did the same with that ancient overcoat. But the wallet wasn't there. With a sense of doom, Montague Pluke realized it really was missing.

'It must have fallen out, it must be in the car,' he said inanely.

'How very convenient, Mr Pluke, if that is your real name. So what is your real name?'

'Pluke. Montague Pluke.'

'A rather peculiar name, if it's real,' said Howell, now with more than a hint of menace in his voice. 'Can you prove that is your real name?'

'Not without my wallet, no. It contains my driving licence, you see, and a credit card, and my warrant card.'

'I think you and I need to have a longer chat in a more appropriate place, Mr Pluke, such as my police station. We have a nice friendly interview room there with all the necessary tape recorders and cameras, with access to all kinds of computer records and police files, and if I am not satisfied, there are some well-appointed cells with all mod cons, where you can sit and contemplate for a while. I am sure that between us we can find out who you really are, what you are doing in Manchester, and in this leisure centre in particular.'

'You could speak to Detective Chief Inspector Sanders from SIOUX, he knows me and we are working together,' and Pluke spelled out SIOUX.

'SIOUX? It sounds like an American Indian reservation to me, I don't know anyone called Sanders in our CID, Mr Pluke, and I have never heard of SIOUX.'

'It is a very secret unit, Detective Sergeant.'

'It must be if I've never heard of it. Come along, Mr

Pluke, it's time for some real questions in a real police station with real police officers. On your feet!'

'But –'

'No buts!'

With Pluke on his feet, Howell patted him down the length of his body to check for concealed weapons, then with Howell holding on to Pluke's right arm with a tight grip, they walked out of the leisure centre as people stared at them. Montague was steered towards a small red Ford in the car park. A man was sitting at the wheel. As Howell and Pluke approached, the man climbed out, opened a rear door and Pluke felt a hand on his head as he was made to duck before climbing into the rear seat. Howell followed and the door was slammed.

'We're locked in,' said Howell. 'If you really are one of us, you'll know the routine.'

'Am I under arrest?'

'Let's say you are helping with our enquiries, Mr Pluke. Now if you are sensible, you'll keep quiet until we get to the police station. Then we can get down to the serious business of establishing just who you really are and what you are doing here.'

'Look, if you ring Crickledale Police Station they'll be able to vouch for me, ask for Mrs Plumpton or Sergeant Cockfield pronounced Cofield –'

'Later, Mr Pluke, later.'

As they were driven though the busy streets, Howell radioed his own Control.

'Delta Seven, Howell speaking,' he said. 'Returning to base with the suspect. He was still at the pool, outside the pool during the schools session. He claims he is a police officer but has given what appears to be a false address and has no warrant card. I've checked records, he has no convictions but is shown as being of interest to the police due to suspected paedophilia in Yorkshire. He's given the name of Montague Pluke of Huddersfield which is the name of a suspected paedophile, but he claims he is a detective inspector from Crickledale in North Yorkshire.

213

Can you run a further check? CRO, PNC, the lot. ETA – fifteen minutes. Over.'

'Received Delta Seven, over and out.'

And so it was that Montague Pluke was driven through Manchester to a police station near the UMIST complex. He had no idea which station it was because the car was driven into a yard at the rear where they disembarked. Pluke was hustled through a swing door and up two flights of stone stairs before being thrust into a small office and told to sit down. He did so, deciding not to protest at this stage. Clearly, there was no point.

The car driver had not joined them but Howell asked Pluke to be seated and then picked up the phone. 'Howell, ma'am, back in my office. I have the suspect with me, he claims to be a detective from another force engaged on murder enquiries in the city but he has no means of identification. There are discrepancies in his story and in view of his claim to be a police officer, I think you should talk to him.'

He then put down the phone and said, 'The boss is coming to talk to you.'

Five minutes later, a very smart and attractive young woman walked in. In her mid-thirties, she was tall and slender with dark shoulder-length hair, a narrow face with dark eyes, good teeth and a very nice figure in a well-tailored dark blue trouser suit. Pluke rose to his feet to greet her.

'Good afternoon,' she smiled. 'I am Detective Chief Inspector Cindy Beckford. So who are you?'

'Detective Inspector Montague Pluke of the Sub-Divisional Criminal Investigation Department at Crickle-dale, that's in North Yorkshire.'

'I'll go into that claim in a moment, but do you know why you have been brought here?'

'It seems I am suspected of being a paedophile at the worst and watching children at the least, but I assure you I am not at all that way inclined.'

'If you are who you claim to be, you will understand

214

we have to check out all reports, Mr Pluke. In recent months, there have been several instances of strange men watching the children during schools sessions at the leisure centre and we have to check every report and every complaint.'

'I can undersstand that, I am aware of recent initiatives in child protection but I was not there to watch the children with any kind of sexual motive in mind. My purpose was to speak to Eileen Bilton from the cafeteria and I was told to sit on that seat and wait until she came for me. I had waited a long time before your sergeant spoke to me. I think she must have forgotten I was waiting.'

'So, if you really are a police officer from North Yorkshire, why are you in Manchester? I knew nothing of your visit – isn't it courteous to inform the local police of your presence? With the reason?'

'I had the consent of DCI Sanders from SIOUX,' said Pluke. 'I am engaged upon a murder enquiry which has links with this city and he said I could come here at any time to make enquiries. He checked with his senior officers.'

'And are you alone?' She did not deny knowledge of SIOUX, Pluke noted.

'No, Detective Sergeant Wain and DC Livesey from my force are also here; I ought to add that our enquiries are rather delicate but their task is to search a house where the victim used to live and to make other enquiries while I was visiting Ms Bilton.'

'So where will they be now?'

'I don't know precisely, but we arranged to rendezvous in the reception of your 'A' Division Headquarters in Bootle Street. Sergeant Russell who works there is aware of our role although I have not spoken to him today. However, he may not know we are in Manchester.'

'Everyone knows Sergeant Russell, he's been on the front desk for years, until civilians took over the job. So what exactly is the nature of your enquiries, Mr Pluke?'

Believing he had got himself into some kind of unexpected mess, Pluke decided to tell the truth.

'I am investigating the murder of Brent Fowler,' he said, and then explained in great detail the precise nature of his enquiries, adding that the discovery of Fowler's body had not been publicized in Manchester, nor had the fact that his body had been identified. DCI Beckford listened carefully, nodding from time to time as Pluke presented a coherent account. When he had finished, she said, 'I know the case, Mr Pluke, Brent Fowler was well known to my officers particularly as the leisure centre lies within this division. But I still need to be convinced that you really are the Detective Inspector Pluke in question. Why are you not carrying your warrant card?'

'I thought I was. It is always in my rear pocket, here,' and he delved down again as if to emphasize its absence. 'I have no idea where it can be, I must cancel my credit card too if it's lost . . . Oh dear, this is so embarrassing.'

'Is there anyone who could vouch for you, Mr Pluke? Preferably in Manchester.'

'Well, my own officers will be arriving at 'A' Division in the fairly near future, to await my arrival at reception. Detective Sergeant Wain and DC Livesey. They can identify me. And Detective Chief Inspector Sanders from your SIOUX unit.'

'You've met Sanders?'

'Yes, we have discussed this case at length.'

'What's his first name?'

'Paul.'

'I think you're genuine, Mr Pluke. Wait a moment.' She dialled a number, then said, 'Hi, Paul, it's Cindy Beckford. I have a gentleman here who claims he's a detective inspector from North Yorkshire, name of Montague Pluke. He claims he's investigating the Brent Fowler murder, he's mislaid his warrant card and we caught up with him in the Dean Road Leisure Centre. Our informant thought he was a paedophile, watching children in the pool, so he

216

was arrested. I'm trying to ascertain whether he's genuine or not.'

She supplied a detailed account of Pluke's experiences and then listened as Sanders provided a detailed description of the Pluke he had met in Leeds/Bradford airport. Then she said, 'Yes, the description fits. OK, thanks, Paul.'

But before the call ended, Sanders asked, 'I'd like a word with him, Cindy, put him on the line.'

'Hi, there, Montague,' said Sanders. 'You've got yourself into a tricky situation! Great stuff, it was just what we wanted, your assisted departure from the pool was noted even if it was not planned. Now, I'd like to make a suggestion. Can you return to the leisure centre, again not as a police officer but as a visitor like you did before? I want you to repeat exactly what you did first time round.'

'What? And get arrested again?'

'Not really arrested. We'd go through the motions and take you back to where you are now. It would have all the appearances of another highly visible arrest of a paedophile suspect . . .'

'Well, I was hoping to delve into the background of Brent Fowler, I need to find out more about him, his background, his haunts, his links with possible suspects. That is why I am really here.'

'We've got all that on file, Montague, we haven't exactly been asleep since he was murdered. But if you do that small job for us, it would be an enormous help and I will supply you with a copy of our confidential file on Brent. It will contain all you want to know, more comprehensive than that disk. Howell will return you to the car park; you must walk in, see the receptionist and ask to speak to Eileen Bilton again. Enter the same particulars in the guest register. You'll be asked to sit on the same bench as before; there is another class of children there now. Eileen will see you this time, explain your request, and then leave. Howell will be waiting outside. Can you do that for us? We believe it could lead to the breakthrough we both need.'

'Yes, I am sure I can do that even if it is all rather baffling to me.'

Before Pluke left with Detective Sergeant Howell, he asked, 'Detective Chief Inspector Beckford, could I telephone my own office to see if my warrant card has been found?'

'Better still, Mr Pluke, I will ring. Don't give me the telephone number, let me find it for myself. That will really convince me you are who you say you are.'

And so she located the number of Crickledale Police Station and asked for the office of Detective Inspector Pluke. She was put through to Mrs Plumpton.

When Mrs Plumpton learned that Pluke was in an office in Manchester with what sounded like a very attractive woman, she took a deep breath, expanded her chest a few more inches but bravely confirmed that Mrs Pluke had telephoned to say Montague had left his wallet behind, complete with his warrant card. It had apparently fallen out of his pocket while he was dressing this morning.

'So, Inspector Pluke, all's well that ends well.'

'Thank you. And now I must return to that leisure centre. Can you ring the reception at 'A' Division to let Detective Sergeant Wain know where I am? Tell him that I may be a while but not to come looking for me.'

'A pleasure, after what you've been through, Mr Pluke. And the best of luck with your new challenge.'

Howell escorted him down the flights of concrete stairs and said, 'Sir, I'm sorry about all this, but you know how it is.'

'You were just doing your job, Detective Sergeant, but it seems I almost landed myself in some kind of soup.'

'Well, it's not over yet, but the best of luck,' and this time he added, 'Sir.'

'I do have my rabbit's foot and a double hazel nut, so I should be all right.'

Howell did not reply. He could not think of anything to say, but hoped this odd-looking fellow could fulfil whatever was expected of him.

Chapter Fourteen

With her legs tired and her feet sore from trudging around Crickledale's cobbled market place and along side streets to find out-of-the-way estate agents' premises, Mrs Fowler realized it was almost lunchtime. How the morning had flown! And how enjoyable it had been. As a result of her efforts, she now had a plastic carrier bag full of leaflets advertising accommodation for rent in and around Crickledale. These ranged from huge wings of country houses which did not interest her, to tiny flats above equally tiny shops which she might consider. In addition, she was pleased to note, there were some modest terrace houses of the kind which suited her, so she would study the brochures and leaflets, decide on half a dozen possible places, and then make arrangements to inspect them.

It was while pondering whether to buy herself something to eat in town as a treat or go home to spread the literature across the kitchen table while she ate her lunch, that she spotted Mrs Pluke near the town hall. Mrs Pluke, carrying a wicker basket full of groceries, was heading towards a small café and so Mrs Fowler hurried after her. She caught up with her just before Mrs Pluke entered.

'Why, good morning, Millicent. What a surprise.'

'Oh, hello, Emily. How are things with you?'

Mrs Fowler explained her house-hunting mission and so it was that Millicent asked her to join her for lunch. They could talk about Mrs Fowler's search because Millicent knew the town so very well and could offer sound advice

219

about which were good areas; besides, Millicent was not having lunch with anyone else today.

Mrs Fowler insisted on paying, a small gesture for Mrs Pluke's past kindness.

Millicent declined, saying, 'Oh but I couldn't let you do that,' and so they agreed to pay for their individual meals. Millicent found herself giving advice about the properties on Mrs Fowler's list but it was inevitable the conversation turned to Brent, particularly when Millicent told Mrs Fowler that Montague had forgotten his wallet this morning. Mrs Fowler knew he was in Manchester with Detective Sergeant Wain because they would be searching her house but she knew they wouldn't find anything. She kept a very clean house and always made sure Brent never left anything lying around. The two ladies could chat in confidence because they were tucked into a corner where the buzz of customers' conversation and the non-stop noise of coffee machines prevented their words reaching the ears of others.

'Brent was like me,' said Mrs Fowler. 'He wasn't one for hanging on to things, I know some people keep all kinds of scrap bits and pieces in case they come in useful one day but we're not like that. I clear stuff away, I can't bear to have things littering the house and Brent was the same.'

'I wish my Montague was like that, you should see the stuff he's collected about horse troughs – books, articles, photographs, even models – and the books he's acquired about superstitions, myths and legends from all over the world! There's books everywhere . . .'

'Oh, my Brent liked photography, he joined the photography club down at the leisure centre, you know, that got him out of the house and gave him a new interest, somewhere he could meet people. He made a nice friend there, but I can't remember his name.'

'Did you mention this to Montague?' asked Millicent. 'When the police are tracing the life of a victim like Brent, they must always delve into their background, their hobbies, places they visit, friends they make, that sort of thing. It helps a lot when people can suggest someone to interview.'

'I'm not sure I told him that,' smiled Mrs Fowler. 'But Mr Pluke and his Sergeant were very thorough when they interviewed me, they almost made me cry, the things they asked and wanted me to remember. I was so upset at having to remember everything about Brent but I'm not sure I told them it all – you can't, can you? You can't remember everything that happened over the last twenty years or more. I know they had to do their jobs. I was quite drained afterwards, and think I told them everything I knew but I do hope they find out who killed him. I really do, Mrs Pluke.'

'Well, I am sure Montague and his officers will do their best. Now, I can recommend the omelettes, they have a variety of fillings and are always very nice.'

And so Mrs Fowler and Millicent furthered their friendship.

Having been dropped off in the car park at the Dean Road Leisure Centre, Detective Inspector Pluke resumed his subterfuge as suggested by DCI Sanders. Sanders had assured him that several of his undercover officers would be on duty within the leisure centre to keep a watching brief on events.

He stressed that when Pluke left, he must not seek the police car in the centre's car park. Although it had taken him there, it would not be available for his return trip. Another vehicle would be used, part of the subterfuge, just in case he was followed or kept under observation by Sanders' target. To locate his lift home, Pluke should walk to the end of Dean Road, check that he wasn't being followed and then find the car which had taken him there. It would be parked to the right of the exit from Dean Road, on a residents' parking area in Springfield Lane. It would be a police car, but unmarked, and it would have a young female driver called Sarah.

221

'Make sure you are not followed, Montague. If you are, I am sure you know how to lose a tail. Whatever you do, don't lead a tail to the police car, keep walking until you've lost the tail, heading towards the city centre. It's well signed. We'll keep you in sight even if you don't see us, we'll find you. I must stress you will be in no danger at this stage, Montague, I can assure you of that. The alternative is that you might find yourself being arrested by my undercover officers, but that will be part of our ploy, in which case you will not leave the complex in the way I've just described. In that case, you won't have to worry about finding a lift away from the place. Your transport in that event will be a police car in full livery, you'll be taken away by uniformed officers. We want that incident to be seen. As you can appreciate, much depends upon what happens while you're there and whatever does happen, we can cater for it.'

'What's the time-scale for all this?' asked Pluke.

'I don't expect it to take longer than an hour.'

'If you are aware of what is going to happen, I'm sure I can rely on you,' said Pluke even if he was rather apprehensive.

'That's vital, Montague. We need mutual trust. What I hope to do is to bring together various strands of our enquiries through your participation in this modest exercise.'

For the second time that day, therefore, Montague Pluke entered the huge complex and headed for the reception desk. As before, the foyer was full of people, some clearly waiting for family or friends either before or after a visit, some just sitting on the settees or chairs and others looking at notices. It was much busier than Crickledale town centre even on market day and no one appeared to take the slightest notice of him. He noted that the reception desk was staffed by the same young woman as previously but she did not seem to recognize him either. He was alone among a lot of people as he approached her. Happily, there was no one else at the counter.

'Yes, can I help you?'

'I wish to speak to Ms Eileen Bilton,' said Pluke.

'Is she expecting you?'

'No, I'm afraid not.'

'So you don't have an appointment?'

'No, but it is important. I wish to speak to her on an urgent personal matter, it concerns a former member of her staff.'

'And your name, sir?'

'Pluke. Mr M. Pluke.'

'Just a moment, I'll check.'

She rang Ms Bilton and explained the situation, whereupon the receptionist told Pluke that Ms Bilton was engaged at the moment but she was expected to be free in about twenty minutes. As before, she told Pluke to sign the guests' register which he did in the way he had done earlier, using his own name but with the Huddersfield address of his publisher instead of his home address. And he entered his own private telephone number. Then he made for a seat near the swimming pool; Ms Bilton would come and collect him when she was free. Pluke made for the same entrance gate as hitherto and the receptionist activated the opening mechanism to admit him; he settled down on the seat as the noise of children enjoying themselves rose from the nearby pool. The area in which he sat was busy too, rather like the foyer with lots of people hurrying to and fro, but no one seemed to be taking any notice of him.

Once settled, he could watch the children splashing and shouting in the water and noted there were several adults in attendance around the poolside. One of them spotted his arrival and clearly made a mental note of the strange man watching from behind the glass panel. As Pluke waited, though, he looked at other things about him – a large plan on the wall which showed further areas of the complex, such as the squash courts, indoor tennis courts, a small swimming pool for toddlers, the gymasium and, he found, a first-floor corridor along which were more club

223

rooms. Clearly, the place catered for a wide range of interests.

So what kind of clubs met here? He was tempted to walk away so that he could conduct further research into that question but felt he must remain on the seat because, evidently, DCI Sanders was using him for an undercover purpose which wasn't totally clear. All he could do was wait for the hitherto unknown Ms Bilton or for whatever else was going to happen to him. He told himself to remember he was not a police officer but, as before, the time ticked away with no sign of her.

Quarter of an hour passed without anyone speaking to him although lots of people who walked past did give him rather strange stares – he wondered if they realized he was upon some very secret undercover police work. Then a loud whistle was sounded and the children began to leave the pool to head for the changing rooms just as another group arrived fully dressed and carrying their swimming bags and towels. The second group hurried past him chattering and laughing as they made for the changing rooms and so another session was about to begin. The man at the poolside, the one who had clearly logged him in his memory, was no longer to be seen, and as the pool cleared other officials appeared. Teachers and staff from the second school's influx perhaps? Half an hour had now gone and the second group of children were pouring into the pool, getting themselves wet and accustomed to the water before the more formal activities started. Forty minutes had now passed without anyone coming to attend to him. Then forty-five.

And the children kept swimming and splashing and shouting. Their session might soon be over too. Then a man came to sit on the bench at his side. He was a large man with broad shoulders, well over six feet tall with closely cropped dark hair and what appeared to be the beginnings of a beard, neatly trimmed. He was dressed in trainers, jeans and a dark blue T-shirt sporting a Celtic cross on the chest. For a few minutes, the man did not

224

speak but seemed intent on watching events in the pool, then he turned to Pluke and said in a rather well-spoken voice with just a hint of a Lancastrian accent, 'Wonderful, eh? Young bodies, so fit and agile. Makes you wish you were young again.' Pluke noticed his large brown eyes.

'We didn't have lessons like this when I was at school,' ventured Pluke, deciding almost instantly that this man was the reason he was acting as some kind of target. He would regard him with suspicion and treat him with great care.

'Missed out on life, eh?' said the man. 'So what do you do then?'

'I'm out of work,' lied Pluke, instantly realizing his presence had become highly important. 'I thought there might be a job going here, in the cafeteria. I used to manage a café in Huddersfield, you see, then I got made redundant, so I thought I'd look for work, it's boring, sitting around doing nothing all day.'

'Then you could watch these kids all day, eh? In their swimsuits. And get to know one or two mebbe?' The man grinned in what Pluke could only describe as a lascivious way. 'Help them to learn to swim? Hands under their tummies?'

'I think I'd be too busy for that if I got the job.'

'But you'd be near the kids though, eh? Very near, near enough to watch them like this. So is there a job going?'

'I don't know, I'm here on spec, I haven't an appointment.'

'Well, the best of British as they say. So what do you do when you're not managing cafés or looking for work?'

Pluke's brain was working fast. He had not ignored the Celtic cross on the fellow's T-shirt; he had not forgotten that Brent had worked here, on the poolside for some of his time. He recalled the Celtic elements of Brent's death and the fact that Brent had talked often to a woman called Ali in his break times. There was Alison Wharram to whom Pluke had spoken and who had mentioned swimming, so perhaps she came here? And she had links with

225

the Hurnehow estate. She'd been to the Hall as a guest, a friend of Dominic. He'd come across another girl called Alicia who might also be the Ali in question and today he'd learned of the club rooms here . . .

What he was now experiencing confirmed to Pluke that this place, this leisure centre, held the key to Brent's disappearance and death, and probably the deaths of the other missing men. What evidence he might not have gained through being taken away earlier might now be presented to him. Thanks to the loss of his warrant card, he'd not fulfilled those original objectives, but now it seemed things were working out better than he'd hoped or expected. He had been catapulted deep into a top-secret undercover operation mounted at very short notice and, quite unexpectedly, found himself speaking to a man who surely held the key to Brent's death. Those good luck charms *had* worked in his favour after all, and were still working, at least for the time being.

In those fleeting seconds, he had not forgotten the sighting by the landlord of the Cockatrice Inn high on the moors above Hurnehow. The sighting of a man called Jake with five others. Pluke's heart began to pound. This was that same Jake . . . he was sure of that. The description fitted even if he wasn't wearing a white sweater. So how had this leisure complex featured in the lives of the others who had vanished? Sanders would have his own views but Pluke must remain cool and in full control, he must think like an undercover police officer . . .

'I study ancient cultures,' said Pluke, trying for the moment to be as vague as possible while angling for Jake to take the bait. 'Superstitions in particular, see?' And he produced his rabbit's foot and double hazel nut. 'Good luck charms, they're to help me get this job.' He did not mention his fame as a horse trough expert in case this man had come across his books, and he knew that if the fellow checked the guest register, he'd be unlikely to telephone the publishers. The phone number was his own. Mrs

Fowler had said Brent got a phone call which had followed his letter.

'Great! There's a Celtic Society here,' said the man. 'We meet here every Wednesday evening, seven till nine. In Room 27. You could come along if you wished. And we have a church group, the Church of the White Kelts, spelt with a K. It has very ancient roots, you may have heard of it?'

'Yes, indeed,' enthused Pluke. 'I believe they demand absolute purity in everyone and everything.'

'They do indeed, well, this is interesting. Look, why not come along and join us?'

'Well, at the moment, I don't live here. I might move into the district if I get this job but yes, if I do I'd love to come along.'

'So where do you live?'

'Huddersfield,' lied Pluke convincingly.

'Well, that's not a very long drive over the Pennines but we're always here, just turn up on the night and ask for Jake. That's me.'

'Thanks, I'll think about it, seriously,' said Pluke, and then a woman came to the bench.

'Mr Pluke? Mr M. Pluke?'

'Yes,' said Pluke.

'Eileen Bilton,' she said. 'I believe you want to talk to me.'

'See you,' said the man called Jake, leaving Pluke. 'We might be in touch?'

'Yes, I hope so,' said Pluke, rising to follow Ms Bilton into her office. 'Might I ask whether our conversation which follows will be regarded as confidential?'

'Anything concerning personnel is confidential, Mr Pluke. Rest assured that what is said between us will go no further.'

'Thank you. And while I am here,' he added, just in case that man Jake did quiz this woman, 'are there any vacancies on your staff? In the cafeteria?'

'Well, not as such although one of our young men left a

few days ago and has not returned, he seems to have disappeared. There may be a vacancy there, in due course.'

'Ah, then that is why I am here. I might keep in touch about a possible vacancy, but my real purpose is to ask about the young man who left. Brent Fowler. He is my nephew, my sister's son. I know she has been here asking about him but she has asked if I can help find him, seeing I am now out of work.'

'Well, if we can help, we will. How do you think we can do that?'

Pluke's skilful pretence that he was Brent's uncle did not elicit any useful information about the young man's fate. Ms Bilton confirmed he had worked in the kitchen of the cafeteria, having been transferred from the swimming pool for what she described as 'administrative reallocation' without revealing the true reason. She said he was a good worker, very reliable, and was particularly skilled at carving carrots into flowers and icing cakes. From her own knowledge of Brent, she knew he frequented the centre in his leisure moments to take part in various activities but she could not help with trying to suggest where he might be. She knew he had disappeared, his mother had been here looking for him as Pluke had said, so Ms Bilton knew about the shooting party weekend to which he'd been invited. He'd told her about it when he'd asked for time off but she couldn't remember the details and had no further information about it. Pluke refrained from saying he was dead, preferring the people here to think he was still missing and unaccounted for. He spent about twenty-five minutes with Ms Bilton, put his name and the Huddersfield address on her waiting list in case a job vacancy arose, then thanked her and left.

As he walked out of her office, he saw Jake standing before a noticeboard in one of the corridors, clearly hoping to engage Pluke in further conversation, but as Pluke walked along, two uniformed constables appeared and seized his arms. Jake saw the incident but merely watched from a distance.

'Just come with us,' one of them said. 'Very quietly, no fuss . . .'

And they marched him outside with Jake still watching.

The enquiries made by Wayne Wain and DC Livesey in the Central Library and some of the nearby branches were almost as unproductive as their search of the Fowler household. They confirmed that Brent Fowler held a library ticket and, after quizzing members of the staff, one young woman could remember him after Wayne showed him the official photograph. The library assistant recognized him because of his interest in photography and his fascination with English country houses. On several occasions, Brent had sought her help in locating books on these specialist subjects and on occasions, during Saturday mornings, had spent a long time reading in the reference section, sometimes saying he was taking his mum for a bus trip to one of the nearby stately homes. He liked to research the house in question before visiting it, so that he could tell his mum all about it. The girl – Anna Meek – thought he seemed such a nice young man, so caring towards his mother. The detectives did not reveal that Brent had been murdered or that his body had been found on the North York Moors; instead, they pretended it was a missing person enquiry and that they were trying to trace him.

'I think he joined the photography club at the Dean Road Leisure Centre,' Anna told them. 'He seemed very interested in that and said he'd been invited to join.'

'Are there many societies in Manchester?' asked Wayne.

'Hundreds of them,' she said. 'We try to keep details of where and when they meet, and who the secretaries are, but we're not told about them all. They cover all kinds of subjects, everything from goldfish care to gold mining.

Quite literally, there's something for everyone, and quite a lot meet in Dean Road's club rooms.'

'We have a colleague who is at Dean Road right now,' said Wayne. 'I'm sure he will be told all about them so we needn't trouble you; we'll remind him when we meet him but if he's not found anything about them, we might return.'

Her eyes said it would be very nice if the tall, dark and handsome detective returned. And so they left, with one factor emerging – whenever Brent came to the library, he was always alone. He did not seem to have many friends, Anna thought, and seemed happy to spend some Saturday mornings in the warmth of the library, and other Saturday mornings visiting country houses with his mother. She knew nothing about his work and had never met his mother, nor had she ever seen him with a girlfriend.

'There's nothing in his library visits that would lead to his killer,' said Wayne. 'I wonder how the boss has got on? Come along, Ed, it's time for something to eat and mebbe a pint apiece, then we'll see what's waiting for us in 'A' Division reception.'

Pluke was alone in an upstairs office at the police station near UMIST, the University of Manchester's Institute of Science and Technology. He was sitting at a table in a small conference room. The room was empty except for a telephone extension on a window ledge and some magazines and daily papers on the rear edge of the table. The two uniformed constables who had arrested him had left – in fact, he now realized, they were really undercover detectives pretending to be uniformed constables for the purposes of this operation.

An arrest by a man in civilian clothes could so easily be overlooked but one effected by a pair of hefty constables in helmets and uniforms was hardly likely to go unnoticed. It seemed that the purpose of Pluke's highly visible arrest was for it to be noted by those under observation by

Sanders and his officers. And so it had been. When the two constables left, one of them said, 'It wasn't really an arrest, Mr Pluke, just a decoy operation. DCI Sanders will be along shortly to see you.'

And then they were gone. Pluke had not yet had any lunch, but was pleased when a secretary brought him a sandwich, a tub of yoghurt and a cup of coffee from the canteen. He was enjoying his late meal while reading *The Times* when Paul Sanders arrived, also bearing a plate with a sandwich in one hand and a mug of coffee in another.

'Great stuff, Montague,' he said as he settled opposite Pluke. 'That went exceedingly well, thanks to you. I know it was very short notice with almost no planning but things seemed to go very smoothly. The bonus is that we got what we wanted. Our fish took the bait. Now, it's a case of waiting to see if he acts upon it.'

'Jake, you mean?'

'That's the fellow. You did well to get him in the frame, we photographed him and recorded his chat with you. From our enquiries, we're even more convinced he's behind those disappearances, all of them. We've managed to establish covert links with the Dean Road Leisure Centre because all the missing men went there for various reasons. And Jake's little girl went there too, swimming with friends; he doesn't know we are aware of his fatherhood. Brent had assaulted her earlier, we've discovered; she was just one of his victims and later on she was murdered and dumped in the canal. Brent was a prime suspect but we couldn't get the necessary evidence. At the moment, we have an undercover policewoman working full-time in the centre, she's been there some time. From the intelligence she's fed back, we're convinced Jake is the key to all this, but we still lack proof. We know he controls illegal immigrants in the city, they're terrified of him. He finds them work where no questions will be asked, and takes a big slice of their wages, threatening them with exposure if they don't do as he says. Some are earning money as beggars in town too, they pay him protection

231

money for their pitches. We are certain he persuades some of them to join him in the executions. They daren't refuse. Jake is something of a mystery man with a very shadowy background. We think he might be an illegal immigrant too, even if he's been around for some time. We're looking into that.'

'I told you he was seen very near the place where Brent Fowler's body was found?' Pluke said. 'We have a good witness,' and he explained about the visit to the Cockatrice Inn with five other men and Brent.

'Could your landlord identify him, do you think?' asked Sanders.

'I'm sure he could,' said Pluke. 'But it would mean bringing him over here to look at Jake without Jake realizing.'

'A nice job for you after we've arrested him!' grinned Sanders. 'You know, Montague, at last I think we're getting closer to Jake. It's not been easy with him committing his crimes outside our police area, not to mention the absence of bodies, so you can see how important Brent is to us. While we're waiting for Jake to take the bait, we'll be digging deeper into his background. He has money, all cash, from his various operations but he's never been convicted of any offence. To our knowledge, he's never been brought to court or even been arrested, and he doesn't mix with the local criminals or drug dealers. Clearly, he's a puzzle. He's not on the DHSS or Inland Revenue's records either. He's been targeted regularly by our undercover units, always without finding any positive evidence against him. Theories, yes, evidence no. He's heavily involved in the Dean Road Leisure Centre, he runs various groups there, and that church of his, all on a voluntary basis which gives him some credibility, and those missing men, the murder victims, were all members of one or other of his clubs. But that kind of evidence isn't strong enough for the CPS to authorize court proceedings, not even to justify bringing him in for questioning. We need more evidence, more facts and much less speculation. The finest thing, of course, would be to catch him in the act. After today, we might just achieve that. You appreciate this affair is not yet over?'

'He has taken the bait. You've got to land him now,' smiled Pluke.

'With your help, Montague, we can do it. He's invited you to join his Celtic Society because he thinks you are a paedophile who's avoided capture; you played your part very well, particularly giving that false address and the spiel about being interested in ancient ways, superstition, Celtic life and so forth. So you'll be wondering what happens next. If he runs true to form, he'll recruit five helpers, probably the same ones he used for Brent – he's got that kind of hold over them and he'll 'persuade' them to join him for another execution, another disposal of an evil person. It will be another occasion for his church to 'purify' society by removing evil people. This time, we'll be ready for him. We are tapping his telephone, by the way, but he's very careful, preferring not to use it for many of his operations.'

'Do you know the identity of his helpers?'

'Not at this stage, Montague, but their presence is strange because you told me only one shot was used to kill Brent, not five. Clearly, only one of them fired a shot. We didn't get that kind of information about the others who've vanished. So why just the one shot? Any idea?'

'Do you remember the firing squads of the past?' said Pluke. 'When soldiers were duty bound to execute one of their own men for cowardice or treason or some other serious military offence?'

'I've heard about them, Montague, but never experienced one, but I'm too young to remember the war, certainly the First World War's beyond my ken. So what's this got to do with Jake Hampson?'

'It was always said that when a firing squad faced the person they were going to execute, with all guns loaded, only one of the guns contained live ammunition. None of the executioners knew who had the live bullet. When the order was given to fire, no one knew who had actually killed the prisoner. I am wondering if Mr Hampson's team works like that?'

'Go on, Montague.'

'Remember that six men accompanied Brent Fowler to our moors but only one bullet wound was found. So who killed him? Who would know which firearm contained the live ammunition? Jake was with them, he was the boss according to our local landlord, but do you think even he has no idea who actually killed Brent? If a live bullet was loaded into just one of those guns, who would know which it was? So how can you prove who actually killed Brent? That kind of thing will puzzle a jury and create the necessary doubt. A clever device, I feel. It also gives Jake a hold over the five men – the threat of life imprisonment if they reveal their knowledge.'

Sanders did not say much for a few minutes as he munched his sandwich and pondered Pluke's suggestions. 'So it's even more important that we catch Jake in the act of executing someone. We need to make our trap even more effective, Montague. Are you prepared to go along with us?'

'Of course, I have a murder to solve.'

'Good. Now, at the moment, there are no recently convicted paedophiles in the city although there is one man who is openly suspected. I believe the killer, or killers, will target that suspect. They see their activities as legitimate purification of our society. The truth is Jake is a dangerous fanatic who will stop at nothing and clearly his recent successes have made him determined to continue.'

'So who is the current suspect paedophile?' asked Pluke in all innocence.

'You,' said Detective Chief Inspector Sanders.

Chapter Fifteen

That Tuesday afternoon, Pluke, Paul Sanders and the others sat in a small ante-room in the Bootle Street Police Station with Pluke still reeling from the shock that he might be the next victim. Pluke had reiterated everything he knew and suspected about the death of Brent Fowler. Sanders was speaking.

'We have enough reliable information to suggest they adopt a similar procedure to tempt each of their victims.' He was sipping from a mug of tea. 'We've established that by talking to friends and relatives of those who have disappeared, and thanks to Montague here, we know the same tactic was used to tempt Brent Fowler. It's the prize-winning scam idea – you know the thing – you've been lucky enough to win a major prize which allows you to take part in some wonderful scheme at no cost to you, and with the potential to enjoy incredible things. I think they'll try that with you, Montague. The fact that you were publicly arrested should be enough to convince them of your "guilt". So if the killers send you a letter to that address in the leisure centre register, will it reach you?'

'Yes, almost certainly. I do get fan letters!'

'More than can be said for most police officers! I hope they never find out you are a police officer but if things go to plan, you can expect the follow-up phone call at home, on the number you left at the leisure centre. We want you to accept the invitation and do as they say, but keep us posted. If things run to plan, you'll be collected in the Ford Galaxy and taken somewhere to be executed. Clearly, although we shall be observing and monitoring the entire operation, we shall not know where that final destination will be. False destinations seem to be given, but the execution will take place somewhere within the locality assigned to that false place, if you follow that. Like Brent was told he was going to a mansion in the North York Moors – it was a false mansion, so it seems, even if Mrs Fowler can't remember its name, but he died on those real moors. In other words, they set the scene pretty convincingly. We know that two others were told they were going to the Peak District or Lake District – and they died there. We think that's a ploy to lull the victim into a false sense of security during the trip – they're being transported to the right place, so they think, everything en route rings true. I must say, though, that we don't know where some of the other missing victims were taken, or died; in fact, we've no real proof they are dead and with more than five hundred people going missing every day, there's no telling how many have been disposed of like this. It means there's a lot of uncertainty about all this.'

'I'll do my best to help, so how will you keep me under observation if they use a stolen vehicle?'

'They don't use stolen vehicles, Montague. We are convinced they use Jake's own Ford Galaxy – after all, while he's using it to drive people into the countryside and back again on what appears to be a friendly outing, he has no cause for alarm, has he? No reason to raise suspicions? If he's stopped for any reason, he can say he's doing nothing illegal. It's just a church outing.'

'But he must have at least one firearm on board!'

'And who's going to search for that unless there's intelligence to say it's actually there? You don't search for firearms if you stop a vehicle because its lights are faulty or to administer a breath test, especially if it's on a church outing. Besides, if the firearms are hand guns, they can be concealed either on the person or about the vehicle, not readily seen without a careful search. If we wanted to find guns on board, we might have to strip the vehicle almost to its nuts and bolts. And you don't do that if you're shadowing suspects with the idea of catching them in the act.'

'Point taken,' said Pluke.

'Their operations smack of ruthless efficiency but I ought to tell you that shortly before the victim is taken away, a similar people carrier is usually stolen in the Manchester area and later found burnt out. That's another device to throw the police off the scent, no less, to establish some kind of false trail if it's needed. They're good at covering their tracks although I'm sure Jake is not aware of our growing interest in him. Our belief is that he's getting too confident due to his previous successes – you know it very well. Give a man enough rope and he'll hang himself.'

'So what are my instructions?' asked Pluke.

'Things are very much in the air at the moment, Montague. Very fluid. However, some things we do know. If you are collected for a trip, it will be in Jake's Galaxy. We know a lot about him now, where he lives and so forth, and so we shall bug it in advance. That's no problem. In addition to a hidden microphone, we'll plant a tracker device in his vehicle so we can follow him – and you – wherever you are taken. He'll never know it's there. If previous incidents are any guide, your destination will be remote and beautiful but you won't be cut off from us. With satellite technology, we can track the vehicle wherever it is. And head it off, by helicopter if necessary. We might even get to the destination before it! I know we will have to act quickly and positively and so I suggest you arm yourself, Montague. Get your Chief Constable's permission to draw a small arm for personal protection – he can contact me in person if he wants confirmation of the reason. Meanwhile, we shall be trying to identify the men who always accompany Jake and, of course, we'll be trying to find out where he obtains his firearms. He has no firearms certificate, by the way, we've checked, so I don't know whether all his zealots are issued with real guns or whether they're fakes. We've a lot to do for this operation,

Montague, but it may please you to know it's now our number one priority and that no expense will be spared to protect you.'

They discussed and analysed the general outline of the plot to trap Jake and once they felt they had exhausted the options, answered the questions and dealt with likely problems, Pluke was advised to return home and await the prize which would be his own murder.

'Before I leave, there is another matter I need to clarify,' he said with surprising calmness. 'I would like to check whether Jacob Hampson – Jake – is on Lord Hurne's Christmas card list. Might I call my Incident Room in Crickledale?'

'Be my guest,' frowned Paul Sanders, wondering how on earth this odd detective could believe that Christmas card lists from stately mansions were connected to organized assassinations.

Pluke made the call and asked for Inspector Horsley. 'Ah, Inspector Horsley, Detective Inspector Pluke speaking. I am in 'A' Divisional Headquarters of Greater Mancester Police in Bootle Street, the CID office. Now, you have the Hurne Hall Christmas card list I left with you?'

'Yes, Montague, it's been entered into the computer and already we're checking each name as you instructed. Twenty recipients accounted for already.'

'Good, then perhaps you could tell me whether Jacob Hampson of Manchester is on the list, and a lady called Alison Wharram – you will recall she is on the birthday guest list but I doubt if Hampson will be there.'

'Hang on, I'll check.'

There was a lull as Horsley accessed the computer to make the necessary checks and then he said, 'Yes, Montague. Both Hampson and Wharram are on the Christmas card list, there's an explanatory note to say he once came to the Hall with Alison Wharram which is why he got put on the list. Their names were together in the visitors' book. They were not married though, and not cohabiting, the note stresses that. Alison Wharram, who was a friend of Dominic, brought Hampson to the Hall as an act of kindness. They're pretty thorough, these country house types, with their records, they do everything efficiently. Alison Wharram is on the guest list for the party as well, as you know.'

'Yes, I've spoken to her and her current partner.'

'So why is this important?'

'Hampson is Manchester's prime suspect for the death of Brent Fowler and others. That list proves he has visited Hurne Hall and that means he would probably know that a nearby patch of moorland was suitable for disposal of a body. Whether he knew about the burning procedures is doubtful but not impossible.'

'So you'll be bringing him back with you then? Under arrest?'

'Not yet, we've no hard evidence at this stage. Manchester Police are working on that. I'll explain when I see you.'

'So what about Alison Wharram? Why the interest in her?'

'I think she is the girl called Ali that Brent befriended at the pool. She's a university lecturer but is involved with swimming events at the leisure centre. She must have spoken to Jake about Brent's love of country estates and so on, and unwittingly planted the idea of taking him there for execution . . . She'll have to be interviewed about that although I am sure she was not involved in his death.'

'Great, I can see your journey wasn't wasted. See you when you get back.'

Sanders smiled as Pluke replaced the phone. 'I liked all that, Montague, you doing the Sherlock Holmes stuff. That kind of old-fashioned detective work still matters, eh? And it still produces results, gives valuable pointers. You can leave Alison Wharram to us, we'll talk to her eventually but not just yet – she might alert Jake to our current interest and we don't want that, do we? You'll have to return once or twice to the swimming pool, just to show you cannot be stopped; let us know when you will be visiting. It's all part of the plan, and then we want to give Jake the prize surprise of his life.'

And so Pluke, Wayne and DC Livesey left Manchester to return to Crickledale where Montague would await an invitation to his own execution.

Pluke went to the Manchester swimming pool twice a week thereafter, sometimes with Jake speaking to him and asking whether he'd got the job. Pluke said he hadn't, but had been told to keep applying because vacancies often arose. And then the letter came about three weeks later, having been sent by post to Pluke's publishers who had forwarded it to his home address. Because that was a Huddersfield address rather than one in Manchester, it seemed they had not decided upon hand delivery. Over breakfast, he studied it with interest, noting the opening exhortation that it was private and confidential and the ten-figure reference number. It looked very authentic but he knew such a document could be produced by anyone with a desktop publishing program in their computer.

It began:

Dear Mr Pluke,

You are one of only six people from this region who have won a 'Lucky Break' weekend for those who wish to improve their lives by learning the best way of harnessing good fortune. There will be lectures and practical demonstrations from world-famous experts on both oriental luck-enhancing techniques, such as the Japanese Seven Gods of Luck, and the popular British methods of attracting good fortune such as horseshoes, touching wood and lucky numbers. The all-inclusive weekend will be held at Pierce Howe Hall in the Lake District, home of the famous item of blue glassware known as Luck of Pierce Howe, itself known to bring fortune to those who possess it.

Accommodation and tuition will be provided at no charge and free transport will convey you to and from Pierce

Howe Hall. The dates are from the evening of Friday 6th May until lunchtime on Sunday 8th May and successful candidates may be lucky enough to win a further five extra days, free of charge. If you wish to attend, you should be in the west-bound car park of Healey Services on the M60 for collection at 5 p.m. on Friday 6th May. Your people carrier will be identified by the name 'Pierce Howe' on red window stickers. It is essential you keep this letter with you at all times; it is your personal document of identification. Further details will be provided by telephone to your home when you have had time to consider this once-in-a-lifetime offer. IMPORTANT: keep this letter close to you; you may be asked to quote the reference number as a means of identification. The letter is strictly personal and the prize cannot be transferred to any other person. This offer will not be repeated and is not available to anyone else. We will contact you within a few days about your decision.

There was an illegible signature at the end but no address or contact telephone number and Pluke had no idea whether this letter could be traced to its source. He thought not. But it could be accurately reproduced on the scanner in the police station which meant a copy could be despatched immediately by email to Detective Chief Inspector Sanders of SIOUX in Manchester.

'Is that anything important, dear?' asked Millicent as she watched him studying it so carefully, almost to the point of forgetting to eat his toast and marmalade.

'It's one of those prize competition letters that everyone seems to be getting these days. I shall take it to the office to see if we can trace its source. One must always be mindful that it might be a confidence trick and that we might have to warn gullible members of the public to be on guard against fraud. Well, I must be off, I can't sit around all day when there is work to be done.'

But he did not tell her about the dangerous mission upon which he would be embarking as a result of that letter. It would only cause her to worry unnecessarily.

'Shall I pop in to see Mrs Fowler today?' asked Millicent.

'That would be nice, I am sure she will welcome a visit.'

And so the Plukes began yet another working day with Montague's forthcoming and very daring duty destined to be shrouded in mystery. To safely emerge from that, he would need all the good luck charms he could muster; indeed, he had already gathered a few such as a stone with a hole in it, and a rowan twig.

In his office, after coping with Mrs Plumpton's overflowing abundance of rounded, almost unconcealed and ever mobile flesh and making several secretive copies of the letter, he called in Wayne Wain and gave him a copy.

'I can understand gullible people falling for this sort of thing,' said Wayne.

'Then I must appear to be gullible,' mused Montague. 'Do you think Jake, or whoever is behind this, has realized who I am?'

'Of course not, sir,' said Wayne with authority. 'If he had, you would not have received this letter. The fact he has sent it means he regards you as a paedophile who should be disposed of. You must have done a good job convincing him.'

'Even if he has discovered I am a senior detective, he might have set a double trap for me.'

'That might be so but I don't think he realizes just who you really are, and I don't think he would risk setting a trap for a police officer. He would be aware of the risks to himself and his own plans. The point is that you've got the letter so you must respond; so much depends upon you, sir. That man needs to be caught and stopped; the idea is that you trap him, not vice versa.'

'And so I will. I will give a positive answer when they ring me, but in the meantime you and I must have detailed talks with Detective Chief Inspector Sanders. There are many plans to be made and plots to hatch.'

Later that same afternoon they met as before in the security offices of Leeds/Bradford airport where Sanders studied his copy of Pluke's letter.

'This is the first of these letters I've set eyes on,' he told them. 'But it fits the description of those we've heard about from the relatives of some victims. So, Montague, if we want to catch Jake and get him convicted, you must be the proverbial fly in his spider's web. Fortunately, we have ample time to get things planned but you must respond and then make your way to that service station car park. Draw yourself a firearm before you go, get yourself wired up for sound and while you are making your preparations, we'll be making plans to guard you every inch of the way. It seems you're heading for the Lake District – any idea where you'll be taken? Do the references to Pierce Howe Hall mean anything to you?'

'I'm afraid not,' admitted Pluke. 'I think that is a fake address but I'm guessing the destination will be somewhere very quiet but reasonably accessible from the main routes. And that story about the Luck of Pierce Howe is false, there is no such place. There are four of those Lucks in the Lake District, but none at Pierce Howe. There is a beck called Pierce Howe with an 'e'; it's in Yewdale, north of Coniston.'

'That could be your destination. We'll check the terrain and access routes to see what we might have to contend with. Right, there's a lot of work to be done. For one thing, we've got to get access to Jake's Ford Galaxy without him knowing so we can plant our microphone and tracker device and then we've got to work out a plan of action to ensure you are not executed. You, Montague, will continue as normal, or as normally as you can, and it might be wise to pop over to Huddersfield or even to wander around a swimming pool in Huddersfield looking particularly sinister or rather too interested in children, just in case any of Jake's cronies are looking out for you. And more trips to the Manchester pool might be wise. I don't think Jake will venture into Huddersfield, he's always operated in and around Manchester, but there can always be exceptions. Then, before that weekend, we need to get our heads together to firm up our plans in the greatest of detail and with armed back-up.'

The phone call to Pluke's home came a few days later and he told the caller he would attend the Good Luck event. And so the very detailed and cunning planning began in earnest.

After listening to Detective Inspector Pluke's story, the Chief Constable authorized him to draw a 9mm semi-automatic Sigsauer pistol and twenty rounds of ammunition from stores, even though he was not an authorized firearms officer. The circumstances were exceptional, he decided after speaking to the Chief Constable of Greater Manchester Police, and they were made more so because Pluke was not going to be protected by officers from his own force. His life would be in the hands of a foreign force, one based in Lancashire to boot.

But, after listening to the Lancastrian Chief Constable's story, the Yorkshire Chief realized there was no alternative. Pluke was going to be the sacrificial lamb, and if he lost his life it would be in the cause of protecting the lives of countless others. Pluke would indeed become a martyr. The Chief Constable took a personal interest in issuing Pluke with a battery-operated radio transmitter which would be concealed about his person; it would include a microphone concealed beneath his tie and the entire device could be tuned into the Greater Manchester Police surveillance unit's system. It would be operated by a switch in Pluke's trouser pocket. Other than wearing a suit of armour, Pluke was therefore equipped to meet his fate. Now he knew how that ancient Lord Hurne had felt when going to deal with the cockatrice.

In addition to his official methods of protection, however, he had also planned his private means which included his rabbit's foot, the hagstone with a hole in the centre, a piece of rowan twig, his double hazel nut, a piece of metal, i.e. a nail which was always guaranteed to ward off evil, and a miniature closed fist made of blue glass which he had found in an antique shop. It had come from an Etruscan tomb, and was widely used in ancient south-eastern Europe as a charm against the evil eye. But by far the most efficient charm against ill-wishers was a piece of wood from the blackthorn bush. Gipsy menfolk always carried blackthorn to protect them against every kind of evil that lurked along the highways and byways, and it was known to be used in several central European states for the same reason.

A small piece of blackthorn was sufficient but Pluke knew that the Irish made their shillelaghs from blackthorn which is a knobbly and very hard wood. Indeed, he had his own shillelagh which he kept under his bed to ward off the attentions of ill-wishers; any burglar daring to enter the Pluke household was likely to come into very close and uncomfortable contact with that shillelagh. Pluke decided it would accompany him as he went to meet his assassins – it was ideal for his protection. As a very young constable having to confront potential trouble, he had been taught to shove his truncheon up his right sleeve with its strap around his forearm. That meant it was hidden from view but if the need arose, he could flick his arm downwards and the truncheon would fly into his waiting fist, the strap around his wrist ensuring it was not lost or pulled from his grip. That was much quicker than having to haul it from the truncheon pocket in his trousers.

He would emulate that system with his shillelagh which was about the same length as a truncheon, if rather more knobbly, for it had a strap too. Thus equipped, Pluke would be invincible. The gun would help too.

On the Thursday before the pick-up at the service area, DCI Sanders rang Pluke.

'I have arranged for a plain police car to collect you from Crickledale Police Station. It will have a young woman driver. It will take you to Huddersfield where you will be dropped half a mile from the offices of your publisher; walk to the offices and wait outside. The same car will

245

come along to collect you – we're doing that just in case you are being watched. It will appear as if you are starting your journey from there. She will then drive you to Healey Services. You will remain in her car until you see the Galaxy – point it out to her. In the car park there will be more of our cars, ready to shadow the Galaxy to its destination, not a difficult task on the motorway or main roads. Your driver will discreetly point out the Galaxy to her colleagues, and from that time onwards it will be our target vehicle, aided, of course, by the tracker device which is now in place. Our observers and operators will have the back-up of others, just in case things go wrong. We are taking no chances, Montague. All those police vehicles will have the latest mobile computer system installed which includes automatic registration plate recognition, video recording, digital communications and on-line database, web access, maps and route finding, radio and vehicle interlink connections and even speed-limit enforcement facilities if we need them!'

'It's not the motorway run that concerns me,' said Montague. 'It's what will happen when we stop in a remote area . . . you can't follow us into a remote area without being noticed, and that is when I am most vulnerable. It takes only seconds to kill a man once he's out of the car. Whatever armoury I possess will be worse than useless if I get to that point, but I will have my blackthorn!'

'We have all that in mind, Montague, every eventuality. We have the use of a helicopter which will keep behind and above the Galaxy, well out of the driver's vision, and our tracking devices will provide us with the general direction of the Galaxy. Once the Galaxy is heading for its final destination – which must be remote if their objective is to be achieved – we shall be able to anticipate its route and arrange interception, either by vehicle or helicopter. Remember it will not be dark at the time, we can keep you constantly in view and will be listening to your conversation in the Galaxy. And that is where you can help. Are you familiar with the Lake District's roads and villages?'

'Fairly,' said Pluke. 'I have made many trips in my search for horse troughs made from local slate.'

'Then questions by you to the driver or passengers would be helpful, asking about the destination perhaps, naming villages, identifying roads, that sort of thing. We might even learn Jake's intended destination, perhaps it is near Pierce Howe Beck.'

'I must be cunning enough to disguise the fact that I am providing guidance to you!'

'Exactly, Montague, although they should have no reason to think they are being shadowed.'

And so the final instructions were issued, digested, discussed, analysed, amended and confirmed. Tomorrow, Montague Pluke would meet his fate.

Chapter Sixteen

At the appointed time, Detective Inspector Pluke walked towards the silver Ford Galaxy in the car park of Healey Services. In his white sweater, Jake was standing near the driver's door and there were other men sitting inside, all in white T-shirts. The car in which Pluke had arrived was now lost somewhere among many others parked here and even Pluke could not identify any of them as police vehicles. But he knew they were there, watching. As he approached the vehicle, Montague put his hand into his pocket and switched on the transmitter, covering his action by extracting his handkerchief as if to blow his nose.

'Ah, Montague. You've made it!'

'Yes, it's all so very exciting!'

'Jake at your service. Well, we're all here and raring to go. In you get.'

Pluke climbed in and was shown to a seat as Jake settled down as the driver. Pluke noted five more men, all silent, all foreign-looking. Mid-European if their features were anything to go by. They nodded and smiled, but did not speak.

'You've left your car here?' asked Jake.

'No, I got a lift, a friend. She's gone already, had to get back home. She'll turn off the motorway at the next junction.'

'Good. Well, off we go. Lake District here we come.'

Vehicles of every kind were constantly moving in and out of the car park, consequently when the Galaxy rejoined the motorway, Pluke had no idea which of the following cars – or even those preceding it – were shadowing him.

There would be other vehicles too, somewhere ahead, ready to take over; all would be in radio contact with one another. Oblivious of the trap into which he was heading, Jake took the Galaxy up to sixty-five and kept it there, not risking a speeding check by travelling at more than seventy miles an hour, and all the time he was chatting to Pluke. He was asking about superstitions, how to make sure good luck came one's way or how the weather could be forecast by folklore, and as they chatted, with Pluke airing his massive knowledge on the subject, Jake guided the vehicle through the traffic and on to the M6 where he turned north. The others said nothing to Pluke, although they chattered among themselves in a tongue Pluke could not understand. During the journey, Pluke asked about Pierce Howe Hall, saying he had never heard of it. Jake said it was a very new privately run conference centre, a former country mansion which was now staging weekend meetings and gatherings for those with specialist interests. Pluke then asked where it was located and Jake said it was north of Coniston Water. Pluke told an untruth when he said he had never been to that part of the Lake District whereupon Jake said the Hall was near Hodge Close in Yewdale. Pluke had been there, hunting troughs and folk tales, and knew there was no such place as Pierce Howe Hall. He did not say so but he knew Hodge Close.

'Ah,' said Pluke, being devious but wanting his words to be overheard by his listening protectors. 'I think I know where that is! Between Langdale and Coniston? A very quiet valley with one or two isolated houses? Where slate is quarried? There was a recent piece in a magazine about it.'

'Got it in one, Montague! A lovely setting. Well, I hope we all learn something from this weekend, especially with you being such an expert. I am sure you will make a valuable contribution to the event.'

Pluke hoped the communications systems were working. Snippets like this should help Sanders and his officers to finalize their plans with great accuracy. That's if Jake was being truthful! But they had plenty of time to check things. The Galaxy turned off the M6 towards Kendal and then made for Windermere, continuing along the lakeside to Ambleside before heading towards Skelwith Bridge. Pluke continued to make comments about the directions they were taking, naming villages and landmarks and saying he recognized the A593 which led into Coniston village.

'Yes, but we turn off before we reach the village, we turn north again, into Yewdale, Montague, towards Hodge Close. Stunning scenery, wonderful at this time of year with fresh green foliage and blossom . . .'

Good, thought Pluke. Jake had confirmed his intended destination and Pluke felt sure Sanders' officers would have picked up those clues, but this is where the landscape began to grow very remote and therefore very dangerous with deep quarries. Pluke must be alert the whole time, ready to take instant action . . . so where was the helicopter? There was no sign of it, no sound of its reassuring presence. And those police shadowing vehicles? Where were they? A pair of motor cyclists overtook them at one stage, noted Pluke. Police officers? Very likely, even if they were not dressed as such. The bikes roared ahead and were quickly out of sight.

Pluke wondered whether they had gone towards Hodge Close. Now the Galaxy was heading south towards the first turn-off for Yewdale, the one marked *Hodge Close Only* which crossed Shepherd's Bridge.

'There is a wonderful tale of the Yewdale Giant,' said Pluke, wondering if any of the other passengers understood him. 'He killed a young woman and her lover in Yewdale, and they fell into Cauldron Dub which was in flood and their bodies were never seen again. The local people behaved like vigilantes, they attacked the giant and killed him, he's buried in Yewdale, his tomb can still be seen. They say the locality is still haunted by their ghosts.'

'I don't like ghosts and know how to prevent them but it's amazing, the things that happen in quiet places,' said Jake. 'We're going up there, I can show you Cauldron Dub later if you like, when we've completed our first commitment. There'll be no ghosts at this time of day.'

'I'd like that,' said Pluke, hoping the listeners had overheard Jake's words. He felt for the reassuring bulk of the shillelagh up his sleeve. It was there, ready for action. 'How far is it?'

'Not far from where we are now, five or ten minutes on these narrow roads.'

A couple of miles or so before reaching Coniston, the Galaxy turned right at the *Hodge Close Only* sign and began to crawl along the narrow lane which twisted and climbed along the eastern banks of Yewdale Beck as it skirted the foot of Raven Crag. Pluke was familiar with the road – he'd been here several times hunting slate horse troughs – but Jake was not to know that.

It was a narrow, tortuous climb which twisted through the tree-lined landscape beneath towering fells, but the road was well surfaced, if very narrow in places. They passed a house which seemed to be tucked into the mountainside. There was still no sign of the Galaxy being followed but Pluke's memory told him there were sufficient tracks for an approach to be made from the opposite direction and for vehicles to arrive ahead of them, and to conceal themselves – like those motor cyclists. Up there were several disused slate quarries along with one still in use nearby. There were some workers' cottages which were now holiday lets, and many huge piles of waste slate which offered lots of hiding places for men and vehicles. Then came the sound of a helicopter. Its loud chopping noises sounded above the trees and then it swept low ahead of them before vanishing over the horizon.

'Mountain Rescue,' suggested Jake. 'Maybe somebody needs air-lifting.'

'A regular occurrence on these mountains, I'm told,' said Pluke. 'Are we far from Pierce Howe Hall now?'

'We've a short stop before we get there,' said Jake. 'Something I want to show you.'

'Cauldron Dub, you mean?'

'Not just yet, that's for later. No, this is something very spectacular indeed.'

'Blue Water Quarry, you mean? The one at Hodge Close?'

'You've seen it? You sound as if you know this area?'

'I've heard about it, that's all, when I was doing research into the folk story of the Yewdale Giant,' said Pluke. 'It's known for its massive depth and sheer slate sides, smooth as mirrors, with deep water in the bottom. The water picks up the colour of the slate, it's very spectacular.'

'Right, rock climbers used to practise there, the only way up or down is on the end of a rope. Legend says it's bottomless which I doubt. I wanted everyone to see it, Montague, it is so spectacular and unique. If you fell in there, there's no way you'd get out without help. These gentlemen have never seen it, I want them to have a look at it. It's just up the road, a couple of minutes from here.'

Pluke was now hoping that all this valuable advance information was being overheard and acted upon by his invisible guardians. At this point, the road wound its way between silver birches and conifers, their trunks determining the narrowness of the carriageway as huge boulders of slate lined the route between the trees. Each was the size of a small van and they littered the sides of the route as the vehicle emerged from the trees on to a plateau. The road continued through it but the left-hand side was composed entirely of surplus and unwanted pieces of slate. By now their speed had been reduced almost to walking pace. The expansive flat area to their left was probably two centuries old, a former dump of waste slate now flattened to form part of this landscape. It was large enough to accommodate several dozen cars but there were no trees on it and therefore no hiding place – although it would make a useful helicopter landing pad. The Galaxy eased to a halt on the roadside at this point.

To the right was Blue Water Quarry, an immensely deep circular chasm in the ground with sheer smooth slate sides and the bottom full of icy water hundreds of feet below. And no fence, no gates, no protection. No one had ever calculated the depth of that water. The helicopter made another pass just as Jake turned the Galaxy and reversed on to a parking area. Its presence above did not seem to worry him as he halted and turned off the engine. Helicopters, civil and military, were not uncommon in these skies, some engaged in exercises and others upon real events.

'This is as far as we go.' Still in the driving seat, he turned to Pluke. 'This is the famous Blue Water Quarry. Out we get.'

Pluke said nothing.

Jake opened his door and climbed out, his hand signals inviting the others to follow and so they did, with Pluke being first and the others emerging behind. Pluke's heart was now pounding – he recognized the intent in Jake's mind. He would shoot him here and throw his body into that quarry, probably weighted down with slate rocks in his pockets to disappear for ever. And there were thousands of small pieces of slate so that Jake could build his ghost-scaring cairn afterwards. Jake led him towards the precipitous edge of the quarry with its sheer drop of hundreds of feet into the blue water below but Pluke held back, not wanting to get too close to the edge. And then Jake made his move.

He dug into his clothing and produced a single shot .22 pistol, shouted something incomprehensible to the others who did likewise. Which of them was loaded? Pluke had no idea.

'Now, Montague Pluke,' he said. 'It is time for you to die . . .'

'Die?' shrieked Pluke. 'Why?'

'Punishment. Punishment for what you have done and

might do to children unless we halt you . . . Society does nothing, the law does nothing, the police do nothing so this is your penalty. Death, the means of purifying our society. You will die right here and then your body will disappear for ever in the water below . . . Stand over here.'

'But –'

'Stand over here!' Jake shrieked almost manically as he indicated a place a few yards from the quarry edge.

He led the way towards it with the gun at Pluke's head and then halted, indicating the point at which Pluke should stand. Pluke deliberately misunderstood and Jake moved closer, edging to Pluke's right but with his back to the sheer drop as he raised his pistol in both hands, the grip of one accustomed to firing a handgun. The others held similar guns but none in the double-handed grip . . . Pluke now knew who would fire the fatal shot. Jake. Jake shouted again and the others formed a semicircle in front of Pluke, facing him with their guns held high . . . There was no sign of help. Pluke must act. Now. He had microseconds.

Jake was facing him, pistol raised at head height. Less than four feet away. Close enough for Pluke. Then the helicopter appeared again, now almost directly above them. Jake hesitated and glanced upwards as it began its descent on to the plateau of slate pieces casting dust and dirt in all directions.

Jake's moment of hesitation was enough for Pluke to react with astonishing speed. He flung his right arm towards Jake's head and the heavy shillelagh sped out of his sleeve and struck Jake between the eyes. As the shock caused him to stagger backwards, Jake raised his own gun-arm and discharged the shot but it went harmlessly into the air at the very instant armed officers rose from the surrounding boulders shouting 'Police, freeze . . .'

But Jake's startled backward step was into thin air. With a cry of alarm and fear, he tumbled backwards into the quarry, screaming as he hurtled down into the bitterly cold water, his scream receding and echoing as he fell into the confines of the quarry. The others dropped their guns and threw their arms into the air to surrender in bewilderment as police vehicles materialized from the trees in all directions and the helicopter landed to release more armed officers. There was no doubt the men were terrified of Jake, but now they were more terrified of the police.

Sanders shouted, 'Great stuff, Montague . . . Come on, lads, get him out of there. We don't want him to drown, we want him to answer for all this . . . and more.'

As the five quiet men were disarmed and led away, a police personnel carrier appeared from a side track in the forest and the helicopter rose into the air. A pair of police officers climbed out of the personnel carrier and prepared to descend into the cavernous quarry on winched ropes now being lowered by the helicopter. Jake had landed in the water and was swimming around, shouting for help, unable to climb out of the quarry due to the high, smooth and very slippery sides.

He paddled water as the preparations to extract him went ahead.

It took almost half an hour to winch him out, wet and slightly injured, but as he stood on dry ground near the helicopter, Sanders said, 'Now it's your turn, Montague.'

Pluke said, 'Jacob Hampson, I am Detective Inspector Pluke of Crickledale Criminal Investigation Department and I am arresting you for the murder of Brent Fowler.'

'You're a cop?' was all Jake said in disbelief.

'Yes, and I found Brent's body. The fire had not destroyed it.'

'Fire? What fire?'

Sanders came in now. 'And there will be questions about other murders, attempted murder today, illegal immigrants, firearms offences and other matters which need clarification. We will retrieve a lot of evidence from your firearm, from your home, from your computer, from telephone records and from these men. Their guns are all fakes, we know that. You do not have to say anything. But it may harm your defence if you do not mention when questioned something which you later rely on in court. Anything you do say may be given in evidence.'

Jake said nothing more.

'We've enough to put you away for a long, long time,' said Sanders to Jake.

'I've had a very busy day,' said Millicent when Pluke returned home after his adventure.

'And so have I,' smiled Montague. 'What made you so busy?'

'That Mrs Fowler has changed her mind again, she's decided not to live in Crickledale after all. She wants to go back to Manchester and we had a long talk about that, and then Mrs Adams has resigned as Gardening Club Secretary right at the start of the arrangements for the annual show. I've been running around all day sorting things out. So how was your day, Montague?'

'Well, I arrested a serial murderer, prevented my own assassination, caught a group of illegal immigrants, dealt with several firearms offences and helped to rescue a man from drowning in the Blue Water Quarry in the Lake District, all thanks to my lucky shillelagh.'

'You will have your little jokes,' she smiled. 'But I think I've earned a nice sherry.'

'I might be tempted to have one myself,' said Montague Pluke, having quite forgotten about the Holy Trough of Blackamoor. It would have to wait until another time.